The scent of his own
gunman entering the c ....ered
that smell and couldn. ..., that he was once more the
target of a gunman's bullet.

Healing from his physical wounds would be the easy part,
grounded in a gratitude for his very survival. Rebuilding his
life would be the hard part. But he was reminded he was
luckier than others whenever he thought of his friend Rick.

Surviving meant learning how to do everything again—from
walking to love. Having Daniel in his life might make it
easier this time. He wanted to believe, but wasn't sure he
could.

MURDER,

ROMANCE, AND

TWO SHOOTINGS

Todd Smith

To Crystal

Todd Smith

A NineStar Press Publication

Published by NineStar Press
P.O. Box 91792,
Albuquerque, New Mexico, 87199 USA.
www.ninestarpress.com

Murder, Romance, and Two Shootings

Printed in the USA
First Edition
June, 2018

Print ISBN: 978-1-948608-96-1

Also available in eBook, ISBN: 978-1-948608-86-2

Warning: This book contains sexual content, which may only be suitable for mature readers, and depictions of two shootings, ptsd, a graphic gay bashing murder and rape of a corpse.

Prologue

FEBRUARY 7, 2008

Ten years without being shot and then another bullet had pierced my body.

It was surreal. Once again, I was lying on a hospital gurney in a trauma center while emergency personnel were in a flurry of activity around me. I was having trouble concentrating. *Focus.* I took a deep breath and looked down at my blood-stained clothes, a seeping bandage of thick gauze pads encasing my right hand, and a nurse preparing to wrap a blood pressure cuff around my arm.

What seemed like a moment later, I startled awake.

"David?" I questioned aloud, looking around the bustling room. I needed him, there and now.

Would David be directed to the hospital I was in? Surely someone, the police, would tell him where I was. Not that I even knew the answer to that question. The ambulance ride was a blur of sirens and EMTs checking my vitals.

A nurse in blue scrubs came by and looked over my chart. I raised my left hand to gain her attention. "Excuse me."

Finally, she looked my direction.

"I have a close friend named David. When he shows up, can you make sure he is allowed to come back? Please? I...I have to see him now!" I must have seemed desperate. I was almost shouting at her.

She narrowed her eyes and nodded as she walked away. All I could hope for was that she would make that happen, even if all the usual "family" protocols were not met.

I lay on the lumpy cold gurney, saying prayers to a god that some said would never hear my calls because I'm a gay man. Yet I wanted divine intervention at the moment, whether it was sanctioned by the Christian Right or not. I kept staring at the large metal clock mounted high on the sage-green wall and thinking, *I won't ask for anything else, God. I really need David to hold my uninjured hand right now, please, with sugar on top.* This was a childhood expression, and here I was, an adult, using it.

Miraculously, as if appearing out of nowhere, David was by my side. Maybe it seemed this way due to the mix of the drugs they had given me in the ambulance, but it didn't matter. He was there, and I could finally find some comfort in the sterile environment of the emergency room.

"It majorly sucks to have this happen to me again." The first words out of my mouth were a statement of the obvious.

"I'm thankful you're still alive, Todd." He glanced around before he pantomimed a kiss and I gave one right back to him. This was all that we could do with nurses staring at us from all sides.

He reached out, took my left hand, holding it tightly, and cradled my fingers in his. The warmth of his skin soothed me. I didn't look at my right hand. At the moment, I kept my sights focused on him.

An orderly came to wheel me into an examining room. He was muscular and silent as the fluorescent lights whiz by overhead.

"An emergency doctor should be in to see you soon," he said as he walked away.

A little while later, the door to my room opened and a man in a white lab coat, his tie askew with wire-rimmed glasses that hung on the end of his nose, came into the room.

After introducing himself and making a brief examination, he said, "We're going to need to have an orthopedic hand specialist in to assess the extent of the damage and what will need to be done to fix it."

"I'm sure that will be painless, right?" I said.

"Probably not, but we have to know this before we can proceed with treatment. But first you need a tetanus shot." A nurse arrived with a tray containing a vial and a large needle, the first of many that I would see while in the hospital. I looked away as the needle made contact with my left arm and I felt the small pinch as the needle punctured the skin. *Ouch.*

The doctor did a quick check of my vitals. "The hand specialist should be here in a bit. He'll do a thorough check of your hand. In the meantime, try to relax and get some rest."

I nodded, and with a smile, he left the room.

I put my head back on the pillow and closed my eyes for a moment. David kissed my forehead. He took my left hand tightly and warmth radiated from his grasp.

The sound of paper flapping on a clipboard above my head woke me. A tall man was now checking on me, his dark hair combed to one side and wearing a white lab coat.

"I'm Doctor Carruthers. I'm the orthopedic hand surgeon who was called in to examine your injury."

He took a moment to check a page on the clipboard, then smiled and said, "So you've been shot. That couldn't have been fun." I guess he was trying to lighten the mood, but to me, it was a bit of a fail.

"No, not really."

Reaching into a box of sterile gloves, he took two out and put them on, then carefully took my hand out of the bandages to exam it.

"We're going to numb your hand to lessen the pain. You're going to feel some sensation as I figure out how serious the wound is."

After giving me a small injection in the area of the wound, he probed my hand, touching the hole meticulously and observing my reactions to better understand the damage that had been wrought by the bullet. I cringed and hissed each time he found a nerve, and David attempted to ease my tension as I clutched to him tightly with my uninjured one.

"It looks like we're going to have to do surgery, but for right now, we'll wrap it up and give you a chance to rest so you're ready for the operation tomorrow." Carruthers took off his gloves.

"Will my hand be back to normal?" This was the question I wanted to be answered right there and then. Yet I knew deep down it couldn't be, which made this all the worse.

"We hope" was all he said as he cleaned and bandaged my hand.

I didn't know quite what to think about his response.

"You'll need to keep your right hand elevated." He demonstrated by placing my hand on a couple of cushions before once again checking the bandage. Then with a "see you tomorrow," he left the room.

At this point, I only wanted to fall asleep. I was exhausted from the loss of blood and everything I had gone through that night. Orderlies wheeled me into an elevator. I jostled as we went in and they maneuvered me to the right; making room for David. The aged elevator moved with the dexterity of an old dog on a freezing cold morning. Then once again, the doors came open and the orderlies wheeled me back out.

I felt a bit helpless since all I was supposed to do, all I could do, was lay there while others moved me from place to place. Ceiling-mounted fluorescent lights flashed above us as we went down a long hallway before stopping at a small room. There was a plain bed with thin white linens. The two of them helped me onto the bed. I guess this was to be my home away from home for the moment.

I thanked them as they headed off. I assumed they had more people to roll around the hospital that night. David was looking into the small closet for an extra pillow that he knew would make me more comfortable before checking out the bathroom to see the condition of the amenities.

I stared up at the whitewashed ceiling, completely drained.

He brought the pillow, tucked and adjusted it under my head, and then shooed me over in the bed. Once I was settled, he carefully crawled in beside me and pulled me closer.

"Sorry about this." I felt the need to acknowledge the craziness of the night. This was a lot to put someone through, and I'd had past boyfriends who would never have made it to the emergency room before deciding to cut their losses.

"It happens." David snuggled in close to the left side of my body. The heat of his body and the warmth of his breath soothed me.

"Not to anybody normal, you know—only me."

"I love you and your bullet-ridden body," he quipped.

"Thanks" was all I could muster.

Ten years without being shot.

Then I began to think back to the first shooting. 1997— what I referred to as *The Year of Living Dangerously.*

First Shooting

Chapter One

JULY 4, 1997

A display of fireworks went off in the distance, lighting up the midnight-blue sky with a fiery red that sparkled as they drifted back to earth. My enduring fascination with them had me smiling at the sight. On this particular night, the Fourth of July, it seemed to add some monumental significance to leaving my home state of Missouri.

It was late, and I was taking the few belongings that I'd brought with me off the bus in downtown Wilmington, Delaware. The place was alive with activity even at this time at night. Outside the bus station, there was a scent of burning cigarettes as the pent-up passengers were finally able to indulge. Once inside, I was surrounded by babies crying and animated conversations between families. I sat down on a long wooden bench and took a moment to gather my thoughts. I had spent the last forty-eight hours crossing half the United States to reacquaint myself with my best friend from high school. Was this the right thing to do?

I had left a lover back in Missouri and headed across the country to stay with Kevin who thought that moving East and starting over might be a good idea. I was doing the opposite of what most people did; most headed West. But I always had to be different, so moving to Delaware to stay with an old friend seemed right.

The bus was behind schedule, arriving late in Wilmington, due to a breakdown outside Harrisburg, Pennsylvania. I'd called Kevin from a payphone at the bus station there.

"I should be in Delaware in a few hours. The bus had an engine problem. I'm looking forward to seeing you again. Not sure if this was the best idea, but what the hell...right?" I'd explained to an answering machine.

I called a cab at the bus station. I didn't want to inconvenience Kevin and could make it to his townhouse on my own. I waited inside, trying to beat the heat of this hot July night.

I walked outside when I saw the cab pull up, and he helped me with my things. I told him the address, and we headed off. He was quiet, no doubt due to the lateness of the hour. The cab smelled of evergreen, probably from an air freshener. It added to the cooling sensation of the air-conditioning, much more pleasant than the warm, crowded bus station. I stared out the window looking at the buildings and streets of downtown Delaware. I tried to keep track of the freeway and then the highways, doing my best to create a mental map of the area.

We turned into a driveway, the headlights of the cab illuminating a two-story townhouse with a garage. He helped me take my stuff out of the back, and I thanked him, then gave him a few dollars. He drove off before I turned my attention to the darkened townhouse lit only by a flickering streetlight across the road.

My palms sweated as I stood in front of the door to his townhouse. I was trying to get up the nerve to knock. We had talked numerous times about me moving in with him, but to finally be outside the door... He was one of my closest friends, but we hadn't seen each other for a long time. It was like we were meeting for the first time again, and I kept thinking, *what am I doing here*?

I pushed the button, the doorbell rang, and all the reasons for being there suddenly felt right. A light came on, the door opened, and Kevin grinned at finally seeing me.

"Let me help you with those bags," he said.

At that moment, I knew this was going to be okay. The sound of fireworks was closer—people in the neighborhood— there were crackling noises and small booms as I closed the door, but I was safe inside, away from the last bombardment of the Fourth of July.

I followed him in and down a hallway. A small kitchen to my left was spiffy clean with a few city skyline magnets on the fridge. A door to my right led to a bathroom with a white porcelain sink and a tub/shower combo. The living room included a large black-box television. We both collapsed onto a brown leather couch with a whoosh. I noticed a picture of Philadelphia on the back wall. Kevin and I always shared an interest in cityscapes and travel. He also had framed family photos scattered about. It was more mature than what I'd had in my college apartment, with film posters, a futon, and a twin bed that I had brought with me from my parents' home.

We didn't say much for what seemed like the longest time. I stared at Kevin. His blond hair was wavy and short, like the last time I'd seen him. He was still as thin as he'd been in high school.

I had always called him my oldest friend, although that was relative. Kevin was the person I'd known the longest who wasn't family. My parents had moved around a lot when I was growing up, and we happened to live in Kevin's town longer than the others.

After high school, I went to a college that was four hours away, and he had gone to a Catholic university near where we had attended high school together. I'd wanted distance from my family. Kevin and I continued to stay close when I came home every summer, back to the little town where I had graduated high school. Now we were back together again, two old friends who had kept in touch through occasional phone calls and summer breaks all those years.

He had moved to the East Coast to take a banking job after college. Wilmington was described as America's Switzerland, with business laws that were less regulated than other states.

He'd called right after my college graduation. It had been a short conversation.

"My roommate moved out, left town. It's expensive to live on the East Coast. Would you like to give Delaware a try in your job search after college?"

"Sure, why not? I'm not doing anything at the moment."

"What about that guy that you were seeing or living with? What was his name?"

I'd paused for a moment. I hadn't wanted to go into a long explanation about what had gone wrong in my love life. "His name...doesn't matter. He's not here anymore, so no worries."

"Okay, it's a deal. See you soon."

"Sounds great to me, Kevin. I can't wait. It'll be like our past summers together. I remember them as some of the best of times."

"Yes, yes, they were."

The phone call ended with those memories.

Now, I was sitting on his couch. "I'm exhausted after the bus ride. Do you have anything to drink?"

"Sure. Here, let me get you a beer."

We clinked bottles and laughed to take the silence out of the room.

Then I asked, "How have you been?"

"Job is going well. It's been too long, hasn't it, Todd?"

A swig of beer and, suddenly, we were right back where we started from.

"You know those summers in high school were carefree," I said.

"Even if it only amounted to us driving around town all night, playing pool, and eating out," he added.

"Simple pleasures, the first taste of freedom and staying out late," I said. "Most of all, time away from our parents."

A few beers later, he said, "I have something to share with you. I've been uncertain how to tell you this so...um...grab your backpack and follow me upstairs."

He opened the door to his bedroom. Asleep in the bed was a man. From what I could tell, he had short curly black hair and was thin like Kevin. He closed the door quietly and walked me over to what would be my bedroom.

I dropped my stuff on the floor, and then we sat on the bed and talked.

"I've been dating him for the last few weeks since my roommate moved out," Kevin said. "His name is Roger, and it seems we're getting serious. He's spent more time here than at his place lately. I know I should have said something before you moved in, but you never know how these things go."

I was stunned. This was not what I'd expected. All I could muster was, "It's great to hear you have someone."

"Roger does travel a lot with his job, so he won't be here every night. I was at the airport in Philadelphia picking him up when you called from Harrisburg. Are you okay with this?"

"I hope it works out for you. I've always wanted the best for you." It might be a little more awkward with three people in the apartment, but I kept that to myself. I honestly wanted his relationship to succeed.

Kevin hugged me and headed to bed. I went back downstairs to bring the rest of my things to my room.

I lay on the bed, staring up at the ceiling and reminiscing about Aaron. We had shared an apartment in college together. It had been small, but I'd loved being close to him like that. He had olive-brown skin and aquamarine eyes that I could feel stare at my body and undress me with a thought. He always seemed to smile with a smirk, and he'd laughed as though everyone would get the joke, whether or not it was funny. Which, in all honesty, should have warned me of the storm that he would make in my life.

The day after I graduated, he'd asked me to sit down because he had something important to tell me. In a pair of casual green Adidas shorts and a ripped yellow T-shirt that gave a tantalizing view of his bicep, he was sweating like he had been working out and completely focused on me.

"So...uh...great graduation ceremony?" he said. "What's next?"

"I guess I'll work at the hotel for a while until I find a newspaper job." I had been working as a bartender while I sent out resumes for future writing positions.

Aaron kept looking at me like he was having trouble articulating what he wanted to say. My answer seemed to give him the resolve to continue, though I wasn't sure why.

"First...I want to say, this is too fucking hard for me!" Aaron huffed.

"What is? What are you trying to tell me?" I wasn't sure if I really wanted to know, but I had to ask.

"I have to go, Todd. You can have the apartment for however long you need it. I'm leaving tomorrow. It's over for me. Ron is helping me move out. I've already paid the rent for June and July. See? I'm not a complete jerk."

He laid it out for me.

"I'm not in love with you anymore. When was the last time we had sex? Do you even remember? You had to realize that this was over."

Tears streamed down my face.

"This is what I hate most about you," Aaron said. "You have these dreamy ideas about how life is going to be. That things would never change between us, but life is change and I've had enough."

I could barely see through my tears. He stared at me. Silence.

Finally, he jumped up. "I have to go. I'll be back in the morning for my stuff. I really... I wish... This dream of our lives together, Todd...was never mine."

He went to kiss me, but I turned away. I couldn't bear it. He walked out without looking back.

I went to bed alone that night, still crying. I was angry and hurt. By morning, I was tearing up pictures of us and then ripping them into even smaller pieces. I didn't want images of him staring back at me in the apartment. They belonged in the trash heap now.

Rick, my closest friend from college who I could turn to for guidance, was starting a new life and a new job as a dining manager at a hotel in Kansas City. He'd never thought Aaron was the right one for me. I called him up.

"Aaron has left me," I'd said.

"I knew he was trouble, Turtle." That was the pet name Rick had given me. "When you introduced me to him in college, I noticed he had a roaming eye. If we all went out together, he would check out the room for hot guys. You were way too good for him. So what happened?"

"You know my friend Ron, right? The one in the architectural program with Aaron? They worked on a lot of projects for classes together."

"The muscular guy with the tats?"

"That's the one."

"Ah. You see, I told you he wasn't good enough for you," Rick said.

"You were right. I've decided I need some time away from the Midwest."

"You're moving away?"

"Yep, I think a fresh start will do me some good."

"Okay. I can understand that. But know this, Todd. If whatever or wherever you decide on doesn't work out, I'm here for you." He paused for a moment. "Damn, I almost forgot. I have to go into work tonight. You stay strong, Turtle."

"I will."

As luck would have it, Kevin called a few days later. By then, I was ready to take a chance, move East, and stand on my own without Aaron. I would show him that I didn't need him. I had all my dreams ahead of me, a writing career, and eventually, with hope, a new love.

It was time to leave the past in the dumpster behind the apartment.

Remembering these things helped me relax as I fell asleep that night, my first night in Delaware.

MORNING, AND I smelled bacon and eggs cooking. Kevin and Roger were both in the kitchen. I had slipped down the stairs without their notice.

Before I made my presence known, a man I assumed was Roger asked, "So how long will he be staying?"

I hung back for a moment, within earshot but out of view.

"Only a short while until he finds a job...maybe a few months. It will be like when we were kids. We'll live near each other again," Kevin said with a hint of excitement.

I moved closer, still out of view, but I could see them now.

"You know, Kevin, high school was a long time ago," Roger said. He put eggs and bacon on two plates, mumbled a curse, and then grabbed another plate from the cupboard. He cracked two more eggs in the skillet. It seemed I had taken him out of his breakfast routine.

Kevin took him in his arms. "This will be all right, Roger. He won't be here long. He will find a job and all will be well."

"I hope you're right."

I walked in.

Kevin looked at me and immediately went into introductions. "Roger, this is Todd."

We did a brotherly hug, all wide-open arms followed by a tight collapse on each other like we'd known each other for years. I looked at him closely. He had dark blue eyes, like Aaron. He was about my height. His gaze was piercing, like he was trying to warn me off.

"Bacon and eggs sound good?" Kevin said, smiling, as if their private conversation had not taken place.

"Sure, sounds fantastic. Thanks for making breakfast," I said.

"Did you line up any job prospects prior to coming out here?" Roger asked.

"I'm going to look at the Sunday paper today and start going through what looks promising. I'm sure something will turn up."

"How were you thinking of getting around?" Roger asked.

"At first, I'll use the bus and trains in the area. I have some savings that will go toward buying a car."

"You know, that's one thing I have never done, taken the bus or the train here."

Roger's voice had taken on a snide tone that had Kevin interrupting. "Let's eat!"

We ate without talking. The bacon was crisp, the eggs scrambled. They both headed out to meet friends later that morning. I stayed behind to look through the want ads, circling any possible opportunities with a yellow highlighter.

THAT NIGHT, KEVIN suggested going to a bar. We all piled into Kevin's car; I sat in the back.

"So what do you think of the city so far?" Kevin asked.

"I like the skyline."

"Yes, I *work* in one of those buildings," Roger pointed out.

To change the subject, Kevin said, "The bar we're going to is a local hangout. I thought it might be good for you to meet people that live in the area."

We parked in front of an older three-story brick building. The bar was up a long flight of wooden stairs.

Kevin was at his best in a crowd. People tended to gravitate to him, and it wasn't long before he was introducing me to his friends. "Hi, nice to meet you," became my mantra as we meandered through the bar. After a while, Kevin and Roger wandered off to speak to someone privately, and I pulled up a barstool to wait.

Aaron and I had gone out to bars together before to see his friends. But I didn't really become close to any of them. They weren't friends I would have chosen for myself, and in the end, they were easy to leave.

My college friends were moving on with their lives. One was to be married, another was moving to the West Coast for graduate school, and a couple I had been close to were having their first child. My friends' lives had become very different than mine. I wanted a chance to strike out on my own and thought Kevin was the person to turn to for that.

I drank three beers and relaxed. I sat alone at the bar while Kevin and Roger continued to mingle.

I was taking off the label of the beer bottle when an older guy came up and said, "Do you mind if I sit here next to you?"

"Sure. No Problem."

He gave me a once-over. He was built, and his tight white T-shirt clung to his muscular frame. I could tell he had dyed his hair blond, making it hard to tell the original color. It made me feel uncomfortable to see an obviously older man trying to look so much younger. Evading the man's gaze, I glanced around and noticed Kevin and Roger dancing. I decided to head out to the dance floor to give it a whirl. The music was loud and reverberating and gave the place an upbeat feel as I made my way toward Kevin and Roger. I danced with Kevin like we used to when we were kids. Back then, there had always been a girl with us. This time, it was Roger.

In high school, we hadn't known we were gay, or I guess neither of us had wanted to face that we might be. It had been a small high school surrounded by cornfields, not exactly a tolerant place if someone was gay.

I laughed a little and then shouted over the music. "It would have been nice to do this in high school, Kev."

"Yeah...it would have been," he agreed.

I was having fun for the first time since entering the bar. A moment later, Roger seemed to lose his balance and "accidentally" stepped on my foot. Given the look I received, I decided to step away from Kevin and head back to the bar.

I sat back down as they danced. I had to face the fact that Roger would be a major part of the household.

A short time later, Roger said something to Kevin, then they both left the dance floor and came over to me.

"We have to go," Kevin said.

"Why? I thought you were having a good time." I asked.

"Roger is ready to go."

I SPENT ALL of Monday searching for jobs. Once I found some interesting prospects, I used Kevin's computer to write cover letters, address envelopes, which I then stuffed with copies of my resume and set aside ready for mailing. By the time Kevin and Roger arrived back from their jobs, I had a stack of them ready to go out to prospective employers.

"How was your day?" Kevin asked.

"I went through the newspaper searching for future jobs here and have resumes ready to mail out, just needing stamps," I answered.

"What do you think about Philly cheesesteaks for dinner?" Roger asked.

"Sounds appropriate considering how close we are to Philly," I said.

Dinner was a quiet affair. They both seemed to be dragging from their day at the office.

Afterward, we all sat down in the living room to watch some television. Kevin and Roger argued about whether to watch a repeat of *Roseanne* or *Seinfeld*. They asked me, and I said I had no opinion. So the argument continued.

I soon realized I wanted to be out of the house and away from the both of them. That was the one thing Aaron and I hadn't done: fight. Arguing would have meant we shared our deepest thoughts with each other. Most of the time, the conversation had been light.

As an architectural design major, Aaron spent most of his time silently scanning his blueprints for imperfections. I enjoyed wandering around the place looking at them. His ability to create was what I loved most about him.

Quiet contemplation was not what I was finding with Kevin and Roger. So instead of hanging around listening to them fight, I decided to explore the neighborhood and learn my new surroundings.

"Kev, I'm taking a walk. I'll be back in a bit."

He turned and nodded and went back to his heated discussion with Roger.

I headed out of the townhouse complex and onto a neighborhood street called Appleby Road, a reminder of apple orchards and homemade pies, which comforted me as I walked along. Small 1970s ranch-style and split-level homes were concealed from the street by bushes and large oaks. It was a hot clear July night with stars glistening in the sky, giving me a sense of peace.

I plodded along, reminiscing about hanging out with Kevin in high school. We would go to the mall and check out the record store for newest hits, then spend hours at Aladdin's Castle plunking quarters into the *Super Mario Bros. 3* arcade machine. Kevin became quite talented at mastering all the different levels. I always looked to him for guidance to the next challenge in the game. I rarely bested him, but his support gave me confidence in myself. Wow, I hadn't played that game in years.

I had gone farther than I had intended. I was standing at a stoplight, debating whether I should turn around and head back or go farther. Thirsty, I remembered a 7-Eleven just up the road a bit. 7-Elevens were new for me, so I thought I would check one out and try a Slurpee. I bought the largest cherry one I could. The store was empty, except for the clerk. I paid with all the change I had on me.

"I've never had a Slurpee before," I divulged.

"Never cared for them," he conceded as he counted out the change to put into the drawer.

As I wandered out of the 7-Eleven, I contemplated my future job prospects. I thought moving to the East Coast, with large cities like New York City and Philly nearby, would allow me to be part of the bigger picture when it came to writing. But in retrospect, I was just happy to be away from the past and specifically from Aaron's betrayal. Roger's presence was unexpected, but I was determined to make this living situation work.

I decided to cut through a brown-brick strip mall that had a mixture of businesses and retail, which were closed in the late evening, along with a few empty storefronts.

I was startled from my thoughts by the ringing of glass being kicked across the pavement in my direction. I glanced at the bottle as it stilled near me.

Out of the corner of my eye, I noticed two teenagers wearing shorts and dark colored T-shirts, pulling out guns and heading in my direction. Their faces were partially covered by their do-rags so it was hard to see what they looked like in the darkened parking lot. They weren't rushing toward me, only nearing with a determined stride of a force to be reckoned with, their guns locked solidly in their hands, pointing at me as they came ever closer.

I glanced back over my shoulder. This couldn't be right. It couldn't be real. I had been lost in thought as I sauntered along, and at the moment, I wasn't sure if I was going to survive the night.

The teenagers were still nearer the storefronts while I was cutting through the center of the parking lot, lit only by occasional flickering lights from the tall lamp poles.

I quickened my pace, still processing what was happening.

"We want your wallet!" demanded the taller one of the two.

"Hand it over now," added the other.

I didn't answer them. I couldn't even make out their faces. The mix of shadows and light in the barely lit parking lot made it hard to truly see them. All I could really see were the shiny metal guns pointed in my direction. They were serious, very serious about shooting me if I did not follow their orders to stop and turn around.

My mind was racing with what to do besides what they had asked. In that instant, with my adrenaline pumping, I decided to make a break for it. The shopping center had an opening that led to the street I'd walked down earlier. I was in decent shape from many strolls like this, and I definitely had the motivation to run the fastest I ever had in my life. Maybe I could get away and be back to my quiet night alone, with the stars looking down on me.

So I ran.

One of them shouted, "You better stop or I'll shoot!" I don't know which one said it, but I was already at a distance. The Slurpee fell in a big splash and red gooeyness trailed behind me as I bolted.

But I couldn't run quicker than a bullet. A loud pop rang out. I wasn't sure what it was. My thoughts were only focused on escaping.

A strange warm sensation radiated through my leg as if something had made contact. Yet, I couldn't really tell what it was. I had to keep moving because they could still be behind me. I came to the road, a little past the shopping center. My breathing was heavy, my heart racing, and my muscles tense; I had to stop for a moment. A strange burning sensation was coming from the back of my leg. I reached behind and my fingers came away wet.

Blood.

Even after seeing that, I tried to keep trudging along, but my leg wouldn't work the same as before. I limped, pushing myself to move forward, but walking became harder and harder. I looked down the dimly lit street that led to Kevin's place. I wasn't going to make it back to the house. It was possible I would bleed out before I made it. At least, that was what would happen in the movies. Or maybe I would lose consciousness. Neither was a good option. No matter how much I yearned to go to Kevin's place, I had to come up with another way out of this situation.

I had to turn around, go back to a gas station near the corner that I had seen earlier, and find help. They might still be behind me, but I had to take that risk or I might bleed out. I couldn't make it to Kevin's on my own, no matter how much as I wanted to be there.

Alone and panting heavily, I stopped for a minute and took a deep breath as I looked down the street toward the gas station in the distance. I had to talk myself into taking action in order to survive. I had to assume that they had taken off after shooting me. This thought kept me on task.

I staggered forward. With each labored step, I came closer to my goal—the lights of that small gas station. I hobbled by the side entranceway to the shopping center, not even looking in that direction. If they were still in the parking lot, I was fucked.

I kept my focus on the back of the white-painted Shell station and limped along like an outcast from some bad zombie movie, blood dripping down my leg.

I finally came to the front of the station, only to realize I couldn't go in, the place was locked and the cashier was behind a glass window. I begged her, "Could you please call 911?"

She seemed unsure of me, but then she noticed that my hand was covered in blood and I had smeared some on the glass. She dropped the cash in her hand, coins bouncing everywhere, and turned to make a call.

I sat below the glass-enclosed counter outside the gas station, feeling a little out of it and not sure what I could do to stop the flow of blood. Luckily, there wasn't much pain. I was sweating, hot, and there was a coppery scent surrounding me.

I didn't see the kids anywhere and guessed that they must have run off. I took my wallet out of my back pocket and looked at it for a moment. I should have given it to them. There wasn't much in it, and that also might have upset them more. If they had shot me from a distance, what might they have done if I'd let them get closer? Obviously, my life did not matter to them.

I was bleeding out while waiting for an ambulance that I hoped would show up soon. I had nothing left to give; it had taken every ounce of my strength just to make it there.

As I sat on the cement step, a guy came up to me and asked, "Are you all right?"

All I could say was an obvious no. My pant leg was mostly red and below me a small puddle of blood had formed.

He stood there staring at me for a moment. Then, he went into action. He took off the white T-shirt he was wearing and created a tourniquet, which helped stem the blood flow. I wished later that I had gotten his name I would have liked to thank him for his kindness. He was a stranger who really paid it forward by helping me.

It seemed like a long while before I heard the sirens of the ambulance. It might have been minutes, but it felt much longer. By the time the ambulance had arrived on the scene, I was going in and out of consciousness and slumped down on the gas station's curb with my head propped up by the hard steel of the building.

Two large burly men came out of the ambulance and toward me with a stretcher. I was glad that they were muscular, which meant I didn't have to do anything. I just let them gather me up like a rag doll and put me on the stretcher.

There was a slight jerk as we headed off. The back of the ambulance was a small space with a flurry of activity. They checked my vitals, gave me fluids, bandaged the wound, and replaced the tourniquet. Other than what they did, my strongest memory of the ride was the loudness of the sirens and hoping I was going to be okay.

One of the two EMTs asked, "Do you have family we can contact?"

"No, they live in Missouri. I have friends nearby who I'm living with...uh...let me think of their phone number." I had trouble concentrating, maybe the shock of being shot made me a little slow with the details.

I struggled to focused on his number. I'd called him a few times in the past, but not every day. Finally, I was able to give it to him.

"They're the only ones who even knew I was out on a walk," I said.

As we came to the hospital, I began to think about my predicament. My parents were a thousand miles away, so they were not going to be able to easily help me. Now I would have to rely on Kevin and, by default, Roger for help during my recovery. These thoughts filled my mind as the ambulance pulled up to the hospital and I was wheeled in to wait in the emergency room. I looked down at my bandaged leg and knew it was going to be a long night.

Chapter Two

I FADED IN and out of consciousness as I waited on a gurney in the crowded emergency room. My mind was a bit clouded, and I was still processing the fact that I had been shot. It seemed so unreal.

After an orderly pulled me into a small whitewashed examining room, I stared up at the fluorescent lights, feeling gross from the mixture of sweat and blood that was on my clothes and body.

"What happened here?" he asked.

"I was shot," I said flatly. Then he picked up a clipboard on the gurney and shook his head a few times as he read.

"I'm...I'm sorry this happened to you," he said. "It's a bit crazy here tonight, must be a full moon. Also, after the Fourth, kids and adults are still shooting off fireworks and injuring themselves."

Then he came closer to me and talked with a softer tone. "Try to relax some. I'll let the emergency doctor know of your condition and he should be here soon."

He left the room, and I waited alone again. I was very drowsy all of a sudden, probably from the blood loss.

Kevin came in, frazzled and notably without Roger. His hair was sticking out in places, he was out of breath, and his clothes were disheveled. His eyes bulged, staring at my leg in bandages.

"Oh my God," he said. "I...mean the police called us and said you were shot by a robber, but I wasn't expecting..." He shook his head in disbelief.

"I know...me neither."

"I explained to the EMTs that your family did not even live in this state and they told me I could come to the hospital and be with you. They let the emergency attendant know that it was okay for me to come back. I grabbed some clothes and headed right out," Kevin explained. "It's busy out there in the emergency room, I'm glad they gave the attendant a heads-up."

Kevin quieted for a moment, then asked, "How are you doing?"

"I was shot in the leg and I'm sore from that, but I feel...lucky to be alive. I...I did everything I could to survive. I walked on a shot leg for a block or two...not sure...maybe more...so I could find help.

"I went to get a Slurpee at that 7-Eleven at the turn-off and decided to cut through the shopping center... That's where the teens came at me with their guns pointed at me. I made it to the gas station on the corner for help. I was lucky that a guy at the gas station knew how to do a tourniquet, doing that probably saved my leg. Can you tell how badly injured I am?" I couldn't tell while lying down.

"It's hard...to tell." He gulped. "But I'm sure you'll come out of this fine." He gave an unconvincing smile.

I smiled back with the same uncertainty.

He grabbed my hand. "Roger is worn out from work and stayed behind at the townhouse. I'm so sorry this happened to you."

I stared up at Kevin. He was all that I had to hang onto at that moment.

A tall man in a white lab coat came in. I guessed he must be the emergency doctor since he didn't bother to introduce himself.

A moment later, an older woman in blue scrubs and dark-rimmed glasses came into the room, carrying a tray with needles.

"I have to give you a tetanus shot first," the doctor said.

He put on sterile gloves and picked up the largest needle, and just as I turned away, it stabbed into my shoulder muscle. *Damn that hurt!* Then he turned to the tray once more with another needle.

"This will numb some of the pain," the doctor said. I looked away once more as he stuck me yet again.

He pressed on my leg, and each time he came close to what must have been the wound, I cringed so badly that I almost came off the gurney.

The doctor stepped back. "It seems that the bullet is lodged in the back of your leg. Sorry but this will cause you pain. The bullet is in between layers in your tendon. You are going to feel it when we take it out, but it has to come out. I gave you some relief with the shot, but you're going to have bite down and bear it." His serious tone let me know that I had no choice in the matter.

I motioned Kevin closer. "Can you hold my hand?"

Kevin's face was pale, but he nodded.

The doctor reached for some forceps. "I am going to have to do some searching around in your tendon in order to pull it out. Wish me luck that this goes quickly. I will try to do this as painlessly as I can."

That didn't sound so good.

A doctor fishing around the back of my leg for a small piece of metal was a strange sensation. I knew it had to come out, but at that moment, I would have been happy if they left it in; the pain became tremendous. Every time the doctor hit a nerve, I clutched tighter to Kevin's hand. I tried to look away, but I also wanted to know what he was doing in my leg. Metal forceps scrounged around in my muscle tissue. I had to look away. It was too weird. Then he hit a nerve and I dug my fingers once more into Kevin's hand.

"Don't squirm around or it will cause more damage," the doctor said in frustration. I kept turning my attention to Kevin. I was trying as much as I could not to think about it. To stay still, but it was hard.

I squeezed Kevin's hand even tighter, and with my right hand, I clutched the bed railing to keep myself in position.

Weren't there stories about people swallowing scissors and having them in their abdomen for most of their lives? I was thinking of telling the doctor to just leave it there. Every movement of the forceps in my leg sent pain and sensations reverberating throughout my body.

I shouted "Fuck!" when I sensed the metal forceps grasping something in my leg, and then the doctor slowly pulled the forceps out.

"I have it."

A bullet was held in his forceps. He placed it in a plastic container. I stared at it until he said, "I have to give it to the police for evidence."

All this pain and blood from such a small piece of metal.

I never saw it again and still wonder if it disappeared, was destroyed, or is in some evidence room as a cold case of the Wilmington Police Department. Even though the bullet was in my leg for only a few hours, the sensation of it will always be with me.

It joined the rest of the evidence, which included my bloodied shorts, shirt, and socks. Blood was on everything I'd been wearing. I learned that once a person is bleeding, it's very hard to control the flow.

The doctor cleaned and sewed the wound closed, then bandaged it heavily. Once he was finished, a nurse came in and connected me to an IV. She had trouble finding a vein at first so she had to make a second try. I didn't say anything, wanting her to focus so she could get this right the second time.

After she left, two skinny orderlies took me to a hospital room. Kevin followed along.

I was groggy and he took my hand.

"I'm sorry, but I have to go. I wish I could stay and be here for you through the night, but I have to head back to Roger. His car is in the shop and I have to drive him to work in the morning."

I took a short breath and murmured, "It's okay. I'm completely drained. I'm going to sleep now and hope when I wake up that this is all some crazy nightmare from watching too many horror movies."

"Rest well." He gave me a small kiss on the cheek. I closed my eyes as his footsteps faded and the door clicked closed. I drifted off, hoping that what had happened wasn't real.

I AWOKE THE next day to find Kevin in the room with me. I was disoriented. An IV bag hung beside my bed. I was hot and sweaty under heavy cotton covers, and when I looked down at a heavily wrapped leg...well, this was not good.

It took a moment for me to orient myself. Oh, that's right, last night—my ill-fated attempt to get a Slurpee.

Kevin and I were silent for a moment. Neither of us knew what to say. I turned on the TV to create some distraction. It was a lot to take in when waking up in a hospital bed. This was also not a part of the welcome I had expected. First Roger, now the bullet. What would be next? I was without words. I didn't know what to say or how to express what I was feeling.

Kevin spoke first to break the tension.

"You really ground your fingers into my arm. I think you drew blood," he chuckled. I had to smile at that.

Then he became serious. "I'm sorry this happened. I wish now that I hadn't let you go out. I should have thought more about how safe the neighborhood is. I was fighting, you know, with Roger...and you know how that goes. I...should have said something. This shouldn't have happened."

He came to the bed, and for the longest time, he held me as we both cried.

Through the tears, I said, "You couldn't have known what was going to happen. You can't blame yourself for everything that went on last night, Kev."

"I know, but I hate seeing you this way."

"Me, too," I said. "But you know, I'm alive, at least...right?"

"Yeah. I couldn't imagine you being chased, shot at... It's crazy."

We both started crying some more. Then he hugged me tighter.

The door swung open and a young nurse came into the room to change my IV and check my vitals.

"I'm giving you a few pills that will help with the pain but probably make you sleepy," she said. "You need to rest to heal."

I swallowed them. In a while, my eyelids began to droop and became very relaxed.

"I hate to say this, but I...I've got to head out," Kevin said. "I have to go with Roger to visit his dad. He has to pick up a few things that he wanted to move into the townhouse, but if you want me to stay, I will."

"No. You go on. I'll probably fall asleep anyway with all the stuff they're pumping into me."

He kissed me on the forehead. "It's going to be okay."

I fell into a deep sleep. Yet in my subconscious, I couldn't find safety. A nightmare unfolded in which the robbers were chasing me and I kept running. Darkness enveloped me. No matter where I turned, they kept coming closer and closer. This time, they were able to shoot me point-blank, and I felt the bullet hit me hard in the chest. Instantly, I was unconscious.

I awoke sweating, scared, and alone. I turned on the television, seeking a safe refuge from those images in my mind. An old episode of *The Jetsons* came on., and I imagined being in the future among moving sidewalks with a blue sky above. I once more succumbed to sleep while Astro the dog talked in rough English with George Jetson.

FUTURISTIC DREAMS WERE interrupted by the ringing of the hospital telephone. I picked it up and struggled out a flimsy hello.

"This is Aaron. How is my little baboosa doing?"

I gritted my teeth and pursed my lips. That one word reminded me how much I hated him and the pet name that he sometimes used for me. How dare he do this now after he'd walked out on me? I held steady; I wouldn't let him get to me. Not now.

"I'm doing the best that I can, Aaron," I said as strongly as possible.

Silence for a moment. *Good.*

"I...I wish I could come out to Delaware to see you, but I'm working at an architectural firm in Denver and, with my new job, it's hard to find time off."

"Yeah, I can understand that."

"What happened?" he asked.

"I was robbed at gunpoint and they shot me in the leg. It was a hell of a night."

"I heard some of the details from Kevin. You don't have to go into it all. I can understand if it's hard to talk about."

"How did Kevin come across your number?"

"He found an address book in your suitcase with a list of numbers and saw my name at the top and thought I should call you," he said.

I clenched my teeth; I wished Kevin hadn't done that, but realized he was probably thinking that hearing from Aaron might provide me some solace.

Aaron, of course, had to talk about the end of our relationship.

"Hey, I know that the breakup was rough, but I still care about you, Todd. I would never wish this on anybody. I'm not a complete asshole. Yes, I left you, and yes, I moved in with Ron…"

That's right. Ron was the third piece in the unraveling of my life. I still had not dealt with that fact. I hadn't talk to him after our breakup. I had been friends with Ron since the start of college and never thought for a moment that we would end our friendship with him having a secret affair with my long-term boyfriend. I had walked away from it all without really thinking about it. God, now he was giving me more shit that I was in no frame of mind to handle.

"Aaron…this isn't helping."

"I'm sorry. I wish that this had all gone down differently, but it didn't. It wasn't working was all. But, fuck! I'm fucking this all up! What I really want to know is, are you all right?"

Am I all right? He'd left me for my close friend, I'd been shot in the back of the leg in a robbery attempt, and he wanted to know if I'm all right. *Asshole.*

No, I realized he wanted me to let him off the hook.

It should have been us in Kansas City together. That was the plan. After three years together, he had walked out on me and I was stuck picking up the pieces. And yes, I should have made better plans, but I had been hurt by his callousness, and here I was running away, into more problems. What was I supposed to say? Should I let him off the hook? I was raised Baptist. We might forgive, but there was no absolution.

"First, Aaron, thanks for calling. I think you were trying to do the right thing. But you hurt me, a lot. I knew at the time we had problems. But stupid me, I thought we could work through them, and now this has been thrown at me. I can't deal with you right now. I'm going to hang up. Don't call again. And also, please tell Ron not to call me either. For now, I will call you if I want to talk."

I banged the phone down, hard.

There was silence in the room again. I turned on the television once more and found a rerun of my favorite sci-fi show, *Quantum Leap*. That was what I wanted to do at the moment. Take a quantum leap backward to before all this happened, and leave Aaron before he walked out on me.

MY MOTHER'S PHONE call woke me up.

"Are you all right? Wait, I know you're not all right. How are you doing?" My mother. Even though she was a thousand miles away, the tone of her voice told me she was having trouble dealing with what had happened to me.

"I'm in a hospital room and recovering now. I guess Kevin was able to fill you in on what happened," I said.

"Yes, some of it. You were shot," she said, "but how?"

I explained what happened with a minimum of details. The bloody trail that I'd left was reduced to being shot in the leg by a robber and making my way to a nearby gas station to have the attendant call 911.

"Do you know how serious the injury is? Are you going to be able to walk again?"

Oh, God. Leave it to Mom to ask a question I can't answer. I tried to wiggle my toes, which of course, caused a serious bout of pain.

"Owww... ow... Ow..." I mumbled.

"Are you all right?" Her voice rose with concern.

I had to stop talking for a moment and hoped she wouldn't notice too much when I laid the phone down for a moment, stared up at the ceiling, and took short breaths over and over. Then I picked the phone back up and hoped for the best.

"Yes. In a little pain here on this end."

Luckily, she went on jabbering about my brothers and sister and how the whole family wished they could come out to see me. My youngest brother, Ben, was still in high school, my middle brother, Nathan, was away from home taking summer classes, and my sister, Karen, had recently had another baby.

"What has the doctor said?" she asked, changing the topic.

"I...I haven't gotten all the details from the doctor. I'm sure I'll be able to walk again, hopefully like I did before." I was comforting her, but deep down, I wasn't sure if my statement was true or not.

"I'm coming out to Wilmington," she said with determination.

My parents did not have a lot of money and the East Coast was a long way away. I decided that I could make it on my own until I was able to go back to see them.

"Mom, Kevin is here. He'll be able to help me along during recovery."

"Are you sure? Dad and I could be on the first plane to the East Coast and right there for you," she said, as if flying was something she did every day.

Along with the expense, I didn't want to deal with the fact they didn't know I was gay. *This is not exactly the best time for me to come out.* I was living with Kevin, and now Roger. They might ask some hard questions about my living arrangements.

"Mom, I will be back home as soon as I can. Don't worry. It will be all right." I tried to comfort her.

"Do me a favor. Keep me up-to-date on what the doctor says about your leg."

"I will, I promise, Mom."

Then I talked to my dad.

"How are you doing?"

"I've been better, but I'm doing okay now. In the hospital, recovering."

"If you need anything, let us know. We both love you and hope you get better soon."

The conversation with my dad was short and sweet, as it always was.

I talked briefly to my youngest brother, Ben.

"You shouldn't have run," he said. "I would have fought them."

I knew that would have probably landed him dead. But I let him rant, because that was how it was with him. It would be useless to get into a long discussion about what I should or shouldn't have done instead. I had been shot, luckily in the leg and not in the head.

Mom came back on the phone and apologized for what my brother had said. "Your brother would say that. Sorry about him. We're all a bit crazed here. I'm also sorry that Nathan isn't able to be on the call. But he told me he hoped your recovery is quick and painless."

They all said they loved me and wished they could come out to see me.

Right after I was off the phone with them, my sister called.

She cried as I talked with her.

"It's okay, Karen. I'm fine." I hoped the tone of my voice gave her comfort.

"You have a new niece, and I want you to be able to see her grow up," she sniffled.

"It's not fatal, Karen. I'll be up and walking and out to see you all soon. I promise."

We'd been close when we were growing up, but like the rest of the family, I had not come out to her yet and she was busy raising two kids.

The phone rang once more. Rick.

"Aaron is a shithead, but he knew enough to call me to tell me you're in the hospital after being... shot?"

I filled him in on all that had transpired.

"Wow. I can't believe this happened to you. Do you think you'll stay in Delaware?"

"I'm figuring that out right now. I only have one functioning leg."

"Man, that is rough. You get better soon, my Turtle," he said with concern. I smiled at the small measure of comfort I felt from his use of his pet name for me.

"I will, and when I make it back home, we'll definitely catch up."

He ended the call by saying, "I have a twelve-hour shift today. Another fun-filled workday for me. If you need anything, let me know."

"I will."

After the phone calls, I kept wondering if my leg really would ever be the same as before the shooting. I was more worried than before.

A nurse came in to check my vitals and to make sure I was comfortable.

"Do you know when the doctor will be in again so I can ask him about my condition," I asked.

"He should be in later this afternoon. Just try to rest and relax," she said.

I did the best I could, but I was feeling the pain again and asked for more painkillers. She returned with a couple pills, which I swallowed, and before long, I was drifting back to sleep.

WHEN I OPENED my eyes, there were flowers everywhere. They covered every surface. All different kinds. Red, blues, and pink ones surrounded me. I wondered for a moment if I had died and was watching my own funeral. *Great.*

Kevin's grinning face greeted me. "Workers from my office sent you flowers after hearing about what happened."

"That's nice." I didn't know what to say or how to feel about the gesture, other than to smile back at him. These people were strangers who gave this gift of kindness. It was definitely much better than thinking I had succumbed to some fatal complication from the shooting, very surreal.

Kevin carefully opened a white paper bag he held on his lap. "I brought you a treat. An East Coast specialty, Italian strawberry ice." He beamed.

I took the frozen concoction and scooped it down hungrily. I hadn't had anything sweet since I entered the hospital. It felt like a strange choice, considering that I had been shot following a late evening run to the 7-Eleven for a Slurpee. I decided to let it go and ate it without comment. He was trying.

He took the remnants of my Italian ice and placed it in the garbage, then walked around the bed, carefully got in with me, and held me tight. This was all I really wanted, the comfort, touch, and warmth of a close friend.

"Thanks for holding me. I know you have Roger, but this is what I needed."

"I know, and I can't pretend to have any idea about what you're going through," Kevin said.

He cuddled me close and kissed me on the forehead. I held him. I knew he had another in his life. Yet a part of me only wanted some kind of physical contact that wasn't painful.

That was the problem. I had gone through so much change: the breakup, moving East, this shooting, and then finding Kevin's love interest had moved into his house. I was so confused. I didn't want to leave the only person that I knew I could trust. If I turned away from him, who would I have to turn to? My parents, to whom I was still in the closet? Aaron, who had left me? It was a mess with no easy way out.

I held onto Kevin. It was all that was keeping me sane.

FINALLY, LATER THAT afternoon, a doctor came in. He wasn't the one from the emergency room. He seemed older. He was tall with short-cropped gray hair. He looked every bit what I imagined a doctor to be from years of watching *St. Elsewhere*. He nodded a greeting before reading the chart at the foot of the bed.

"So will I be able to walk again?" I asked.

He hesitated before saying anything.

I wanted an answer instantly. Those seconds of silence were long and arduous. *My stroll for a Slurpee would end with me in a wheelchair.* That thought scared me to my very core, and I felt anxiety shoot all the way down to my toes.

"You should be able to walk again," he said at last. "But how well will depend on your recovery. This injury will take some time and rehabilitation."

I took a deep breath. I was so relieved that I didn't care much about anything else he said.

"Will this be a complete recovery?" I didn't want any permanent damage that would change my life as a reminder from this horrible night.

"It should be, but I can't make promises on these things," he said. "You were lucky the bullet just went through muscle and not bone, or it would have been much worse. We want to observe you for another day to make sure that you have enough fluids in your system. You lost a lot of blood before the ambulance arrived."

He checked my vitals and made notes before going on his way.

I was relieved after he left. I wanted so badly to be up and out of bed, but I was stuck for the time being.

I had to ring for the nurse whenever I needed to go to the restroom, and that was a painful trip at best. I would have to figure out how this was going to work when I was back at Kevin's. I hated thinking how I needed help for a while. This was not how I had wanted my new life to begin in Delaware. I had yearned for this to be a fresh start after Aaron left me. Now, I was depending on Kevin, which is a lot to ask of a friend.

KEVIN AND ROGER visited me the next morning. Kevin carried a teddy bear with a crutch and a cast on one leg.

I took it in my arms, laughing and rolling my eyes. "Really, I'm not a kid, Kevin."

"I know, but I saw it in the gift shop and felt I had to bring you something to make you laugh," he explained.

The hospital was releasing me, and I would need to ride down in a wheelchair, which made me feel even more like an invalid.

The *St. Elsewhere* doctor came back in.

"I bring you crutches!" he said.

He seemed to have taken a page out of Kevin's book on how to make me feel less unnerved. He called my crutches my "new friends" and had Kevin demonstrate how to use them before handing them to me for some fumbling attempts at mobility. Fun times I was having.

The doctor waited for me to be seated before he said, "Recovery is expensive, but you will need to do all physical therapy."

Now this was something else I hadn't thought about: how to pay for it all. I only had a little money with me. Nothing that would even begin to pay for a three-day hospital stay, surgery, and everything else.

I cringed at the thought of all the expenses. I should have already been thinking about this, but instead, I'd focused on my leg and not money concerns.

The doctor gave me a moment to process everything, then said, "In Delaware, there is such a thing as victim's compensation assistance. I can have the nurse bring you the paperwork. You can fill it out and mail it in."

Sounds great. He left, and a few minutes later, the nurse came back again, a stack of papers in her hand.

"I hope they come through for you," she said.

I thanked her, figuring I could forgive her for all the shots and IV changes.

After taking two pills out of the bottle and handing them to me with a small cup of water, she instructed me to take them every four hours.

I swallowed, hoping it would do the trick.

The doctor and nurse were gone. I was now in the care of Kevin and Roger.

Roger was doing his best not to look at me. I assumed that this responsibility they had inherited was not to his liking. He gathered up all of the flowers that Kevin's friends and coworkers had sent to take to their car. He bunched them all together tightly in the box. I kept the teddy bear in my arms. I didn't want him touching it.

"So you're ready?" Kevin asked.

"Yeah, I guess." I hoped I sounded convincing, because I wasn't feeling it.

"You guess?" He tickled me a little, just so I would laugh. At least my mind was off the pain for a moment.

Roger came back somewhat perturbed. "We need to head to the house before traffic becomes a bitch. Is he ready?" he asked Kevin, ignoring the fact that I was in the room and perfectly capable of answering. Just to show his bitchiness about the situation.

Kevin helped me into a wheelchair. I cringed in pain. Before I left the room, I had him give me another glass of water and painkiller. *Prescribed amount be damned.* One couldn't possibly make it worse, or they were going to have to chop my leg off to make the pain stop.

We headed to the car that Roger had pulled around to the front. I hobbled in with the help of an orderly, and we were off. But I was scared as hell. Strangely enough, part of me didn't want to go. After the shooting, I had this sense of fear, like the minute I went back to the townhouse the kids who had tried to rob me would hunt me down and shoot me again. A crazy thought, but it was there in the back of my mind.

I was now on high alert. If I went outside of the townhouse at night with them, I would look around making sure there was no one in the shadows with a loaded gun. Any loud noise I heard in the distance could be a shooter. A loud conversation while you're at the mall could lead to a deadly confrontation that you would need to duck and cover. I was now hyperaware of my surroundings, twenty-four seven. It was mentally exhausting. I didn't say anything about it to them, of course, since I didn't want to appear insane.

IN HINDSIGHT, THIS was probably PTSD (Post-Traumatic Stress Syndrome) caused by the shooting, but in 1997, this was not talked about except for people who had been in a war situation. At least that was what I was aware of back then.

I'd grown up stubbornly thinking that I could handle anything on my own. I had come out to Delaware, clear across the country, alone. Yet, I was not prepared for a traumatic event or the repercussions that it caused to my psyche afterward. This is why I wrote this book so others know that if they are ever shot at and survive, they should get help immediately. Don't fight it. I didn't know this at the time and that was why I struggled so much over the next few months.

SINCE I HAD been shot in the leg. I couldn't walk for a few months after the shooting. I had to make sure I completely recuperated. No matter how I felt mentally, I wasn't going to let myself down physically. I didn't want to be in a wheelchair or limping with a cane. I was going to be upright, standing tall. It took all my effort just to make this possible. I not only had to face mental anguish I also had to survive the pain of doing physical therapy in order walk again. It was a lot to take on and I would never wish this upon anyone. These were the struggles I was now facing.

Chapter Three

THE FIRST NIGHT back at the townhouse, I slept on the couch. This was the only place that worked for me, since I couldn't easily manage the stairs using the crutches.

I had my left leg elevated with pillows, which was uncomfortable, but it was doctor's orders to aid healing. The pain had intensified, possibly due to the added activity, and I was having frequent muscles spasms. I wanted to saw my leg off in order to make the mind-numbing discomfort go away. I took a couple of extra painkillers to help me finally fall asleep.

I longed for the comfort of dreams, but my subconscious was the place of nightmares.

I was alone in a darkened alleyway. I could sense someone behind me, but I didn't dare turn around. In my fear, I imagined guns pointing at my head and shadowy figures looming large from the impenetrable blackness.

So I ran.

I tripped over a cement embankment, bashing my head on the hard concrete. A haze of red veiled my sight for a moment as blood trickled down from my forehead.

I stumbled along. They should have been on top of me by now. Hard pounding footsteps were all around me in every direction. This time, I couldn't find a place to go, only darkness without any stars.

Lights shone in the distance. I ran toward them. I kept tripping over my feet, and my vision blurred from sweat and mounting blood on my brow.

Then what sounded like a thunderclap sounded and white-hot pain pierced my leg. More blood. Everything was so red.

I fell hard and couldn't get back up this time. I dragged my limp body forward with my arms. They had to be coming for me.

When I looked behind me, the shadowy figures moved all around me. Were they running away or coming to finish the job? I couldn't tell.

Please, God, make them stop.

Inch by inch, I pulled myself forward with only my arms, my body scraping against the hot summer cement.

I couldn't stand. I pushed ahead until I dropped from exhaustion, my body limp, like a ragdoll left on the ground. Then the shadows were on top of me, above my head. The barrel of a gun pushed into my face. I was going to die...

I awoke gasping and shaking and soaked in sweat. I needed to clear my mind, so I turned on the TV and came across an old episode of *I Love Lucy*. An episode where she makes this huge loaf of bread. I watched, feeling the remaining tension ease.

Footsteps sounded behind me, and for a moment, a wave of anxiety swamped me, only to realize that Kevin had come to check on me.

He sat next to me and held my hand. "Hey, how are you doing?" He seemed to sense that I was off.

"I had a nightmare. You know, about that night. I needed to take my mind off it so I thought I would watch some Lucy. I'm sorry if I woke you."

"I thought I heard you call out and decided I would check on you." A worried look crossed Kevin's face. "Is there anything I can do to help?"

"No, unless you have some kind of magical spell that will take the soreness away."

"I wish I did." He chuckled as he touched my hair.

I looked up at him. "Kev, I really feel horrible because the only thing I'm capable of accomplishing right now is lying on your couch, hoping that the blinding pain eventually goes away. How are Roger and you dealing with my sudden incapacity?"

"Do you remember the first time we met?" Kevin asked.

"In math class," I said. "I was having a hard time of it."

"I told you I could help, right?"

"Yes, and I wouldn't have passed without you; either she wasn't a good teacher or I was really, really bad at math."

Kevin snickered. "Maybe both. Well, I'm here for you again, Todd. Lie back down. I can stay awhile."

I laid my head on his lap, and he stroked my hair. It was better than all the painkillers in the world.

After a time, I fell asleep, only to wake briefly as Kevin gently rearranged me before returning to his room. As sleep once again took hold, he pressed a kiss to my forehead.

This time, I dreamed of him.

We were in high school this time and practicing kissing each other since we wanted to learn how to do it. This involved lots of tongue and laughing and tickling, of course. We stopped because we didn't want anyone to think that we were gay, including ourselves.

MY FIRST THOUGHT when I woke was that I really needed to pee. I grabbed my crutches, and as I was about to stand, one skidded away and I fell. A shot of pain went through my leg as I landed hard on the floor.

"Fuck!" I shouted.

Kevin came rushing down the stairs and found me lying on the floor, trying to get up.

"I need to pee and...can you help?"

"Sure, as long as I don't have to hold it and aim it for you," he said, with a chuckle.

I rolled my eyes at him in response. This took the edge off my humiliation although it came rushing back as he half carried me to the bathroom. This was a bit humbling for me.

My butt cheeks were facing him and I was having trouble peeing. Finally, I thought about water and concentrated and it began to flow. I hated for him to be there waiting on me to finish peeing. God. What had I gotten myself into?

"Are you going to be all right if we leave you alone at home?" he asked after settling me back on the couch.

I could tell he was hesitant to leave me after what had just happened, but I didn't want to become a burden. I had to find strength within myself.

"I'm still working out how to use the crutches properly, but I don't want you to miss work. I can't expect you to watch over me every waking hour of the day. If I have to, I'll crawl to the bathroom. I can do this, I promise."

Kevin continued with his concerns. "It's just that I feel like shit for leaving you here. Tell me again that you're going to be fine today, please? It's stupid, I know, but if I come home and you're lying on the floor, I'm going to feel like crap."

"I'll be—"

Before I could finish my sentence, Roger came in the living room from the kitchen.

"What's going on in here?" he asked.

"He fell and I helped him to the bathroom," Kevin said.

He looked at both of us, unconvinced that he was hearing all of the details. "Breakfast is ready. Will you be joining us?" he asked in a slightly condescending tone.

"I'm good, thanks."

"You need to eat, Todd. I'll bring you some breakfast." Moments later, Kevin came back into the living room with eggs, bacon, and a slice of toast on a plate. "I'm going back to eat with Roger and after that we are heading off to work. Remember, just give me a ring if you need anything."

"I think I can do this if you leave a sandwich in the fridge for me," I said. "I just need to practice around the living room with the crutches."

"I'm only a phone call away, understand?" He kept staring at me like I was a child. I felt like shit about it all.

After Roger left for the day, Kevin gave me a quick kiss on the forehead and looked into my eyes. "Just a phone call away," he said firmly. He seemed to want confirmation that I wasn't going to fall again.

I nodded, shooing him out of the living room. With a wag of his finger and a stern look on his face, he walked out. *This must be as hard for him as it is for me, although he doesn't have the actual wound to show.*

I practiced with the crutches. I stood and sat from the couch and wobbled around the living room. *Okay, this isn't so bad. My arms are going to be buff after lifting my bodyweight daily.* I grinned.

I made it to the chair by Kevin's computer desk and pulled out the want ads and victim's compensation assistance paperwork. At least the shooting hadn't affected my ability to type. Those skills were what I needed most.

I filled out the victim's compensation paperwork first, answering questions about how serious the injury was and if it was currently affecting me. As I looked down at my heavily bandaged leg, this all seemed easy to answer as true to fact. After spending the morning on paperwork, I found stamps and envelopes and put it together for Kevin to mail out. It would be an anxious wait for that to come through. If not, I would have to borrow money from my parents.

That afternoon, I began what would become a daily routine for me. I worked an entire assembly line of typing cover letters and resumes, then licking and sealing envelopes. This was my occupation during my first week home from the hospital: job-seeker.

I had bouts of discomfort but didn't let that stop me. Sending out resumes was the only thing I could do at the moment. At least I was accomplishing something. I only hoped that they didn't respond too soon, because I would have to be using crutches for a while.

THERE WERE ALSO rules for recovery I had to follow. Once a day, Kevin helped me clean the wounds. He undid the bandages meticulously. We learned this had to be done carefully after the first time he had done it and I shouted "Fuck, Fuck Fuck!" while he unraveled it. Unwrapping it too fast would cause me to have the sensation of needles pressing into my leg. Once the bandages were off, he would dab the wounds with alcohol. Even with light touches, it felt like someone was taking a serrated knife across my leg. Every morning, I took a deep breath to prepare myself for wound care.

I continued to have to elevate the leg as I slept to keep proper blood flow, which was not easy to do on the couch. I couldn't spend a whole day sitting, either.

Kevin and Roger were mostly gone while I remained home alone. They had lives: work, social engagements, or errands. Roger made dinner in the evening and Kevin brought me a plate.

Every night, they seemed to have an outing they had to attend. I wasn't sure if Roger was intentionally finding something to keep Kevin busy so he'd be separated from me, but Kevin seemed to want to please Roger so away they would go.

I found solace from the TV, constantly searching for old comedies so I could escape from the pain and the dark world outside the window.

TWO WEEKS AFTER the shooting, Kevin took me to see the doctor. In that time, I'd become pretty adept with the crutches. I would go thumping with them back and forth across the house.

I wondered if the doctor would give me the okay to use the stairs with them. I desperately wanted to move on with that phase of my recovery so I could sleep on a bed with fluffy pillows and soft covers and not on uncomfortable couch cushions.

The orthopedist, Dr. James Whitaker, was in his late-fifties, wearing a standard issue white coat that seemed to be the fashion for all doctors. I hadn't been in a doctor's office in years. I worked to stay in top physical form and had been until someone thought I needed a hole in my leg.

"So what happened exactly?" he asked me. "The hospital sent me some information on you, but I need a few more details."

"In a quick synopsis, a few weeks ago, two men tried to rob me. I was shot right here in the leg." I pointed to my thick web of bandages for emphasis. Showing him was easier than going through the whole bloody and terrifying story.

He gave a nod and said, "How are you doing now?"

"I have the pain pills that were given to me by a doctor at the hospital. Actually, I don't remember him very much. You would have to ask Kevin. I was a bit out of it. It still hurts like hell when it acts up, and that's when I take an extra one."

"Do you need more painkillers?" Doctor Whitaker asked.

"That would be great." The leg wasn't bothering me at the moment, but flare-ups didn't come with any logic.

"Now, you will have to be weaned off them. We don't want you to become an addict." He stared down at me.

"Sure," I said.

Great. Another thing to worry about. I could become addicted to painkillers. I had a hard time imagining myself as an addict. Did he think this was self-inflicted? Like I had wanted to be shot in the leg in order to obtain painkillers. All I wanted was some escape from the burning and throbbing my leg would give me at any point of the day or night, and he was giving me a lecture. Didn't I deserve some respite from it?

"Here's the prescription for the pills. If it becomes worse, you can take more, but be aware of how many you take," he said.

"I understand." Yet I felt resentful, like I was being judged unfairly. What I really came for was to learn how I was recovering.

He took me through a number of exercises, pointed my leg this way and that. Each time he touched it and checked my reflexes, I grimaced and told him to stop. It was torture.

He scribbled on a clipboard, making notes of all of his findings.

I asked, "Do you think I can climb stairs yet?"

He looked up. "Sorry, son. Not yet."

Dammit! I wasn't his son and his calling me that didn't endear him to me. I guess my couch potato days would need to continue.

The doctor added, "You'll have to come back every few weeks for follow-ups, and I will let you know what you will be able to do as the wound heals."

"Thanks." I was unhappy with the news, and yet what could I do about it? Nothing.

I returning to the waiting room and told Kevin, "It sucks, but I won't be able to go up the stairs. I need more time on the couch for recovery. This is a longer process than we first thought."

We headed to the car with only the pounding of the crutches on the ground to break the silence. We both knew that my current condition was difficult for the household. They wanted to enjoy the TV and couch in their living room, and here I was in the middle of things. I knew I was pushing Kevin and Roger to the limit. I felt awful.

Kevin finally broke the silence as we neared the townhouse. "I'll make him understand. He can't blame you. We don't have much choice in the matter. Don't you worry about it."

We pulled into the driveway. Kevin tried to smile, but I could feel his uncertainty in how he looked away and stared for a moment at the front door. He would have to go first and hold the door for me so I could return to my roost on the couch.

I was causing them problems, and all I could do was take a deep breath and hope my recovery would go quicker.

KEVIN THOUGHT IT would be good for me to meet some of his friends and enjoy a moment of fun by having a barbecue. The food would include all the staples: hamburgers, hotdogs, pies, and cake. Roger would tend to the grill. They would have a cooler filled with bottled beer and soda and a table outside for liquor and wine. Kevin borrowed lawn chairs from neighbors and friends. I could already picture myself sitting down outside with a cold beer in hand talking to a handsome stranger, but then I looked down at my leg and thought I survived a bullet. That has to seem cool, right?

Most of all, the gesture was sweet and one of the reasons why Kevin remained a close friend even if we had been living a thousand miles apart. The days went by slowly as the party date came closer. I spent all of my time on job searching and walking in and out of the house to the backyard with crutches. I wanted to be able to stand part of the time at the party.

Finally, the day came and his friends surrounded me. They all told me how sorry they were about this happening. Kevin handed them a black Sharpie, and they signed a giant Get Well card one by one. I didn't really know any of them, but at least strangers cared.

I drank beer after beer. Kevin told me to stay off the pain medication if I wanted to drink, which I agreed would be for the best. I did worry about medicating through alcohol, which was probably not the best trade-off.

"How are you doing, Todd?" Roger asked as he flipped a burger. Roger manned the grill like a pro; his shirt and face were covered with sweat from the heat of the summer day. Sweltering while he was grilling was the first genuinely nice thing he had done for me.

"As best as I can be." I tried not to look at him too closely. I hated that I was in this situation and had no power in making it better.

"We all hope you recover soon," Roger said.

I tried to see the world from Roger's perspective: I had come into their life in rather quick fashion and inhabited the couch for a month. That would be hard for anyone to accept, along with the fact Kevin and I had known each other so long.

A blond guy sat next to me. He was muscular and about my height.

"I assume you don't feel the best about Delaware," he said.

"A bullet is not the best welcome to a new town," I said.

"No, a bullet is not. I'm Don, by the way. Kevin has talked more about you than probably anyone else since I've known him."

"He should. We've known each other forever," I said.

Don's eyes were like the clear blue of a midwinter sky. He was wearing well-matched lime-green shorts with a laurel-green T-shirt. His arms were muscular, his face a sun-touched shade of brown, and I could see a hint of chest hair along his neckline.

I hoped that he was flirting with me.

"Do you know where they put the magic marker?" Don asked with a husky deep tone.

I handed it to him. Our hands touched. "I'm going to sign this with my phone number, so if you start to feel better, you can give me a call," Don said. "I actually have to head out early. I'm an artist and have a gallery showing tonight."

I imagined him wearing a tight white T-shirt with paint specks everywhere. I bit my lip.

Yet, my dreamy thoughts were quickly overrun by reality. He was leaving now.

He came up and gave me a bear hug. I felt his unshaven facial hair touch mine. Even if he was only being nice, physical touch from this beefcake made me a bit giddy.

I watched as he left the house, even his backside was perfect with a well-rounded butt. I took an ice-cold beer out of the cooler and rubbed it across my face as a relief from the heat.

I sat back and looked at the phone number. I would definitely have to give him a call. Sure, this was not a date, but at least someone had shown an interest in me.

After everyone headed out, I talked to Kevin about Don.

"He is cute, and those blue eyes," Kevin said as he gathered up dishes. I felt bad that I couldn't help with the cleanup for a party held for me.

I kept looking over the card and the well wishes written on it, filled with names but only one phone number. "What do you know about him?"

"I don't want you to get your hopes up. He is a bit of a flirt and he's had plenty of men after him. What I will say is that he is a nice guy. Just don't fall for him." Kevin gave me a serious look.

"I won't." But I already wanted to dial that number; maybe I would give him a call when I was better.

KEVIN CAME HOME early from work for the next appointment to the orthopedist since I couldn't drive with only one fully functioning leg and wasn't sure I could manage a bus.

I gazed longingly at the stairs. Hard to believe I could miss walking up and down stairs. I was hoping I would be allowed to try them. Doctor Whitaker constantly warned me not to overdo it and, if I had pain, to stop and take a break.

While waiting for the appointment, I spent most of the morning sending out more cover letters and resumes. I hoped I would hear a response or an interview soon. Each day I had a little less savings for a car and without a job I had no source of income.

After Kevin pulled in the driveway, I grabbed the crutches from beside the couch and was standing up with them when he came into the townhouse. I was even able find my way into the car without too much help. I was trying to convince myself of how well I was doing.

The waiting room was filled with the usual magazines and patients with casts and an assortment of bandages on their limbs. I wondered what their stories might be: someone else like me who had been shot, or was I the only one? It occupied my mind until my turn came.

"So how are you doing with the leg?" Doctor Whitaker asked.

I told him the usual. "I'm still walking around with crutches."

He scanned my leg for signs of improvement, made me wiggle my toes, and tested my reactions, touching around the wound. I wasn't sure what he was looking for. He made me stand up on the leg briefly, which of course caused me some pain.

The doctor began to unravel the bandages. He did it with care, probably knowing that I would have some discomfort. He slowly turned the leg around to the back where the bullet had entered. I gazed at the wound. This one was smaller and did not seem as red or caked in pus as the other. The stitched incision on the front still looked like a nasty bloody mess.

"You need to take better care in keeping the front wound clean. I know it probably hurts, but this is important," he warned.

Doctor Whitaker stepped back for a moment gazing at both legs together, "Your left leg is smaller than the right. That happens while you're not using it. Once you heal, I'll have you do physical therapy so you can go back to using it."

He tested my reflexes. "How does this feel?"

I said *ouch* each time as he checked the leg's tenderness.

"That might have hurt, but it looks like your leg is healing," he said.

"That sounds great. So can I go out of the house and upstairs?" I asked, hopeful.

"Not until the stitches have been taken out and few days of healing is allowed," he said. "You're going to have to keep bandages over the wound, keep an eye on the stitches, and be careful, most of all."

The examination ended with Doctor Whitaker taking off his gloves and saying, "You will need to see me in a few weeks to take the stitches out."

After we went back into the car, my leg stung all over with the support of the stronger bandages gone. Luckily, it was a short drive from the doctor's office, because I had been optimistic and left the pain pills at home.

I hobbled in, and Kevin handed me the pills and a glass of water. I sat down and turned on a rerun of *I Love Lucy*, the episode in which Lucy works at a chocolate factory with Ethel.

I fell asleep and dreamed that Kevin and I were working at the factory. We worked feverishly to keep up with the conveyor belt to package the chocolates. We couldn't keep up and began eating the chocolates and throwing them at each other and laughing.

I awoke in the middle of the night, still laughing. I hadn't felt that comforted by a dream in a long time. Everything up to the dream had been a nightmare. I went back to sleep, returning to the world of black-and-white and not the modern world of full-color troubles.

THIS TIME THE visit to the doctor involved the stitches being taken out.

We waited briefly before being shown back.

Doctor Whitaker undid the bandages on the leg and touched and prodded my leg, which caused some stinging but not as bad as before.

"It is healing nicely now, I'll take out the stitches and then a few days later you can start to do the stairs. How's that sound?" he asked.

I nodded.

The stitches coming out did not hurt too bad. A few times there was a piercing shot of pain as he wrestled them off.

As he wrapped it back up, he cautioned, "Take good care of the wound; as your body adjusts you might feel some bouts of pain."

I left knowing that now I could start to contemplate going more places.

Doctor Whitaker had said to expect some discomfort the first few days, and he was right.

On the first night, I lay on the couch in a fetal position and wallowed. The *discomfort* wasn't easing, even with extra pills.

The next night, I awoke in even more pain. Of course, the pills were by the chair near the television. I should have remembered to have Kevin put them by the couch.

I thought I could limp over without the crutches. But I slipped and landed with a crash, managing to scrape the wound on the carpet causing blood to spurt out of it.

"Fuck!"

"What happened?" Kevin cried as he rushed into the room.

"I fell."

Blood ran down my leg, and he rushed to grab some bandages and rubbing alcohol. His touch was tender as he dabbed the wound to clear away some of the blood before he rewrapped it up.

"All cleaned up," he said, smiling.

I was relieved.

"Does it hurt?" Kevin asked.

I didn't want him to worry, but I had to be honest since the leg felt like someone was stabbing it with a small knife. This would keep me up all night.

I answered him quietly, trying not to sound dramatic. "Yeah, do you mind grabbing the pills for me?"

Kevin came back with them and a small glass of water, then helped me onto the couch.

I felt guilty, as always. This was such a slow and tortuous process for both of us. I kept having setbacks, and he watched over me. I felt awful, and it was a struggle to stay optimistic.

And as if Kevin read my mind, he said, "It will get better, Todd. Your physical therapy starts soon. After you complete all of your treatment, you will walk like you did before the shooting."

"Yeah, you're right."

Once he had made sure I was comfortable, he headed back to bed, upstairs where I couldn't go.

I lay on the couch, staring at the ceiling. I wondered if walking normally was going to be possible.

AFTER A FEW torturous days with the wound, the pain finally subsided so I decided that it was time for me to move onto the next challenge. I was going to try the stairs.

Kevin stood at the top. "Are you ready?"

I stared up at him. Time to face my first roadblock on the way to recovery. If I could do this, I could once again have a bed of my own.

"Here I come." Looking up, I imagined each step I took feeling solid beneath my feet. Advancing one by one without a tumble or all-encompassing pain.

I didn't dare look behind me. I was going to do this.

"You're halfway," Kevin said.

"Thanks." Only a few more to go. Luckily, the crutches had improved my arm strength.

I finally made it. Kevin caught me in his arms and high-fived me, face-to-face and smiling together at the accomplishment.

I went back down the stairs more easily, since I knew I could do this. It felt like I was on the way to normalcy.

This was the first time since the shooting that I'd had some freedom in my life. After all this time being dependent on others, I was able to make it on my own to my bedroom.

While they were at work the next day, I put on my tennis shoes and began practicing with the crutches around the inside of the townhouse. I was making progress. Yet, I was still afraid of pushing too hard and falling, and had some fear of leaving the house alone, since they hadn't caught the kids who had shot me.

After a few days and seeing how well I was doing, Kevin decided to take a long lunch with me to talk. We went to a small deli.

"Life seems to be heading in the right direction for you now," he said.

"Yes, seems that way," I said, wondering where this conversation was going.

"How are you feeling?" he asked.

"Better, but it still feels like a bad movie. I can't believe all this has happened to me."

"Yeah, I know," he said. "How's the job search going?"

"I've sent resumes out, but nothing yet. Although, right now, it's for the best. I haven't been able to go very far with how much I've had to endure with the leg," I said.

"I know." He reached out and held my hand tight under the table. He must have realized that someone across the way was staring at us, since he let go. It felt nice to have him comforting me that way.

The sandwiches we had ordered showed up, and we both ate in silence.

"How does it feel to be out of the house?" he asked as he finished the last bit of sandwich.

"I haven't seen this much sun in ages," I said.

"It's a nice day." He turned more serious. "Have you heard back from victim's compensation? Bills for your care have been coming in, but I assume that they will take care of that."

"I haven't yet, but I can't imagine it being a problem, since there's plenty of evidence of what happened."

We finished our sandwiches and headed back to the townhouse. I was still uncomfortable about leaving their place on my own. With him, I was fine, but eventually I would have to leave their place without them—the next step to recovery, both mentally and physically.

I FINALLY MANAGED to set up a time to follow up with the police about the possible suspects. I had put it off, hoping I would remember more.

"Do you want me to stay?" Kevin asked as he put on his tie for work.

"No. Maybe it would be best if I worked alone with the officer and concentrated on what they looked like."

"Okay. But if you want me to come back, give me a call. I can arrange my schedule to do it," Kevin added.

Roger seemed a bit annoyed by the statement. He was heading off for work at the same time, and I was pretty sure his sympathy had reached his limit. Kevin gave him a glance that I read as "Don't push it."

The doorbell rang not long after they left for work. The policeman had broad shoulders, looking very official with his dark sunglasses on. "I'm Officer Scott Seagle. I'm going to ask you some questions about what happened that night."

"Sure... no problem." I hoped I didn't seem too nervous. We sat down at the kitchen table. I put my crutches to the side and he took out a small notebook and a pen then looked up at me.

"Can you describe your attackers in detail?"

"They had dark skin, as far I could tell. You know, high-school age...I think. One was over six feet tall and the other a little taller than me, probably five-foot something. I'm just basing this from the few seconds that I saw them. To be honest, I only had a moment to look at them."

He jotted down what I said, then opened a small briefcase that I hadn't noticed and took out a stack of photos wrapped with a rubber band.

"I would like you to look through these for possible identification." I went through them several times. I stopped on five photos I thought looked most like my attackers. I wanted to be sure, but I wasn't.

"That night is such a blur. Their faces in shadows...the gleam of metal guns...pointed at me. It is so hard to remember what they looked like in great detail," I confided.

"Just do your best as you look over the ones you put aside."

I picked up two photos for closer inspection.

"I think it might be these two, but it's really hard to tell," I said with honest conviction. "What happens next?"

"We will bring them in for questioning, if we find them. If their story doesn't seem to pan out, we will go further." He separated the photos that I had pointed out from the others, then closed his briefcase. I thanked him for coming as he left.

I wasn't holding out any expectations that they would be caught. I sat at the window as he went to his cruiser. *This always seems to work out better in police shows than in real life.*

Chapter Four

A MONTH AND a half after the shooting and I was on my way to my first physical therapy session. I was becoming more confident at using my crutches, and as a result, I had decided to take the bus to my appointment. It was difficult to face my fear of the outside world, but I had to do this if I wanted to move on with my life and attain my goal of walking without crutches again.

I made my way using the crutches the two blocks to the bus stop. The bright sunshine seeped into my skin, giving me a sense of lightness and comfort.

The bus came to a halt near the hospital. I grabbed my crutches, stood up, and managed my way down the bus steps and into the building, then through a maze of winding hallways and up an elevator to the rehabilitation center on the fourth floor. I was more than a little winded when I showed up.

Monikah Sheridan, a physical therapist, checked me in. She had short dark hair and smile on her face, which provided me comfort.

I introduced myself and told her about what happened to me.

"Hi, I'm Todd. I'm here because I was shot in the leg in a robbery attempt. That's everything in a nutshell."

I hoped that didn't weird her out since I said it so matter-of-factly.

"I'm sorry to hear that, Todd." She didn't seem stunned, but I realized I was probably not the first person in rehab that had been shot.

I pointed out the bullet wound and the incision where they took the bullet out. "It's still sore."

She explained. "My job is to get you back to walking. It is time to give your muscles a workout. I promise not to overdo it, but no pain, no gain."

We headed for a balance beam with the side rails. She stood at one end. Her eyes affixed on me. She guided me forward, one step after another. The sensation of sharp needles shot through my leg with each movement, but I was determined.

"Keep it up. Don't stop. Your muscles need to get used to working again," she said.

I moved slowly, but I was doing it. When I slipped, I stopped moving, waiting for her to help me out. She didn't.

"Come on, Todd, back up. You can do it. I know you can."

I looked her straight in the eyes and felt her encouragement. This was not going to be easy. But I had to do it if I didn't want to spend the rest of my life with a cane or a walker or even a wheelchair. None of these options gave me a future I wanted. I got myself back up and made it all the way to the end.

"Now turn around and do it again," she said.

Easy for her to say, harder for me to do. But I kept going. I didn't want to stop. I wanted my mobility back to the way it had been before; I wasn't going to let two kids with guns take away my ability to walk.

At the end of the session, I was breathing heavy and sweating. Both my legs were sore since my right leg overcompensated when it came to exercising the left one. This had been the toughest workout I'd had since the shooting.

"If you need some time to wind down, don't worry. You did well today," Monikah said. "Next time we meet, you will do even better. Now, here are some exercises to work on at home."

"Homework, great."

She laughed. "If you want to walk without the crutches, you have to strengthen those leg muscles." She handed me a sheet of paper filled with black-and-white images of leg muscles going in a multitude of directions.

Sure, no problem. I sat for a while as others worked out. Everyone was cringing; I felt better knowing I wasn't the only one. Monikah went back to the check-in station, and when a woman on crutches came in, they headed to the balance beam.

I didn't want to watch her struggle. I also needed to be on my way. The bus would arrive in about ten minutes. At least public transportation was available to take me from place to place.

I took a final look back as the lady stumbled a little. I was feeling for her at the moment, and not sorry for myself.

Since my legs ached from the workout, I slowly went up the steps onto the bus and sat alone to head back to the townhouse. I was making progress. I was really doing it, making my way around the world again on my own two feet. Well, two feet and a pair of crutches.

MY FIRST JOB interview came three months after the shooting. I was able to move around for longer periods with the crutches, and I was well on my way to recovery.

The job was a reporter position at a small newspaper, but not near the townhouse. I had to take two buses to find my way to it and was exhausted by the time I arrived. I was committed, though. Monikah kept telling me I was becoming stronger through the physical therapy.

I crutched up to the door and laughed to myself. Of course, there were stairs. What? Was I expecting this to be easy? I hobbled up and did the best I could with the crutches, down a hallway filled with framed copies of the newspaper.

The managing editor was a slightly overweight man with gray hair and glasses. Inevitably, the first question was about the crutches, as he looked over my resume.

"I won't be walking this way much longer. I...I took a fall." I didn't want to talk about the shooting. I didn't have the strength to go into all the bloody details.

He looked over the resume but seemed put off by my injury. "Your only experience was working on the college newspaper?"

I wasn't going to let him stop me with the "first job concern." I showed him my portfolio, which included many news clips of stories I had written.

He went through my newspaper clippings as I hoped for a hint of his opinion.

He kept staring at my crutches, which was frustrating me, since I couldn't deny the condition I was in.

The interview ended by him saying, "I'll contact you if I need more information. We do have other candidates to interview."

Somehow, I knew he wouldn't be calling.

This became the routine as I looked for jobs. I didn't have a car and couldn't obtain one without a job. My savings was also depleting. Most of all, the crutches were always held against me. This was the first time I saw how rough life could be for those who might be considered handicapped.

Yet I stayed the course. I knew I could do this. I had to keep going and not let it get me down.

But the meagerness of my bank account told me I would not last much longer in Delaware.

I needed something positive. I hadn't spoken with Don since the party. I knew it had been awhile, but I wanted someone to talk to that was outside the Roger-and-Kevin world.

I called and, when he answered, said, "Hi. This is Todd. I was wondering if you wanted to maybe go out on Friday this week." It was only Wednesday, which I thought was enough advance warning, but I could sense hesitation.

"Sorry, but I've got plans," Don said.

"Oh, all right. How about Saturday?"

"Uh...the same thing, sorry."

I realized how desperate I sounded, so I ended the conversation quickly. "Let's try some other time."

"Sure." But I knew he was only being nice and went back to looking through the paper at help wanted ads.

Soon Kevin came home by himself. "Roger is going out of town tonight."

I told him about Don. "I must have sounded crazy and desperate on the phone."

Kevin took it all in and made a suggestion. "Would you want to go out?"

This perked me up a bit. At least I could have a night away from all my worries.

He drove to one of the few bars in town, which included going up a flight of stairs, of course. I'd never noticed how many places had stairs until I had crutches.

I took in the layout. Two guys were on the dance floor, and everyone else was scattered about. I bought a beer while Kevin talked with someone he knew from work.

I looked away from the dance floor as Don came out of the bathroom with another guy.

This was fine with me. It's not like we were dating. He'd flirted with me a bit at the party. That was all.

I decided not to think about it and focus on talking with Kevin. I laughed and enjoyed myself for a while, but eventually, I broached a serious subject. "I'm running low on money. I'm not sure what I'm going to do. Should I head back to my parents until I am on my feet again?"

"It is up to you. You've been through a lot. They still don't know you're gay, right?"

"No, they don't."

"This would probably not be the time to come out to them," he said.

"I've managed to keep it a secret for this long. I can probably do it a bit longer if I went back home," I said, and gulped down my beer.

Kevin looked up for a moment, then said, "You can borrow money from me for a little while until you find a job."

"Let me think about it. All of this isn't going so well." I looked out on the floor where Don danced with the other guy.

"I know. I wish I could make it all better for you."

A few drinks later, I was looking at gay newspapers put out at the front of the bar and discovered a large ad for Atlantic City, which I'd never been to. It wasn't that far away. I took a copy with me.

Once we reached the house, we sat on the couch together, watching reruns. Just as I was becoming sleepy, I flipped once more through the gay paper and thought about Atlantic City. I showed Kevin the ad.

"That sounds like a great idea, Roger likes Atlantic City!" Kevin said.

"Yeah, it will be a way to do something fun and exciting and away from here."

"Let's do it!" he said.

I pictured large casinos and trying my luck at slot machines. Maybe I could win big. I knew it was spur-of-the-moment, but what could go wrong?

I WOKE UP Saturday morning energetic about the trip to Atlantic City. I couldn't wait.

Of course, the trip began with problems, which included a traffic jam on the expressway due to an accident. Kevin and Roger fought.

I tried to think positive. These were only minor hiccups.

The day was cloudy, and I wondered if rain might be in the forecast; I'd forgotten to check before we headed out. That might make the walk from casino to casino along the boardwalk less enticing.

Finally, blinking lights and tall glass buildings appeared in the distance. We found ourselves in yet another traffic slowdown, which led to more fighting until we arrived at Caesars.

Roger pulled the car into a tall parking garage. Kevin glanced back at me. "Are you ready to gamble?"

I definitely was. Kevin opened the door for me and I got out with my crutches. I followed behind them to the doors. Inside, the air was cool and crisp. Surrounding us were rows and rows of slot machines, and way in the distance, I noticed poker tables. There was a sea of people, gray-haired women and men wearing casino T-shirts and young couples walking around with beers in their hands, laughing with each other.

Kevin and Roger headed to the far-off poker tables, while I tried my hand at a nickel slot machine. I had been in some Native American casinos back in the Midwest, but this was the first time I'd been to such a huge casino. There were

Roman statues and the slot machines had all sorts of themes, from country-western to African safari and even the Village People.

This is going to be fun. Yet, almost immediately, I ran into problems. I kept having trouble maneuvering through the crowds with my crutches.

I sat down and played for about thirty minutes and lost all the nickels I had on me. I went to play a quarter slot and did the same. Luck was not my lady that night.

I went to find Kevin and Roger, but couldn't locate them anywhere. I kept bumping around with my crutches until I was almost at the point of exhaustion, so I sat in a deli in the front area of the casino.

I finally saw them, but I was mad and asked, "Where have you all been?"

"Roger wanted to wander the boardwalk," Kevin said.

"I wish you had told me first. I've been looking all over for you."

Kevin looked down. "I'm sorry, Todd. We weren't thinking."

Roger said, "Kevin, I want to check out another casino along the boardwalk."

I decided to tag along to at least have a change of scenery.

Outside, the air was damp and there was a chill from the sea. A cool mist hung over the boardwalk. I had trouble balancing myself, slipping around a bit with the crutches until finally we came to another imposing structure, the next casino.

The casino had animatronic cowboys that were able to move better than I was. I felt strangely jealous of their ability to spring to life, compared to me in my current condition. I went to a cashier and obtained more change and tried my luck at nickel slots again. The losing streak continued.

I lost Kevin and Roger once more. I was boiling mad and tired. We had been in Atlantic City several hours at that point. I finally came across them at the door to the casino.

"I need a break. Do you mind if I head to the car?" I said.

"Are you okay?" Kevin asked.

"I'm exhausted."

Kevin handed me the keys, but he and Roger kept arguing about something else. I should have told them I wanted to get the heck out of there but couldn't get a word in.

"Let's head to the new casinos toward the end of the boardwalk," Roger said to Kevin.

"We have been here awhile already... Are you sure, Roger?" Kevin said.

"Yes. Todd can make it back to the car on his own."

Roger had a determined expression, and I knew he wasn't backing down.

I was left with the keys and a long hobble down the slippery wet boardwalk through the throngs of people in the casino and finally to the car. My leg was hurting, and when I unbandaged it, I found it red and throbbing. I took a few pills and soon fell asleep.

I awoke to find that it was 1:00 a.m. and we were still at the casino. I couldn't believe it. I had been forgotten.

Nothing I could really do but wait until they returned. I sat up and stared out the window at the people coming and going from the casino, checking my watch over and over as time trickled by.

My leg was hurting, I kept trying to massage it but to no avail. The trip to Atlantic City was a reflection of the bad luck that the East Coast had become: the shooting, the job search, Kevin and Roger. I had gambled everything for a change, and I'd lost. Now what?

I fell asleep again and woke to the sounds of the door opening and closing. The time was 5:00 a.m. and I couldn't believe it. We had spent the whole night at the casinos and I had spent most of it in the car in pain.

I decided I had to say something. "I wish you two had thought about how bad this was for my leg…"

Roger cut me off. "Our luck was bad the whole night through. You're not the only one with problems."

Kevin looked back at me and shook his head, silencing me. I was stuck with soreness all the way back to Delaware.

Chapter Five

MY JOB SEARCH was going nowhere, and my savings were all but exhausted. The victim's compensation fund was only for my medical expenses and nothing else. I was going to have to make decisions on my future in Delaware. But first, Doctor Whitaker would have to give me the prognosis on ditching the crutches.

I decided to see the doctor on my own, using the bus system once more. The last time I'd seen him I'd had the stitches taken out. Ouch.

I continued to use the crutches and still found it difficult to completely control my muscles. Yet I felt like I was moving forward.

I told him in the examining room. "I made it here on my own using the bus system."

"Impressive," he commented with a grin, which comforted me.

"I was wondering if I could wean myself off the crutches. I want to head back to my parents in Missouri to rehabilitate on my own. Am I at that point?" I asked.

I'd finally said it out loud. I hadn't talked to Kevin about wanting to leave. I was waiting for the right time, though I wasn't sure when that would be.

Doctor Whitaker pushed on my pressure points. I didn't squirm much this time around compared to the past. He watched me walk without the crutches. I staggered a bit but was doing it.

He had me stand on my healthy leg and then the "bullet leg." I didn't realize at the moment, but that was how I would think of and speak of that leg forever more. I was actually able to balance on it.

"You can probably spend most of your time without the crutches," Doctor Whitaker said. "You will need to bring your strength up on your left injured leg. Make sure to follow what the physical therapist prescribes for you and if pain flares up see a doctor."

"Will I have complete recovery?' I asked.

"The leg won't ever be perfect, but you will be able to walk again without having to use crutches or a cane. I know what happened to you was horrible, but as far as your ability to walk again, think of yourself as lucky."

I was so overjoyed that I wanted to hug Doctor Whitaker, but thought better of it.

As I came out of his office, I couldn't think of myself as lucky. Lucky in that I could walk again on my own, maybe. Lucky as far as what happened to me? Not so much.

I KNEW THAT this was probably the last time I would do physical therapy in Delaware, so I tried riding the bus on my own without the crutches.

Of course, Monikah noticed me walking in without them the minute I stepped through the door.

"Impressive," she said. "Why don't you work out on the bicycle for a while, and we'll see how you do on the balance beam?"

When I first started the exercise bike, I found it hard for me to be on it for more than a few minutes. By that point, I was able to ride it for long stretches of time.

The best part of the bicycle was that it faced the window. I could see a park outside, and every time I was on it, I pictured myself out there, walking like normal. This was my favorite daydream. I knew that soon I would be able to take a long walk once again.

Monikah came over and saw me sweating. "You can stop. You were really giving the bike a workout. Now let's head for the balance beam."

I walked on the beam without having to use the side rails for balance. I was at top form, finally.

"Good, you might not need to come back," she said.

This seemed like the right time to explain to Monikah that I had decided to go back to the Midwest. "I'm heading back to my parents and want to work on my physical therapy back home. Do you have some exercises you recommend that I should do once I'm back there?"

She gave me a packet full of them. "You've made remarkable progress, considering what happened to you."

I had only told Monikah the barest essentials of the shooting. I was uncomfortable talking about it. She'd not pushed the subject, respecting my privacy.

Monikah gave me a quick hug. "You've been an excellent patient for doing all of your exercises, staying on task, and not yelling out profanities like some patients when they fall down or struggle."

I blushed. "Thanks."

I gave her another hug. She had really helped me find my way back to using both my legs.

"Goodbye and good luck, Todd, as you heal," she said.

Luck. That word kept popping up over and over. I would need it. One last conversation to be had. A talk with Kevin.

I DECIDED TO do it at lunch, after telling him about the positive news from the doctor and Monikah.

He looked somewhat somber. I waited until after we'd ordered to tell him how I felt. "This isn't working, Kevin. I think it might be best if I head back to my parents. I feel that Roger wants me out of your place... Am I right?"

He nodded. "Todd, you know you mean the world to me, but with you in the townhouse, our focus has been on you. Roger brings up the fact you're not paying rent, electricity, and the water costs. And after everything, I know that's not possible right now. This has been a difficult time for me and Roger, and he told me point-blank that if you don't find your own place soon, he will leave me."

That thought stuck in my mind. I didn't like Roger that much, but I didn't feel like it was my place to tear someone's relationship apart, especially after Aaron.

Just as important, I felt I was becoming a burden in Kevin's life. I didn't want to become dependent on him. That would only strain our friendship even more.

"Maybe it's time for me to go," I said with as much composure as I could.

"I wish that wasn't the case," Kevin said.

I could feel him staring at me. He wanted an answer that would stop us from separating. Our friendship had always been strong, no matter what was happening in our lives. Now, we were testing those limits to the utmost and feeling the bands stretch completely out.

So I did what a true friend always does. I hugged him and said, "Going back to my parents will be the best thing to do under the circumstances. No reason for you to feel bad."

I wanted to face the future on my own terms again, even if that meant going home.

PLANNING HOW BEST to return to my parents' house became my main occupation. I would be going back wounded, without money, and with a sense of loss, but I still hadn't told them I wanted to come home.

Roger and Kevin had gone out that night. I was alone in the house. It was time to make the fateful call.

The phone rang three times, and when I was sure that nobody was home, my mother answered. "Hello?"

"Mom, it's Todd."

"How are you doing?"

"I'm doing okay."

"No, you're not. I can tell it in your voice. What is it, hon?"

"Mom, I'm coming home." Those four words were really hard to say, a lot of emotion was wrapped up in this decision. What else could I do?

"It makes the most sense, hon, after everything that has happened," she said.

I told her how much progress I had made in my recovery. "I'm off the crutches now and I can walk around without them for a pretty long time."

Privately, I had made the decision not to take the crutches home. I didn't want to deal with them on the bus. This would be the longest time I had been without them, yet at some point, I had to move on. I was going to say goodbye to them, hopefully forever.

She confided that she wished she could have come to see me when I was in the hospital. "I fretted over this decision with your dad. But we didn't have enough money to fly out to Delaware on such short notice," she said through her tears. She provided me some encouragement. "It will be fantastic to see how you're doing. I'm so glad you decided to come back home. It will all work out."

"I'll call you when I head out. Dad will need to pick me up at the bus station in Columbia, Missouri."

"Love you, dear."

"Love you, Mom." I hung up. Silence again. I had graduated college, but now I was going to be living off them until I found a new start in life. This was a low point for me. Delaware felt like a huge mistake.

KEVIN WALKED ME through the bus station in silence.

Roger wasn't with us since he had to work late and this gave us a chance to say our goodbyes.

Before I went out the door of the townhouse, Roger had said to me, "I will do my best to be a good boyfriend to Kevin."

In a way, it gave me some comfort, but my uncertainties remained.

The day was freezing cold. Earlier, I looked behind the townhouse into a field and thought I'd seen frost.

Kevin handed me a cigarette and lit one too.

"You know I haven't smoked in years," I said.

"Me neither. I thought we might want to, considering what has gone down between us." He took my hand and put it around his shoulder. "I didn't realize how hard this was going to be. Are you sure you're going to be all right without me?"

I stared up at him. "I will be home with my parents. What could go wrong now? Besides, they live in the country. Unless a hunter is in the woods mistaking me for a deer, I should be fine as far as being shot again."

I stepped away and kept going through the bags. I wanted to make sure I hadn't left anything behind. The more I looked, the more uncertain I became about what I was really searching for. The bus would be here soon, and part of me wanted to stay.

Even when things had gotten this bad...Kevin was still like a brother to me.

I had to say something. "Kevin, are you sure about him?"

Kevin looked down, as if he didn't want to answer. He kept kicking at the curb on the side of the road. His blond hair had grown long since the day I'd come to stay with him. It looked like the summer had aged him as much as it had me.

"He's not perfect, but I want to give it a chance," Kevin said. "That being said, don't ever hesitate to call me. We can't let this come between us."

"But this is more than the shooting, Kevin. I want you to be all right without me and with him," I said.

"I'll be all right, I promise," he said.

The tears in his voice demonstrated how much the situation hurt him with crystal clarity. Even in this fucked-up situation, where leaving was the best choice, I still cared about Kevin and he still cared about me. Maybe it wasn't the kind of love that created a long-term relationship, but it did make for a long-term friendship.

The bus pulled up, and Kevin helped me find my way on. He wouldn't let me carry my bags onto the bus. We hugged, and neither of us wanted to let go. I kissed him on the forehead, and he did the same to me.

We both smiled, then separated.

I stared out the window as the bus headed off, tracking him until he disappeared from sight.

AS THE BUS crossed the state line, I thought about the previous day. I'd walked to the scene of the crime by myself without crutches, wanting to face my fear, standing tall and on my own terms.

Early November, a bright sun-drenched day, but a cool breeze flowed around me. Four months before, my life had fallen apart. That was the best way I could describe it. I hadn't found a job and had barely made it out of Kevin's apartment.

I'd tried, going on more than twenty interviews, but all they'd seen were the crutches and someone who hadn't healed.

I'd learned a few things, too. I'd experienced what it's like to use public transportation on a daily basis and seen how the world looks at someone who doesn't have the full use of their legs. These were lessons I would carry with me the rest of my life. Most of all, I learned I can survive a bullet in the leg.

It had felt unreal to be on the spot of the shooting, although there was nothing to mark the incident. My blood must have disappeared after a few rains or from someone hosing off the pavement.

No one had noticed me standing there. People all around me were going into shops, a normal day for them. Yet I'd had a fear that somewhere in that sunny, crowded day, I could be shot.

Kevin hadn't wanted me revisit the place that had brought me so much pain, both physical and mental. He'd felt it would be too soon. But I had to touch it, to feel the space, to take it back, reclaim all that had been taken from me.

I'd also hoped that my memory would be better, that I would suddenly see them clearly, their faces no longer veiled images in my mind.

Yet... nothing. Guns. That's all I could remember. Guns pointed at me and the popping noise. Blood. But not their faces, nothing that would make them pay for what they had done.

The police department had told me that no one had confessed to the crime against me. That was it: no justice.

I didn't want to be bitter, I just wished to move on. But all of this had taken its toll on me. Even while physically better, mentally, I was still picking up the pieces.

Going to the spot where the bullet had entered my body, I crouched down, which was not the easiest thing to do, I was already sore from the walk.

Forever tied to that moment, every day for the rest of my life, my leg and me.

The kids who did this to me would be arrested at some future time, I thought to myself. Their nonchalant attitude toward shooting someone was going to take them down in the end. No one gets out of this unchanged. Not even me.

Standing up, a lingering fear went through me, as though death had passed me by.

I wanted to hold onto the memory, in case the police called me out of blue one day and told me that they had the perpetrators in custody. I knew that wasn't going to happen, but didn't think it would hurt to hope for the implausible.

I lost track of the miles heading home, as I thought about my future. Hopefully, things would be different. Would I find a job I'd enjoy, find a new lover? Suddenly the world seemed open to new possibilities and hope. Perhaps it would be as they always seemed to say, that time would heal all wounds.

Murder

Chapter Six

I LEFT THE bus at the Columbia, Mo., station and waited for my dad, shivering in the cold. Late fall was in full swing, and trees were barely holding onto their leaves against the dark blue sky. The cold winter months would soon be upon us.

My dad showed up about a half hour later. He seemed older to me. His salt-and-pepper hair was even grayer than the last time I'd seen him, and he had lost some weight from the way his jeans slouched around his waist.

He stared at me for a moment, then cleared his throat, gave a quick tight hug, and asked, "How are you doing, with the shooting and all?"

"I'm doing fine." This was my pat answer for most things related to the shooting. I didn't want to deal with the memories that still haunted me in my sleep.

"That's it?" he said, seeming to hope I would open up a bit more and share with him how I was really doing, but that was not our relationship at the time. I wasn't out and I held back from them my true thoughts and feelings on almost everything to protect that secret.

"I'm sorry if I'm a bit terse, Dad. It's been rough. The doctors say I'm improving and I should be able to walk without much pain if I keep working at it."

"That's good to hear." Dad then turned his attention to my bags and put them in the car. "Are you ready to head home?"

"Yeah."

With the trunk full, we were on our way. "Your mom made a pie for you."

My mother makes a pie for every occasion, so I guess this one called for it. "What kind?" I asked.

"Apple."

That ended our conversation. I wasn't good at talking with my parents and I was uncomfortable about living with them again. What I really wanted to do was reconnect with Rick. I needed a close friend back in my life especially after everything that happened in Delaware.

My mom was outside the house when we arrived. She ran up and squeezed me tight the minute I got out of the vehicle. Her once-black hair had touches of gray. Her glasses hung at the tip of her nose, as she watched me for hints of the anxieties I was hoping to hide with a partial smile.

Mom was wearing an old red sweater and faded jeans that were almost white from wear. She had beads of sweat coming off her brow. I assumed she must have been working around the yard. The screen door screeched open and slammed hard behind us as we all walked into the house.

"I thawed some tomatoes that came from the garden for dinner," she said, before the cooking began.

My mother had always had a vegetable garden. My memories of her are filled with her hands in the soil, planting some lettuce or tomato plants.

"How are you feeling?" she asked.

"I'm fine, Mom."

"You always say that. You know you can't be fine."

This was going to be a difficult conversation. "Considering everything that has happened, I'm holding up as best as I can."

I walked out of the kitchen and headed to the living room. I sat down in a soft leather chair and turned on the television, hoping she would get the hint that I didn't want to talk.

It didn't work. "Did they find the shooters?" Mom asked, stirring ingredients in a pot.

Mom was determined if nothing else. I could feel her giving me that spill-it look across the open distance between the kitchen and the living room. It was impossible to hide given the small house with close quarters.

"No, they haven't." I flipped channels on the remote, deliberately bypassing the news with all its reports of violence.

"I hope they do. They deserve to spend a long time in jail." She grabbed a potholder. "Do you have any job prospects?"

"Not yet, Mom. I just got here." I turned up the volume in hopes this would end the conversation. I didn't want to discuss anything.

This time, she yelled over the now-blaring television. "You should drive down to Bennett where I saw ads in the paper for jobs. And turn down that TV. It's too loud."

Dinner was a quiet affair. I tried to ignore them as much as I could by looking at the help-wanted ads in the paper.

"Todd, stop being difficult and say something," my mother entreated.

"Mom. It stinks, is all. I know I'm being difficult. I'm sorry. It's been a lot to get through." I kissed her on the forehead and hugged my dad.

"I love you both, and I appreciate you helping me out right now. I...I need some time to think."

I turned away from them and fled to my brother's room, since I didn't have my own since they'd moved into this house after my high school graduation. It was near the Lake of the Ozarks. The room was filled with photos of Nathan in college football gear, and I felt even more out of place.

AFTER A FEW days of settling in with my parents, I called Rick.

I had also managed to work out a plan for a car. My dad had a rusty beige Dodge pickup that he no longer needed since he'd recently bought a new truck. When I found a job, I'd pay for the truck in installments until it was paid off.

Now I could see Rick. I told my parents that I really needed to see my friends.

"It will probably be good for you to see them," mother said. "Just give me a call when you get a chance so I know that you are okay, especially after the shooting."

I promised I would.

I called Rick right after talking to them. "I'm back in Missouri, living with my parents until I find a job. Do you want to meet up?"

"Turtle, I've missed you. I'm actually off tonight, I know it is short notice, but would you want to meet up?"

I was ecstatic. "Yes, of course. I can't wait to see you."

As I drove the next three hours to see him, I reminisced about Rick. He was the first person I came out to. I'd met him when we were both working at a hotel as banquet servers during college.

The banquet manager had introduced us to each other on our first day, and for some reason, he had known right off I was gay. At the time, I had come out to myself but hadn't talked with anyone else about it.

While helping me put tablecloths, silverware, and plates on tables, he'd said, "Todd, we need to talk," and gazed down at me.

He had a slender frame and looked like a young John Waters. His belt would even slip down sometimes. He would have to tighten it so it would hold up his pants. Rick was also as pale as the white china plates we used on the tables.

I followed him to a back room, and he'd came right out and said it. "You're gay."

My eyes bulged. I was aghast. I wasn't out to anyone yet, but the way he said it so matter-of-factly took me by complete surprise.

"Why...would you think that?" I asked nervously. I had been found out.

"Are you?" he asked.

"Yes...but..."

"Sorry, I guess I can be a little forward at times. Would you like to get together sometime outside of work?"

I cocked my head and considered his proposition. I wasn't used to hanging out with someone else who was gay. Especially since I wasn't even of drinking age. Yet, I was curious, and he seemed nice and so sure of himself. Maybe he was the right person to learn about the gay world. So I decided to meet up with him.

"Sure. What should we do? I'm not even twenty-one yet."

"We can go to a coffeehouse," he said.

"When?"

"Tonight?"

"O...kay." I almost couldn't believe what I was saying. I'd never done anything like that before. But I had to make the first step at some point to meet others like myself.

We finished with the banquet about 10:00 p.m., and Rick stopped me on the way out of the hotel. "Are you still up for it?"

"Uh...sure. I don't have other plans. I have to meet other gay people sometime, right?"

"Oh, honey, it will be fine. You got me now to show you the ropes," he said.

I went straight back to my dorm and picked out an REM T-shirt and faded blue jeans. I wanted to look hip for our get-together.

I arrived at the coffeehouse and looked for Rick. He wasn't there yet. The barista was busy making coffee concoctions. A few couples were talking about classes.

"I'm never going back to algebra class. The teacher hates me," one girl said. Her dark-haired pencil-thin boyfriend held her hand as she vented her frustrations.

I struggled to keep my nervous thoughts at bay while listening in on the vocal dramas going on around me, but to no avail. My energy manifested itself in the tapping my foot on the flaking enameled floor. I wondered what gay people talked about? I was pretty sure they discussed fashion, like Meshach Taylor in *Mannequin*, but I was never good on the subject.

Rick came in, wearing a brown leather jacket and a blue-and-white striped shirt with a red scarf. Rick put his things on the back of the extra chair, then sat down facing me.

I blurted out, "I know nothing about fashion."

"What?" he asked.

"Isn't that what gay people talk about? In movies...on TV shows...and I'm clueless on this subject."

"Todd, look at me."

I looked him straight in the eye.

"Relax. We're just like everybody else. Okay?"

I took a deep breath and nodded my understanding.

"Would you like another cup?" he asked.

"Sure. Thanks!"

He came back to the table with two steaming coffees and set one on the wood-grain table before me.

"Now, let's talk. Are you...out?"

"Uh, no. You're the first to know. I haven't even told Kevin, my best friend from high school."

"You should. It's good for you to get it out in the open." He touched my hand.

I pulled back. "I thought we were only hanging out."

"Do you want it to be something more?" he asked.

"I... maybe. But there are people all around us. What if someone sees us?"

"So what? We're in a coffeehouse. I doubt we're the only gay people here."

Rick looked to his left. I followed his gaze and noticed the two other guys holding hands under a table. I guessed he was right.

"Do you like me?" he asked.

I was uncertain. I had no idea how I felt about dating a guy. He was all right-looking and friendly enough, but I had only known him from one shift at work.

"I think you're handsome," he said.

"Thank you." I blushed. "Do you have gay friends at school?"

"A few."

"You know you're the first to know. I'm not comfortable yet talking about being gay and all."

"It gets easier," he said.

"Do you mind if we head back to my dorm room?" I asked.

"Wow, you move fast."

"No... I'm not used to being out in public talking about being...gay."

"Okay."

We walked back to my dorm room from the coffeehouse, which was only a few blocks from the college.

When we arrived, I unlocked the door and we headed up to my room.

We sat on my creaky bed. I had a single room with only the barest of furniture. A chest of drawers, a falling-apart recliner that faced a small TV I had brought from home, and a desk with a wooden chair that came with the dorm.

I showed him my posters of different city skylines: New York, Los Angeles, San Francisco and the Golden Gate Bridge, all places that I hadn't been to yet but dreamed of seeing.

"I've never been out of Missouri," I said to him.

"I moved here from San Francisco. It is a beautiful city. Although it's expensive to live there," he responded.

"Is that why you came here? The expense?"

"Not the only reason. I also came here to get away from the memories of my past relationship. I was totally in love with a guy named Lance. We met in high school. I sat behind him in English class, and when we had a segment on Shakespeare, we studied together, reading the lines back and forth. A very gay romance, right?

"After graduating, we moved in together. Found jobs—I worked as a waiter and he as a travel agent. One time, we flew to the Bahamas on the spur of the moment. I almost lost my job. It was a crazy magical time. I woke up every morning in his arms, but it didn't last. One day, he woke up and kissed me on the lips." He stopped for a moment and gazed up at the San Francisco poster. His face had become pale and his eyes welled up with tears.

"With that kiss, he told me he'd had enough of me, then grabbed my clothes and put them in a suitcase. He wanted me gone. Three years, and he wanted me gone. He didn't love me anymore. That...hurt."

I didn't know what to say. He turned and looked at me with warm tears streaming down his face.

"That really sucks," I said, hoping my direct response comforted him.

"That was probably the most painful thing that has ever happened in my life. I didn't have any place to go. My sisters were married and had kids, and my mother felt that once I was out of the house living with a gay man I was old enough to find my own way in life. I begged him for a little money until I figured out what to do next. Luckily, he complied. I would have been homeless otherwise."

"I can't even imagine," I said to him.

He wiped his tears away and took a deep breath and continued on. "Yet, I stood strong. I decided it was time for a change, so I headed to Missouri and enrolled in Midwest College in their hotel/restaurant management degree program. I had spent summers with my older aunt and uncle in Kansas City so I was familiar with the area and far away from my past pain. And that is where I met you." He gave me a kiss on the head. "Why did you choose this college?"

"It's only a few hours away from my parents, close enough I can see them when I want, but not so close that I could head home every weekend."

"Do they suspect you're gay?"

My mouth opened and I took in a breath. "No, I hope not. They're Baptists. So not ready for that conversation. How did your parents react when you told them?"

"My mom raised me on her own. I think she knew since a very young age. I remember sitting down with her and we had a conversation when I was...must have been high school. I told her I was gay and she would have to understand that from now on."

"How did she take it?"

He was quiet for a long moment. "I love my mother. That is all I will say about that."

We sat on the bed together. He went for my hand, though I wasn't used to a man touching me in an intimate way. The hairs on his hand caressed my sweating palm. I was nervous and he wasn't.

He gazed into my eyes and gave me a kiss.

"That's the first time a guy has kissed me."

"How was it?"

"Nice." I told him simply. Yet, I wasn't sure if I was head over heels for him. The kiss was tender, but I didn't feel an emotional punch like what I would see in movies.

"Do you think we can call it a night?" I asked.

"No problem. I know you're new to this."

"Thanks."

"Nice to talk to someone who...is gay like me," I said.

I kissed him goodbye and lay back in bed thinking about him and the night. "Wow, I met a gay person," I said to myself just before I fell asleep.

We spent a few more nights together, going out to the coffeehouse and seeing movies. We were becoming close.

After one such night, I asked him up to my room again.

"Can we sleep together, but not have sex just yet? I've never been in bed with a guy, except for sleepovers when I was a kid and we only talked and went to sleep. I—"

He stopped me from going on. "If you want to be in bed with me and not have sex, that's fine. No pressure."

"Thanks."

He took off his clothes and I did too. We were both in our underwear, and I was nervous.

I snuggled up to him. "Do you mind holding me?"

His body was warm and his naked chest rose and fell with each breath. This was the closest I had ever been to a man since I was a boy at slumber parties.

Yet, I was still uncertain what my true feelings were about him. That thought plagued me as I fell asleep.

I awoke to the sound of the morning news on the local TV station.

"Wow. I fell asleep with you here and slept all night."

"Yep." He gave me a small peck on the cheek.

"Ah, shit, I'm supposed to be at the library this morning to work on a group project." I was a bit embarrassed. I had forgotten all about it.

I scrambled over to the closet and quickly found a shirt. My jeans were on the floor next to the bed, and I threw those on. In a matter of seconds, I was dressed and ready to head out. I put my hands in my pockets to find no keys. I began searching the room for them until I heard a rattle. The keys danced on the end of Rick's finger as he held them up for me to see. Rick had found them.

I kissed him. "Thanks. I'm sorry I have to leave like this."

"It's okay, Todd. I liked spending time with you."

"Rick, also thanks for being a friend while I figure this all out."

"Don't beat yourself up about it. You have your whole life to learn what it is to be gay." He gave me a smooch goodbye.

I closed the door, unsure how to feel. I needed to tell my best friend Kevin that I was gay. He'd know what to do about all of this.

After the meeting about our project, I called him. "Hey, Kev, I-I need to tell you something."

"What is it, Todd? Sounds serious."

"I'm...I'm...gay!" I clinched my teeth and wondered what he would say after my declaration.

"Todd, can I tell you something?" he said finally.

"Spit it out, Kev."

"I'm gay," he said.

"Oh my God. Really?"

"Yep."

"Wow, that is great to hear. I mean…it's nice to know. Did you tell your parents?"

"Yeah, I told them, and they said they knew already. Are you going to tell yours?"

"Hopefully, I don't have to. You know, they're Baptists. Kev, can I tell you something else?"

"Yeah."

"I kissed a guy. We've hung out a few times. We work together at the hotel. His name is Rick. He's super cool, but I don't know how I feel about him. He's a little older and wiser about this whole gay thing. I like him…just not sure as…someone to date."

"Todd, take it slow. You'll figure it out. You always do."

A knock came on the door and someone called out, "Are you ready to go to lunch?"

"Oh, shit, I forgot. Rick and I are going to eat down at the college cafeteria."

"Go eat. I'm sure whatever you decide, he'll understand. If not, at least you know now, right?" Kevin was always like that with his answers.

"Thanks, for the advice, Kev."

Rick came into the room and we had a quick smooch. I was still not feeling it. Maybe it took time.

Over the next few weeks, we spent more time together. Yet, we didn't have sex.

One day, we had a talk in my dorm room as *The Simpsons* played in the background. He was giving me lots of kisses on my body. He really wanted to go further.

"I don't know how to say this to you, Rick. I like you…a lot. You're becoming my closest friend, but I'm…I'm not *in* love with you."

He pulled away. I could tell I had hurt him. I didn't want to have this conversation with him, but it had to happen. He had to know. Even if I lost him as a friend. I needed for him to understand this.

The smile left his face. "That hurt, Todd."

"I'm sorry. I had to say it. I do like you; I'm just not attracted to you in that way. But I would like to stay friends."

He jumped out of bed. "I have to think about this."

"What do you have to think about?"

"I have to go." He walked out the door, and I wondered if I'd ever hear from him again.

ABOUT TWO WEEKS later, he called. "Do you want to go the coffeehouse?"

"I've missed you, Rick. I'm sorry I hurt your feelings."

"Thanks for saying that. I still think a lot of you, Todd. You're a sweet, cute guy. And that's what made this so hard to get past."

"I really enjoy spending time with you. You're my best friend here at college. Can we hang out again?"

"Do you want to play checkers at the coffeehouse?"

"Sounds fun. I really... really missed you."

"I missed you too, Todd."

From that moment on, the awkwardness of our short time dating went away and we became best of friends.

RICK KNEW ABOUT the shooting, so at least that part of the conversation could be avoided. I needed a familiar face in my life. I was smoking a cigarette when he showed up at the gay bar.

I looked him over for a moment. He was thinner than I remembered his dark hair was cut short, making his face seem even more narrow, and wearing a plaid shirt and dark-blue pants. He hugged me and gave me a kiss on the cheek. Then held me at arm's length as he studied me for a moment.

"Where were you shot?"

"In the leg." I pulled up my pants and pointed out the healing scars. We both looked at the wound. He focused in on the scar and touched it ever so lightly.

"Does it hurt," he asked.

"Sometimes I'll take an occasional ibuprofen for it, but it is much better than it was."

I let the leg of my pants fall, and we sipped our drinks.

"How are you doing, Turtle?"

"I'm falling apart." I tried to make light of it. "What do I do now?"

"I wish I had the answer, Todd," he said. "I'm a dining manager at a hotel. It's one crazy day after another. I have trouble with people skipping work and constantly have to find someone to fill in when they don't show. Not so sure about my hotel/restaurant management degree now."

"So we are both really being screwed by life for the moment," I said.

Rick did what he always did. He found a way to make me laugh. "Come on to the dance floor with me, babe!"

"Sound's great!"

He took me in his arms, and we floated around the room. He kept dipping me.

I couldn't help but giggle the whole time we were boogieing to "Another Night" by the Real McCoys. When we sat down, he seemed a bit taken back.

"I didn't hurt you, did I?" he asked.

I was a little sore, but the last thing I needed to do was make him feel bad. I only wanted to enjoy the night together.

"Nope, I'm still in one piece. What should I do, Rick?"

He stared at me for a moment, put his finger up like he suddenly had a thought, then walked away and came back with a gay newspaper.

"I saw a job ad for a reporter in here."

I opened the paper, and in the front section was the ad. "That sounds like a good idea, Rick. Maybe I shouldn't have let you go so easily."

"You say that now, but we both know that you can be quite the crazy one!" He smirked.

"Do you want another cocktail?"

"I was waiting for you to buy one for me," Rick grinned.

After a couple of more songs, he wanted me to drive him to a hillside that overlooked the city. When we arrived, spread out before us were the gleaming lights of Kansas City with the Scout statue, a Native American on horseback, looking behind us. It was our favorite place to go.

"I love coming up here," I said.

We sat on the front of my car, throwing rocks down the side of the cliff. Rick talked about what was really going on at work.

"Earlier, I didn't tell you everything. I got into a fight with one of my supervisors and he's making it impossible for me."

"That sucks."

He threw a beer bottle over the cliffside and it shattered into pieces on a rock below.

I leaned in to put my arm around him. "I don't know what to say about life, Rick. I've only just become able to walk again without aid. I've pretty much fucked everything up the last couple of months."

"At least you have an excuse, with the shooting," he said as he stood up and tore apart a tree branch that was lying next to the car.

"Yeah, super excuse. That makes it fine and dandy," I said. "But I can't seem to get past that night. I keep having trouble trusting anybody. I can't seem to move on. Most of the time, I feel like I'm losing my mind."

"I support that! Let's lose our minds together!" He leaned into the car to grab some more beers.

After handing me one, he held out his beer bottle and we clinked them.

"I'm going to apply for the job and see what happens," I said.

"It'll all go well, I'm sure. Life has a way of eventually working out for you. Me, I keep scraping by without ever going anywhere." He lay down in my arms. I wondered why we never made it as a couple. Maybe I was too fearful of things working out, of letting someone get too close.

I pulled out a sleeping bag and we both got in. We would have to leave this dead-end road with the early morning sun. Yet, being with someone on this starry night gave me comfort.

I awoke holding Rick in my arms. He made me feel stronger just by being near him.

I kissed him on his head. "Shit! We have to go." I realized I had forgotten to tell my mother I wasn't coming home that night. "Mom's going to be pissed at me! I have to call her as soon as we find a gas station with a pay phone."

When we found one, I dialed the number and hoped for the best. "Mom, I'm so sorry I didn't call, but I stayed the night at Rick's."

She hesitated a moment. "Why can't you call before you do these things, Todd?"

"I know. I know."

"Todd...I'm so afraid. When I don't hear from you—"

I answered with more feeling this time. "I'm really sorry, Mom. I needed to spend time with Rick. You know he's my closest friend, since Kevin is all the way back in Delaware. He made me feel better."

"Todd. All you have to do is let me know what is going on and I will be fine."

"I promise not to do this again."

"Don't promise. Just do, Todd. Why must you make me worry?"

"I don't know."

"I hope that you figure that out soon."

I could hear the uncertainty in her voice. I decided to stay positive. "I have... Well, I'm headed home now."

I let her go, knowing that I needed to find a job and move out. I didn't want to keep disappointing her.

I pulled out a cigarette and offered one to Rick. He didn't take it.

"She keeps wanting to know all my moves," I said.

"She senses that you're struggling. Your mom cares," he said.

"I know. It's rough for her too. She wasn't able to make it out to visit me, and I think she feels guilty for that." I deeply inhaled the cigarette. I felt a little high from it.

"You'll need to talk with her when you move out and help her understand that from now on you'll be all right," Rick said.

"You're right. Well, I need to head home. We'll have to get together again, Rick. This was...really nice."

I pulled out the ad again. This was going to be my ticket out of this fucked-up existence. I promised myself I would use all my power to make this newfound dream possible. I put the clipping back into my billfold so I wouldn't lose it. Time to move on.

WHEN I'D FIRST come out to myself and to friends, the gay publication in Kansas City had been the first thing I read that told me I had rights. Back then, I'd rarely seen gay people on television, and gay life seemed limited to the back room of an adult bookstore and magazines featuring a shirtless muscle-bound guy staring at you from the stands.

The whole process of applying for a job with the newspaper had been quick. I'd mailed out the application and heard back a few days later. My parents were at work and I was home alone when I got the call that they wanted to interview me.

Neely Fromm, the associate editor who managed the Kansas City office of the newspaper, was the one who called and asked a few preliminary questions before offering me an interview. I told her my experience of working for the college newspaper and how much I had always enjoyed reading the publication. We set up a time to interview on Friday.

As I waited for my appointment, I was excited at the idea of working for a newspaper that gave a voice to our rights. This made me feel stronger about myself, even if I didn't make it further than this.

The office was small and filled with copies of the paper and posters of AIDS services, gay pride festivals, and a large one proclaiming, "Being gay is not a choice but a way to be fabulous." I chuckled to myself at that one.

Neely signaled me into her office and promptly started searching for something. She kept going through her desk over and over, papers flying everywhere.

Neely was short in stature, had chestnut brown hair, and was wearing torn blue jeans. She could easily have been mistaken for a one of the Indigo Girls. She wore small, thin, wire-framed glasses and seemed to be trying to keep me in focus as she searched.

"Our publisher Oscar Wright faxed me your resume. It should be here," she said.

I tapped my foot while I waited. I wanted this job so much. I was about broke and going to have to borrow money from my mom and dad.

"Aha," she said, waving my resume proudly in the air.

Then she sat down at her desk, which was overflowing with papers, and warned, "I want you to realize that, along with reporting, you will have to sell ads. Are you okay with that?"

It wasn't something I was ecstatic about, but I wanted this job. If that was a prerequisite, I was going to do it. I also wanted the paper to be a success, so I agreed.

She looked over my college articles and asked, "Are you out?"

"I'm out to my friends, although not to my parents."

"You should do that, but it is a difficult process. My family was not happy at first, but now my dad and I are closer than we ever were."

I gave her my references, and she glanced over them.

"You can have the job after I check your references and with Oscar. What do you think about that?"

"Thank you, Neely. I needed this." She'd made me the happiest person in the world with those few words. Finally, after months of barely making it along, I had found success. I needed this job for more than money. It would help me feel better about myself since I could be more comfortable being gay. Most of all, Neely seemed to be someone I could confide in as a friend, considering she had practically given me the job on the spot.

One thing, though. I wasn't ready to tell my parents everything about the new job and me being gay, especially after all that had happened to me recently. Luckily, Kansas

City was far enough away that they would not drive up for a surprise visit. They also could see how gleeful I was, and I hadn't been that way in a very long time.

"What kind of newspaper is it again?" my mother asked as she unpacked cans of food from a large paper grocery bag.

"A paper for those in the city, arts and entertainment related," I said.

"Oh, are you going to feel safe in the city?" she asked.

"Yes, I'm going to be renting out a bedroom for now until I can find an apartment. They are an older couple." I didn't explain that they were an older gay couple, Tom and Bob. I had found them in the very newspaper I was going to be working for.

I'd had a long conversation with one of the guys, Tom, who immensely enjoyed reading the newspaper I worked for. He'd said to me, "You can make yourself at home as soon as you move in. You'll have full use of the kitchen as long as you clean up after yourself. You only need to put down the first month's deposit and the room is yours."

HAVING SECURED A new job and apartment, I was eager to move out of my parents' house.

My mother had me sit down with her at the dining room table to talk. "We're fine to assist you in starting over after everything that's happened. Don't worry about paying us back quickly." Always the mother, she grabbed some cleaning supplies to take with me in my move.

"Thanks, Mom."

"Are you doing better, Todd? Tell me that you are. Otherwise, I'm going to worry every day you're gone. At least lie to me," she said, half smiling.

I looked directly at her with full attention. "Mom, it's been difficult. Don't get me wrong. But finding this job puts me back on the right track."

"You have acted happier since you found out you had this position," she said. "But understand it's my job to worry. Make sure to call me when you can so I know you're doing okay."

"I will," I said.

As he helped put my things in the truck, Dad said, "I want you to promise me that you're going to stay safe."

They both turned to me for the answer.

"I promise not to stay out too late or take long walks at night," I said to them.

They thought it was too soon for me to move out on my own again. I was becoming exasperated.

"Are you really sure you're ready to be on your own again?" my mother cautioned.

I gave her a hug and said, "The 'bullet leg' is functioning the best it has since the shooting. It's time I restart my life once more." I kissed her on the forehead.

My dad put the last box in the truck. "You know we're here if you need us."

I hugged him, then turned to the truck and jumped in the driver's seat. "Everything's going to be great from now on!" I said.

I drove out of the gravel driveway to the blacktop road. I was on my own. I wanted to prove to myself that I could move on without anyone's help. No Aaron and no Kevin, just me.

I smiled to myself as I listened to "I'm Coming Out" by Diana Ross. Finally a brand-new day.

Chapter Seven

IT WAS THREE months of long hours writing stories at the newspaper before I decided I needed a fun night out on the town, and Rick obliged. We headed out for the bars, both of us aware that this could end in mayhem. But I needed a moment of excitement unrelated to work.

We went out to the largest gay dance bar in town. It had once been a theater featuring "Tony 'n' Tina's Wedding" for what seemed like forever before closing and being transformed into a dance club. The place practically shook with vibrating music and gleamed with strobe lights. On Saturday nights, it was packed with a wide variety of gay men, fag hags, and a few straight men who had been talked into going there so their girlfriends could have a good time.

Rick waded through the throngs of people to bring me a vodka cranberry with lime, my favorite cocktail, and looked out at the dance floor. "What do you think of the men tonight, Turtle?"

"A lot of skinny young twinks, it seems. But that's not what I'm looking for." I thought of myself as an otter/cub. "I want to meet someone a bit older and huskier."

I had another vodka cranberry and began to unwind. "Rick, you're in your thirties now…"

"Oh, don't say such things."

"I know. I shouldn't bring up your age. But do you ever think of settling down again?"

"It is hard to find the right guy," he said. "I had Lance... and that fell apart. You had Aaron and you know I warned you about him being trouble."

"Yeah, love can be tough," I added.

Rick grabbed me and signaled me toward the dance floor. The music was fast and furious, but the next song had a slower beat. I took him close into my arms, and we danced back and forth. Eventually, the drinks made us tired, and the house lights came on and it was time to go. The bar was within walking distance of where we both lived.

"Do you think I'll ever find another guy like Lance," Rick asked. His eyes were glazed over. I was half carrying him.

I took a deep breath, and we sat down on the front stoop of his ground-level apartment.

"I don't have an answer for you, Rick. But I do know, you will always have me as a friend."

"Thank you. You know I care deeply for you. I was so glad to hear that you were coming back. I really missed you."

"I missed you, too, Rick."

Then he passed out. I carried him in, took off his clothes, and put him to bed.

Rick was crazy sometimes and a bit hard to take other times. Yet deep down, he had a good heart. It might have been bruised and battered by life, but it was beating strong and trying to survive in this world. I watched him sleep for a moment and had this unsettling feeling that something was wrong. I felt a tingling sensation in the hairs on the back of my neck as I walked home in the early-morning dark. Suddenly lightning flashed and a loud crack of thunder sounded. A strong wind came up and the sky opened up and rain began to pour. I ran. Something was coming, but I didn't know what it was and it haunted my dreams.

RICK WORKED LATE that Saturday night at his new job as a banquet manager at a swanky new hotel in town. I was proud of him; he was making good money – more than I was.

"I can't go out on weekends as much, but honey, I can treat you to a night on the town more often during the workweek," he told me.

I decided to head to the gay bar that was frequented by burly hairy men called bears—the kind I was attracted to. The bar was dark, with soft lighting, and had a small dance floor decorated with a leather wall.

I'd had two beers and was feeling a bit buzzed when what could best be described as a "Latin bear" came in—short jet-black hair, tanned, and burly. He had a tight T-shirt that hugged his upper body. I also noticed a thatch of chest hair below his neckline, which I loved to see on a man. He glanced at me and then walked over to where I was sitting. He kept looking me over while I did the same to him. I figured I should say something, but he made the first move.

"Are you here alone?" he asked.

"Not now, with your sexy self talking to me," I said.

"Oh, so you think I'm interested in you?" he said in a flirtatious manner.

I noticed him giving me the once-over. "I think it's a distinct possibility."

"You're in luck," he said, offering his hand to shake by way of his introduction. "My name is Erik."

"Todd, and you're lucky. I like you too," I said.

"So you can be a bit coy."

"I'm not that easy." I decided I wanted to learn more about him. "What do you do in your daily life?"

"I'm a financial counselor at a hospital. How about you?"

"A reporter for the *Gay and Lesbian Times*."

"Ah. A journalist, interesting. Would you like to come over tonight for...more conversation."

"Sure, why not?" I followed him out, and we headed to his place.

That night, we made love.

I awoke in the morning in better spirits than I had been in a while, but alone in bed. The scent of eggs cooking wafted in to me.

"Todd, would you like some eggs, bacon, toast, and sausage?" he shouted from the nearby kitchen. The bedroom door was open to the kitchen/living room area.

"Sounds awesome," I yelled back.

I sat down at the table, and he soon came over with a full breakfast plate.

"I hope you had a good night," he said.

"Yes, I did."

"That's great to hear. Would you want to meet up again this week?"

"Sure. I love a man who can whip up a nice spread like this for breakfast."

He winked at me, and we ate. He was wearing only a light white T-shirt, and his arm muscles flexed as he took each bite. I had to keep stopping myself from staring. He even made me a sandwich for work, and we left with a kiss. I hadn't felt this blissful in a long time.

I headed into work that day with a spring in my step.

"I see someone had a fun night," Neely said, looking at me over her glasses.

"Yes, I did," I said with a grin. Then I went to my desk and did my best to ignore her.

"Did this night involve staying over at someone's house?" she asked as she tried to look like she was working diligently on her computer.

She was my boss. But she was becoming more than that—a good friend.

I turned on my computer. "He's a handsome Latin bear, and we are going to see each other again this week."

"Good for you," she said.

We both went about our jobs, me whistling. I felt good about life. Finally, after the long ordeal, I was moving past awful summer and difficult fall. I began to see signs of spring, with plants blooming and trees budding, and my mood improved with the changes in the weather.

ERIK WAS A hairy monster, which might be the best way to describe my relationship with him. Before long, I moved out of the rented bedroom with the older couple and into Erik's one-bedroom apartment. In that time, I even paid off the truck to my parents and bought a used white Chrysler Neon, which was cheaper on gas and easier to get around with than the truck. My parents were glad to hear that I was doing well.

I referred to Erik as a "roommate," and luckily, they didn't ask any more questions. I buried myself in his hairy chest on hot summer nights. Erik's muscular arm curled around me as we watched episodes of *Buffy the Vampire Slayer*. He loved cooking, and he spent a lot of time in the kitchen making dinner each night. Home-cooked meals were one thing worth becoming used to.

While I was busy seeing Erik, Rick and I spent less and less time together. He would call and talk about the trouble he was having meeting guys. I kept putting off hanging out with him, which I shouldn't have done. I could tell he was going through a spell of loneliness, while I was basking in the warmth of my new romance.

The phone rang at midnight one evening, and Rick was on the line. Erik didn't want me to answer, but I was determined to get Rick through this.

"Todd, can you come pick me up? I...I don't think I can drive. I'm at the...bear bar in town," he slurred.

"Can you call a cab?" I asked.

"Please, Todd, can you help me, please, please, please..."

I dressed while Erik taunted me. "He can find his own way home."

"I have to go. He's been there for me when I was falling apart, and I need to be there for him." I hurried out of there. Rick meant the world to me. This might have annoyed Erik, but Rick and me had been friends for many years by this point.

I headed into the bar. The place was mostly empty. A barback was clearing bottles from one table to the next. The music was even off. I was lucky they'd let Rick call me and not the police to have him thrown out of the bar. I asked the bartender where Rick was.

He pointed me across the room. Rick sat propped up by a wall near the cement dance floor, asleep with beer in hand. I lightly slapped his face to get him to wake. He flapped his hands at me to stop.

"Rick, you need to wake up so I can get you home," I said.

"I don't want to leave," he insisted.

"You have to. Otherwise, they're going to throw you out."

"I don't care. Why don't I have anyone? Why do I end up at a bar alone?" he slurred as I tried to prop him up.

"We have to go, really. I don't want you to be in trouble." I dragged him out of the bar.

We went as far as the steps outside and sat for a moment. "What's wrong, Rick?"

He slumped over. "I'm not getting it together, Todd."

"You will. I did."

"Why am I a fuckup?"

"You're not. Stop beating yourself up. It's the beer that's talking and not you. Maybe you should cut back."

"Why? Do you think I'm a fuckin' alcoholic?" he screamed.

Part of me did feel that he was going in that direction, but in his current state, it would not have been productive to push it. "We need to head home."

"All right."

I helped him into my car and we headed out. I took him to his apartment and put him to bed.

"Will you stay the night with me, please?" he begged.

"I can't. I have to head home to Erik. He's not happy that I came out when you called."

"It's always about him now, you and Erik. Go...Go now. I want you fuckin' out of here!"

I left. I knew he didn't mean it, but he was jealous. I thought that next time he called I might have to let it go to voice mail.

Yet I also knew that in Rick's past, he had faced family and relationship problems. He didn't go into great detail, but through the years, I understood that what he had gone through had taken its toll. I wanted him to know that I would be with him in his darkest hours, because I had been there myself.

I stared down at a keychain he'd bought me on one of our adventures together in college. I wished that life was like that again.

I reminisced on the time Rick and I had taken a road trip. It'd been all his idea, after knowing each other about a year and being comfortably in the friend zone. We spent a lot of time together, watching movies and going out to eat, but I'd recently turned twenty-one and he thought we should do something spontaneous to celebrate.

"We need to get out of town and have some fun," he said. "Oklahoma City has a gay-friendly resort. Let's go."

He had brought out a brochure that included photos of half-naked men around a hot tub and young guys dancing around in soapsuds with flashing lights. The resort even had a country bar with men dressed in western wear, cowboy boots and hats, looking like they had attended a Garth Brooks concert.

"Are you sure about this?" I said.

"Come on, Todd. You're always doing schoolwork. Live a little for once." Rick waited for me to answer.

I should have been studying for a test I was scheduled for after spring break but decided this once to take a chance with him. "I guess we can do this."

"Yes! Out of your shell, my little Turtle. Besides, neither of us have plans for spring break, and we don't have money for a beachside resort. God, we would have to go all the way to Florida for that."

"You're right. You think your car can make it?" I asked.

"Sure, it will."

"We can go, but maybe I'll do some reading for my test on the way down."

"Todd, sometimes it's good not to be so stuck in your studies!"

"Okay, okay," I said.

A few days later, we were heading out. He honked his horn for me to get moving.

I yelled out my dorm window, "I'm coming. I wanted to make sure to bring a jacket. Do you think I should bring swim trunks?"

"Yes, we'll definitely be spending time by the pool!"

"You think we might do some swimming?"

"Sure, something like that. Come on, Todd!"

I did like to swim. I put my backpack full of clothes behind the seat and we were off.

We talked a lot about our lives on the way down. I wanted to know more about his past, which he'd never shared.

"What was your happiest memory?" I asked him.

"Wow, that's a deep one. Going to the beach in Half Moon Bay with my sisters when I was little. It wasn't something we did often with my family. Just the occasional trip we would take. My sisters and I would spend the afternoon wandering around the beach and looking for sea creatures or gathering shells. That was the best of times of my childhood. What's yours?"

"I loved to spend the day hanging out with Kevin in high school. Not like we really did anything. Just go to the stores, or drive around and eat fast food. Rinse, repeat. Even though neither of us knew we were gay, the time away from my parents and with him gave us space to relax and be ourselves as much as possible."

We stopped at a small café on the way, and some hunky backwoods guys walked in.

"What do you think?" Rick asked.

"Have you ever seen *Deliverance*?" I acted like I was strumming a banjo.

"Yes, but we can look. Am I right?" He stared at them, but I turned away and rolled my eyes.

We ate some burgers.

"They are handsome, aren't they?" He gestured to the table to the right of us again. We both peeked once more. Their arms flexed as they ate their fries.

I nodded.

He kept looking at the guys, even as we left the

restaurant, just to taunt me.

"Are you trying to get us hurt?" I asked.

"You need to relax a bit, Turtle."

Then we were back in the car, heading for Oklahoma.

"When do you plan on having sex? You borrow all my porno movies, but you haven't acted on it yet, have you?"

He was right. I was a virgin. "I want to fall in love."

"Oh, dear. That again. Why can't you think of sex as fun? You need to start somewhere. Besides, you'll meet many a bastard before you come across the right one and well... even sometimes... that doesn't work out."

Rick and I made it to the hotel that evening. The bellman was a stocky guy who looked like he could carry us both along with the luggage. He was nice eye candy.

"Here, let me help you with those," he said.

He took our bags. I was going to stop him because I didn't have much money, but Rick caught me before I did. We couldn't help ourselves, staring at all his moves as he put the luggage on the cart. Each time he reached for a suitcase, it was a sight to behold. He followed us to the check-in counter.

I gazed around the lobby with walls of fake marble and tropical plants placed all around. There were men in all directions, in little groups talking. There were a few leather couches pointed toward a large television behind us. Most of all, at least it seemed clean.

The front desk clerk was a slender guy—young with blond wavy hair. "Do you have a reservation?"

"Yes," Rick said and gave him our information.

"The pool and bar are open until 1:00 a.m."

"Wow, late hours," I responded.

"We'll head there after we're finished checking in," Rick

decided.

We went into the metal elevator and then down a white painted hallway with red carpeting. Our room was furnished with two beds and the same red carpeting. It had all the usual furnishings for a moderately priced hotel: a small TV, a little bathroom with a sink and a tub and desk with a phone. It was like the Holiday Inn just across any interstate but filled with gay men. I put on swim trucks, and Rick did the same, and we went in search of the pool, which turned out to be a party scene.

A number of guys were in the hot tub and others in the pool. They were all in very tight groups, making it hard to tell what was going on since they were so close together.

"What are they doing?" I asked.

"Uh...you know what they're doing, Turtle." Rick laughed.

"Oh my," I said.

"Let's go to the bar and buy some beers."

The bartender was wearing a leather vest but without a shirt underneath, and some leather underwear that were open in back.

"Two Bud Lights," Rick ordered, and once we had our order, we walked back by the pool. "What do you think?"

"I...I'm not sure how I feel about all of this," I answered.

"Watch and learn," he said. "Maybe you can pick up a few things."

I did indeed watch the action going on in the pool. I decided that after three beers I wanted to move on. "I think I've gained new insights into a lot of activities I can have with one guy or, in this case, with a group of guys."

Rick laughed so hard he almost fell off his chair. "I'm sure you did."

"I'm going to check out the country bar in the complex,"

I said.

"Go right ahead. I'm staying here."

At the country bar, they were line dancing, and boots scraped across the wooden floor with each kick. The bar had a mechanical bull that a guy with chaps was riding on. He was bouncing all over the place, I was surprised he didn't fall off. He was very drunk. I sat down by the bar and ordered another beer. I was not coordinated enough to dance like that with a group of people and I would kill myself on the bull.

A man around my age, wearing a red checkered shirt, cowboy hat, and leather cowboy boots sat next to me. "How are you doing tonight?" He gave me a once-over.

"Okay... This is my first time here," I answered.

"It's a lot to take in. I know. You're kind of cute. The name's Tim." He was not shy about checking me out. I had never had a guy appraise me like that before. I actually blushed.

"Thanks. I'm Todd."

"Would you like to dance?"

"I can't do line dancing, but maybe some two-stepping. I grew up in the country, and the girls always dragged me to school dances. Guess they felt safe with me since it never went past being friends."

"We can two-step."

After another line dance, finally a slow song. He led. I was a little drunk, so I worked on not stepping on his toes. I managed to keep from it except once, and he laughed at me when I did. He pulled me in closer and gave me a kiss on the ear. He twirled with me. After dancing, we went back to the bar.

"That was surprisingly fun," I said.

"I'm good two-stepper, right?"

"Yep, you are. Thanks for making us look good on the

dance floor."

We talked a little more about our lives. He lived in Oklahoma City and worked as a store clerk in the men's section of a department store in the mall. He was in college, majoring in business. I told him I was in the journalism program back in Missouri.

"Would you like to head to my room?" he asked.

I wasn't sure what to say, but he looked like he could be a Baldwin, the ones with the sexy dark hair. "Sounds great," I finally answered.

I went back by the pool first. Rick hadn't moved from his chair, where he could see most of the pool.

"I'm going up to spend some time in his room," I said.

He looked at me and gave me a sly grin. "I thought you were out to find love?"

"Not tonight, Rick."

A few hours later, I knocked hard on the door to our room. "Rick, I don't have a key with me," I all but shouted. It opened a moment later.

Rick was standing there, looking half asleep. "What happened?"

"I'm not a top," I said.

He laughed—and even snorted. He was beside himself. I began to laugh too.

"Uh...I don't know what to say to that," he said.

"I know," I said.

"At least, now you know," he added.

"You're right." And we went to sleep.

I encouraged Rick to check us out the next day. I was embarrassed, but Rick kept telling me I had no reason to be.

"It was your first time. You're being way too hard on yourself," he said.

"Maybe, but still, I want to go."

"Okay, okay," he said.

We headed down the road. Rick gave me the play-by-play action from the pool, which sounded like a porn show in real life. "I drank too much to take part."

I wasn't sure if I believed him. At least what happened in the pool kept my mind off my first time.

This was the nicest thing that Rick had done for me. He gave me space to get over my shyness and never brought the night up again, unless I did. He was a true friend. Still was after all these years.

Chapter Eight

AFTER THE NIGHT I picked him up from the bar, Rick didn't call me for a while. I kept thinking that I should give him a ring. When I hadn't heard from him in about a week and a half, I decided to make the first move.

I called his phone. No pickup, but this was not unusual for him. I left a message and headed into the office.

I thought I would hear from him when I returned home. I hoped he understood that I was not deeply bothered by his jealousy of Erik.

Erik and I were in the honeymoon phase of our relationship, when we needed to spend extra time together and were still getting to know each other. So far, he had been a boyfriend that I could depend on. He seemed to make the extra effort to pick up dinner if I worked late or make a scrumptious meal for the both of us.

His only issue so far was my need to help Rick out of this funk, and he thought I tended to be negative about life when I was stressed. Erik didn't like it when I wanted to vent about a rough day or even discuss the past shooting in Delaware.

The night I showed him the scar on the back of my leg, he touched it and I flinched.

"It's like having a funny bone, but it's on the back of your leg," I explained. "The wound only gives me occasional trouble if I sleep on it wrong. Like a charley horse that's a bitch to go away. I have to shake it about and eventually it subsides, and then I take some ibuprofen afterward to keep away any residual pain. Yet, the real wound is here." I pointed to my head. "I sometimes fear being alone in the night, and I'm always conscious where I am at and what's around the corner if I go down a street and nobody is around. That sort of thing stays with you always."

He responded by tickling me, and we kissed, and from there, it led to sex. That was Erik's way of dealing with anything serious.

After another unanswered call to Rick, I began to be concerned that maybe I had caused a rift between us. I would have been more worried, but it was not unlike Rick to be distant for a while. He was like that. He had his own life and his own way of dealing with his issues. Yet, in the back of my mind, I kept wondering if something more serious had happened.

I discussed my fears with Erik as he was making dinner after a few weeks of not hearing from Rick.

"I'm sure he's fine. You know it might be for the best if you gave him some distance," Erik said as he prepared spaghetti noodles.

"I know you don't like Rick. I've received that message loud and clear over the time we've been together. But as I've said before, he's always been there when I needed a friend. I'll go by his place tomorrow and see if he's in."

Erik reiterated his stance. "I think you should give him his space. He obviously wants some time alone from you."

I was quiet during dinner. No matter what Erik said, I knew something was wrong.

That night, we watched the evening news, which reported that a body had been found in a ditch behind an apartment complex. The unknown victim had been beaten almost beyond recognition.

The newscaster said the victim had been at a bar that I knew Rick sometimes went to.

"Do you think that was Rick?" I asked Erik.

"That's crazy," he said. "You're reading too much into the news. Rick only wants you to feel sorry for him; he'll call when he needs you again. Don't worry."

But all I did was worry. Was it him?

AN UNKNOWN NUMBER appeared on my phone. I let it go to voice mail, then listened to it.

"I'm Officer John Dillings with the Metro Squad. I need you to call me back as soon as you can."

I put it off for an hour as I watched another episode of *Buffy the Vampire Slayer*. The number came across my phone again, and I answered.

"Hello."

"I'm Officer John Dillings. Am I speaking to Todd Smith?"

"Yes."

"When was the last time you saw a Rick Forsyth?"

I was beginning to feel uncomfortable. "I...I haven't spoken with him for a couple of weeks. Why?"

He hesitated for a moment. "I'm sorry to tell you this, but Rick was killed Saturday night. Do you know of anyone who might want to cause him harm?"

"No," I said quickly. The realization of what he had just told me had me shaking. Tears rolled down my cheeks, and all I wanted to do was curl up into a ball and weep.

"I know this has to be a shock, but I need you to answer a few more questions." He paused, then asked, "What was your relationship with him?"

"He was a close friend."

With these questions, I wondered if I could be a possible suspect. He didn't know our relationship; I might have been friend or possibly a jilted lover. I was going to have to be careful with my answers.

"We went to college together. He is...was a great guy." I struggled saying it in the past tense. I couldn't believe it. He was really gone.

"The police found his billfold on the ground next to him, under the deck of an apartment. He was somewhat disfigured. We need to have his identity confirmed." He paused again, giving me time to dread what I knew was coming. "I'm sorry to have to ask you this, but can you identify him for us from a photo we have?"

I thought about this for a moment. I knew there was nobody else they could turn to since his family lived in California. No matter how much I didn't want to see Rick this way, I had to.

"Yes."

"Thank you. I'll be by in the morning. The forensics department has done an autopsy so I'll come by with photos."

After hanging up, I retched. *It just can't be. This isn't possible.* How could violence shove its way back into my life and this time claim Rick?

I went to bed, but sleep was impossible. Rick was dead. It was so much to take in. How could this have happen?

Hours later, I was exhausted from my tears and about to fall asleep when I heard the door open. Erik had finally made it home late.

"Rick's dead," I said simply.

"Are you sure?"

"The cops called while you were doing overtime. They want me to identify the body from a photo in the morning. I can't believe this. Right now, all I want to do is call him up and say how sorry I am that I haven't talked to him in a while."

All he said was "You know, he did have a drinking problem."

I was shocked by Erik's reaction. How could he be so cold? This was my longtime friend. Of course, Rick had a drinking problem, and it could have possibly led to his death. But he was human... I still couldn't believe I was putting him in the past tense.

"I'm not going to be able to sleep tonight." I went into the living room. Erik didn't follow me, obviously sensing that I wanted to be by myself. He'd never liked Rick, which was fine, but I was friends with him. Shouldn't that mean something to him?

I watched old episodes of *Golden Girls* until morning, drifting between wakefulness and sleep. I felt very alone in the world with Rick gone.

The world was a dangerous place once more.

ERIK CAME INTO the living room in the morning. "Did you sleep in here all night?"

"Not really. I just found out my friend is dead. It sort of kept me up."

He walked into the kitchen, ignoring the comment. "I was thinking of making eggs. Do you want some?"

"No, I can't eat. Maybe some coffee."

I was mad. Not that Erik could do anything about the current situation, but that he was lacking empathy. He didn't seem to understand that this was throwing me into an emotional pit.

He started the coffee, scrambled eggs, and sat down at the table. He motioned me to sit with him, and I poured myself some coffee.

He gobbled down the eggs like he normally did every morning. Nothing seemed to faze him.

When he finished the last of the eggs, he asked, "So when are the cops coming by?"

"Probably around 9:00 a.m. I told Neely I'd be into work late today and would explain more when I came in."

"Sounds like you have everything under control," he said as he grabbed a jacket. He gave me a quick kiss goodbye before heading out the door and closing it with a definitive click.

I sat with my coffee for a moment and then cleaned the kitchen, like I did most mornings. I somehow dropped his glass of juice in the process, shattering it. I went to sweep it up and managed to cut my finger, making blood pour out. I had to run into the bathroom to grab a bandage.

Eventually, it stopped bleeding. I kept staring at the cut on my finger. I wondered if the cop might think I was somehow involved with the injury on my hand.

A crazy thought, no doubt drawn from watching too many crime shows. None of this made sense, it was all so insane.

I listened to some Madonna as the time ticked closer to the police officer's arrival. It made me feel close to Rick. He was always flamboyantly gay, but that should not be a crime. I needed to know how this could happen to him.

OFFICER JOHN DILLINGS, who I had spoken with the night before, was hard-bodied and tan. I thought Rick would have enjoyed the fact that such an impressive man was investigating his death. At the same time, it felt really weird to think of that.

Officer Dillings was hoping I could provide him with some clue as to why this had happened. He began to tell me what took place the night Rick was found dead but paused in his story to warn me that the details were graphic and would be hard to hear. There was no way to avoid the facts.

"Rick left the Good Times bar late Saturday night. A white truck came by, and he got in. We think they took him to the apartment complex where a horrified woman found him dead under a back deck. His pants and underwear were pulled down to his thighs, and one end of a seventeen-inch piece of metal rebar was in his anus. Part of one ear was burned off, his body was singed, and bruises covered his head and upper body. Also a toupee was found near his body."

He stopped as my tears flowed. He went to grab me a Kleenex and waited quietly while I got my composure back. Rick had never talked about the toupee. I'd only really noticed it once when we were drinking and it had been a little off on his head. I never said anything to him about it because I respected his privacy on this issue.

Officer Dillings picked up a photo and paused before handing it to me. For a moment, I didn't recognize him. His head was completely bald and it looked like someone had cut his face into pieces. His body was partially burned, like he had been set on fire, and his eyes were wide open, even in death. Pain was evident in them, staring at me from the photo. The image of his bruised face and the cuts above his brow would haunt me for the rest of my life.

"It's him," I managed to say. I hadn't wanted to accept that he was dead. *How is this even possible? This has to be someone else.*

He explained to me that they thought Rick probably knew his killers, possibly from his job.

"Yet, we're having a hard time gaining details when we talk to people there. Do you know of anyone who would harm Rick?"

"No. Although Rick had a way of hooking up with strangers. The way he did it wasn't always the smartest." I said.

"Officers have already searched his apartment for clues, but nothing showed up. If you hear of anything, let me know."

"You'll be the first one I tell. Is it okay if I go to the apartment? Rick left me a key and I want to feel close to him."

"That's fine. The officers have already gone through everything," he responded.

A short time later, he had packed up his notes and the photos and handed me his card. As I showed him to the door, he said he was sorry for my loss and to be sure to call if I could think of anything that might be a lead.

As he drove away, I suddenly felt very alone.

I wondered if they would really find the killers. I didn't have much hope. This was a gay man who was sexually violated and murdered. Who besides me really cared about Rick in this city?

I knew I shouldn't feel this way about the cops, but this was tough. They had never found the boys who'd shot and robbed me in Delaware. I just didn't have hope with the evidence they had. Nothing in real life is like *Law & Order*.

I SAT ALONE in the apartment in silence for the longest time before I decided that I would talk this out with Neely at work. She was the one I could turn to for help. Especially with the way Erik had responded. I headed into newspaper office with my eyes still watering.

"What's going on?" Neely asked as she turned away from the computer.

"My friend Rick was killed in a gay-bashing over the weekend. I...I can't believe this is happening."

She came over to my desk and held me in her arms. "Do they know who did it?"

"No." I told her about my conversation with the cop. "They suspect that maybe Rick had met his killers through work." I told her that Rick had his issues. "He was flamboyant as far as being gay. Sometimes, he made bad judgments in who he hung out or hooked up with, and this might have been one of those times. But why would this lead to his death?"

Fury sparked in Neely's eyes like I had not seen before.

"We need to let others know about this crime. It can't go unpunished," Neely said.

"I'm sorry. I can't write today. I'm having a hard time dealing with the fact that he is dead and was brutally murdered."

"I understand. We will work together on a story about Rick and this awful crime," she said. "I can't believe this happened to a friend of yours."

"I wish there was something more I could do. But to be completely honest, I'm also scared of these people. When it comes to being gay, there are some people in society who don't care whether we live or die."

"Why don't you head home and take some time for yourself."

"Thanks, you're the first person who seems to understand how painful this is for me." That's when I began to cry. I let it all out. I'd held it all in, but now it poured out of me in torrents. Though as quickly as I'd started, I stopped. When I was able, I said, "It hurts so much. I need a little time to think."

Neely nodded. "Take all the time you need."

I felt proud to be her friend. She would look into this, and we would find the killers. Justice would prevail. They wouldn't get away with this. In my heart of hearts, I desperately wanted to believe that.

I CAREFULLY UNLOCKED the door to Rick's apartment, which was completely silent. This was strange to me since whenever I came over there, music was always playing.

It felt like it he had just left, with dishes still in the sink, ready to be cleaned, and the mail still scattered across the floor where it had fallen after being pushed through the slot. The cops might have searched, but they thankfully hadn't torn up the apartment.

On his refrigerator door was a list of family members with phone numbers. His sister's name, Samantha, was at the top. Time for me to build up the nerve to talk with them about what had happened.

I picked up the phone, took a deep breath, and dialed. A woman answered. "Hello?"

"It's Todd, I know the cops have already called you, but I just had to reach out to you too."

"Todd, I'm glad you called. Rick mentioned that you'd moved back." I could sense a hesitation in her voice as she asked me, "Can you tell us anything more than the cops?"

"Sorry, I only know what they've told me. I just wish I had been with him that night so I could have stopped him from getting into the truck." I stopped when she began crying, and gave her time to pull herself together.

"Do you think the police will find whoever did this?" Samantha asked.

"I hope so. I...really thought the world of Rick."

"Thanks for saying that," she said.

"How is the rest of the family dealing with this?" I asked.

"My sister is heart-broken... It's so horrible. And Mom... it's been really rough on her. You know she's not in good health."

"I didn't know that. Rick was never good at letting me know about how you all were doing."

"Yeah, that was the way...he was."

She wept some more, then ended by saying, "We're going to try to make it out there in a few days. I'll call you back with more information."

"All right... I...I'm...so sorry."

"I know." And then she cried some more as she hung up the phone.

I thought I would feel some closure talking with his family, but all I felt was horrible.

I did what any gay man would do for a friend: I did some cleaning up. I wanted the apartment to look decent for their visit. I removed all the adult magazines and videos too.

Finally, I took one last look at the apartment. I kept thinking Rick would come through the door. It was so hard to believe he was dead.

I PRESSED PLAY and watched *My Best Friend's Wedding* with Julia Roberts. The last movie Rick and I had watched together. I wanted to relax and remember all the times we had rented movies in college. He would bring out the wine and make popcorn. Simple comforts that would never be the same again.

Erik came home and noticed I was watching the movie by myself.

"Were you able to reach his family?" he asked as he went into the kitchen.

"Yes. That was the hardest phone call I've ever had to make."

"What would you like for dinner?" Erik asked.

"Really, hon, I'm not hungry."

"You know, you can't keep letting this bother you," he said. "It didn't happen to you, and remember, Rick did have a serious drinking problem."

"I know. You've reminded me of it over and over."

He left the kitchen and stood above me. "Well, I'm going to go out and grab some Chinese takeout. Would you like to order some as well?"

"No, that's fine," I said.

He grabbed his coat and headed out. He came back an hour later and tried to make me eat. Erik was nice enough to bring back some sweet-and-sour chicken with rice, but I had no appetite.

Erik sat on the couch, and I rested my head in his lap. He lightly brushed my hair. I guess he finally got the hint that I only wanted to be held.

BEFORE I LEFT for the office the next day, I received a phone call from Samantha.

"We're going to be out to see you this next Saturday. His niece, Jessie, is also coming along," she told me.

"I'll be here for you," I told her. I'd never talked with his niece, so it would be interesting to meet her in person.

I arrived at the office and started to work editing some short articles that Neely had left on my desk.

"Are you ready to do the story on Rick?"

I looked up and didn't say anything for a moment. "I'm ready as I will ever be," I eventually answered.

"You said you had a photo of him."

I'd almost forgotten she'd asked for that. I opened up my briefcase and pulled out a picture of Rick, wearing his favorite short-sleeve blue-and-white striped shirt.

"This was taken only a week and a half ago. We went antique shopping in a little Amish community north of here. He kept commenting that Amish farmers were well built and corn-fed. I told him to stop looking at them like that and I remember saying to him 'Jeez, Rick, this is conservative farm country up here.'"

I realized I was telling her more about that day and him than necessary. "You're wanting only the facts, right?"

"I can gain that from the police report. Tell me what you miss most," she said.

I paused for a moment. "Rick had a quirky a sense of humor. What I will miss are the evenings of red wine and watching old movies we rented at Blockbuster." I smiled in remembrance, then continued, "He would open up some cinema guide and find an odd detail about a movie. Like the fact that *She's All That* was released on the anniversary of Freddie Prinze Jr.'s father's death. Rick had an eerily sense of sharing these strange deadly factoids."

I stopped for a moment, and then she said, "Go on."

"I loved being in the moment with him. He made you feel at home in his apartment."

"This is the sort of stuff that goes missing with the facts."

"Most of all, I remember his acts of kindness. You might show up at his place and on the table would be some small knickknack, like the small clock he found at an antique store that he couldn't find a place for, and he'd want you to have it. Or he would make reservations for dinner for the both of you on a whim. He did these sorts of things for all those he was close to."

"That's great to hear," she said. "That's what I'm looking for."

"I hope it helps," I added.

Neely's article came out shortly. I wish that there had been an outpouring of love in the community. But what the article did bring was a television reporter knocking on the door when I wasn't home.

Erik answered the door while I was at work.

Erik had had it with Rick and his death. He told the reporter that I didn't want to talk and not to come back. He'd shared this information with me without looking away from the television. This led to us having it out about Rick's death and our relationship.

"Why did you tell her that?" I asked.

"Because, I feel that you're so focused on Rick that you've forgotten about me," he said.

He was probably right about that, but it did not excuse what he did.

"Erik, did you at least get the reporter's name or who they were with?"

"No, I didn't," he said.

"How could you not have done that? You know with all that's happened to me in my past, with the ones who shot me never being found, it's important to me that Rick's story is known so his killers might be caught."

"I think you need to let this go for us," he said.

"I'm sorry, Erik, but I can't." I turned my back on him, slammed the bedroom door, and fell asleep from exhaustion.

SANDRA BULLOCK KEPT me company this time with *While You Were Sleeping*. I opened up a wine bottle and poured two glasses. It was time to commune with Rick, one last night alone with him—or at least the memory of him.

I pulled out his cinema book and began to commune with him about the details. I wanted it to be like a normal night. I even popped popcorn.

"Did you know, Rick, that the home in the movie was real, and it was an early 1900s house in La Grange, Illinois? If...you were alive, we could drive up there and see the white-painted beauty and wraparound porch in all of its splendor. Also, Matthew McConaughey was up for the role, but Bill Pullman was cast instead. And thank God. Could you imagine the movie with him? Not!" I chuckled.

After I found a few more details, the book dropped to the floor and I fell asleep on the couch.

When I woke up, I headed straight to the office. There was no call from Erik so I felt no need to head home.

That weekend, I went to Rick's apartment once more. Samantha said I could go through Rick's possessions and keep what I wanted. I decided to go with things that reminded me of him. I took all the romantic comedies that we had watched together, some of which I had bought for him, still wrapped in plastic and waiting for us to watch together once more.

He'd had an infatuation for Marilyn Monroe. She'd died before her time, like Rick. I kept his poster of Marilyn in different poses.

He'd bought it at a flea market. We'd always checked out secondhand stores.

"Wow, this is a find, Todd," he had said.

I had looked at it with him. "It's well done and nicely framed."

"I'm getting it." He'd left with it, so happy that day, and we had gone straight back to his place and put on the wall.

I flipped through a large photo book of images of her. I remembered doing this when I'd come to his apartment the first time.

Rick had also enjoyed large books on historical Hollywood, especially about those who had died in their youth. I picked up his books and videos on the Titanic and put it all in my car, along with some of his favorite records, like the Carpenters. I even found a yellowed newspaper clipping about the drowning of Natalie Wood, her death still a mystery to this day.

Rick had always seemed to have an infatuation with an early or violent death. It made me think something deeper in our minds or the world might connect us to a possible future.

I put the mementos of Rick's life in the back of my car and arrived at the apartment late at night.

Erik watched as I brought in the boxes. "What is all this stuff?"

"It's Rick's life," I said.

"We don't have room for it," he said.

"I will make room," I said as I stacked the boxes on what I considered my part of the bedroom.

"You can be so difficult at times," he said.

"That's your problem," I said.

He stomped out of the apartment. I took out a hammer and nails. In the corner that I called my own, I nailed up the poster of Marilyn. She was staring at me, and I felt that Rick's presence was now there with me.

I MET RICK'S sisters and niece, who'd flown in from San Francisco, at his apartment on Sunday. Arlene, the oldest, had gray hair and a kind face, reminding me of a photo I had seen of Rick's mom. Samantha was the youngest; she had brown hair and was really thin like Rick. Jessie was in her twenties. She wore black pants and black shirt and reminded of the actress Christina Ricci with her dark hair.

They gave me huge hugs.

They went through his things, telling me more about him and sharing stories of his life. An air of sadness hung over the affair, all of us aware that this was the only way we could have met. We reminisced about him.

"He was always so generous," I said to them. "If he saw a Superman coffee mug at a thrift store, he would buy it for me since he knew how much I liked comic books."

"Yeah, he was always buying stuff for people he cared about, even though he didn't have much money," Samantha said.

"Rick found a beautiful porcelain doll for me once. I still cherish it," Arlene added, as she put together some knickknacks.

Arlene held up some pottery pieces. "I made these for him. Although I'm not the best at pottery making, and to be honest now that I really look over them, not my best work. But I'm going to take them. It will make me feel close to him since I wasn't able to say goodbye to him in person."

His niece, who had been mostly quiet, teared up. "I wish... I really wish I had known him better."

She turned to Arlene for a moment, and they all hugged each other for comfort.

After they had gotten their composure back, I asked, "How is your mother doing? Better?"

"No. Sadly, she's really not doing very well, and this trip would have been impossible for her," Samantha answered. She showed me a weathered black-and-white photo of her. She was wearing a long dress, her hair dark and held back with barrettes. I couldn't really sense who she was from the old photo.

"Are you going to have a funeral for him back in San Francisco?" I asked.

"His wishes were for a cremation. We're going to scatter him over the ocean at Half Moon Bay. It was his favorite place," Samantha said.

She pulled out a bunch of pictures with them together on the beach. He was so young and happy, jumping around in the waves with his sisters.

"I wish I could make that, but I'm sort of low on money. I recently bought a car," I said. "Although, if I ever make it out to California, I promise to say goodbye to him at Half Moon Bay."

"That would be nice," Jessie said.

Arlene flipped through a large mass of disco records, showing me each one.

"Rick would turn up the volume and we would dance around the house. Mother hated when he did that."

She put an ABBA record on Rick's stereo and the apartment filled with disco beats and the yearnings for "Waterloo."

They went through his books, magazines, and records. "We're going to split these amongst ourselves," Arlene said.

"I found a few books, CDs, videos, and posters I wanted to keep. It's one of the few ways I can hold onto memories of Rick," I said.

"He would have liked that you had those things," Samantha said. The three cried again. I tried to comfort them as best as I could, but I wasn't sure how. How can you truly make people feel better when their brother and uncle was killed in such a horrific way?

I decided to leave them with their memories and let them go through the rest of his effects in private. I was about to walk out when Samantha asked me to talk about a favorite memory I had of Rick.

I showed them the photos that I had taken of us antique shopping.

"We had so much fun on those trips to neighboring small towns. Rick loved to look for fun, bright pieces to put in the apartment, and would haggle with the store clerk until he got it down to what he thought was a fair price. He bought a small green glass lamp the day I took this picture," I said.

I showed it to them and said, "Arlene, you should take the lamp."

I told them what really frustrated me the most. "The police keep trying to hedge away from calling it a hate crime, but with the brutality and the way Rick was found, how could it not be? I keep thinking that it can't be true—that he disappeared somehow. The body wasn't his and I'll run into him coming out of a restaurant around the corner. It all seems so senseless... I can't believe he's gone."

We all held each other. I hadn't meant to go on about his death. After I dried my face with a Kleenex, I decided it was time for me to go and give them some space to grieve on their own.

Before I left, Arlene told me that they could take pictures and such back with them, but not the furniture and kitchen stuff.

I gave them a final hug goodbye. I was going to have to use Erik's truck to haul it all out. He was not going to like that.

Chapter Nine

A NOTE ON the fridge when I arrived home said, "Dinner is wrapped in foil on the second shelf. I decided to go out to the bar with Alex and Joe."

I microwaved the meal. The divide between us was growing larger. I had spent too much time in closing the chapter on Rick. Yet in this painful process, Erik was nowhere to be found. I turned on the television and watched an episode of *Will and Grace*. At least Will had time for Jack, no matter what shenanigans he found himself in. I fell asleep on the couch with the TV on.

The front door creaked open—late, judging from the DVD clock glowing in the dark. Erik headed for the bedroom without even giving me a kiss good night. The light to the bathroom came on and went off. He fell into bed. Not a word was spoken between us.

In the morning, I searched for the right words at breakfast. "I need to borrow the truck."

"For what?" he asked.

"We have to take Rick's stuff to the AIDS Center. We're donating what is salvageable, such as his furniture, clothes, and kitchen stuff."

"Why us? Why you?" he asked.

"There isn't anyone else," I said.

"Why not his family?" He scarfed down some bacon.

"They flew here and were only able to take what they could pack onto the plane along with...his remains," I said. "I think that is enough, after what they've gone through."

"I'll let you do this," he said as he stuffed his mouth with eggs. "This is it, though. You're pushing me, you know."

I knew it. We were not in a happy place. Yet I was sure we would be, after we were past this rough patch with Rick's death.

THE GRASS IN front of Rick's place was frosted white that Sunday. It was an early burst of winter on this fall day. A cold mist came down. We both wore gloves and heavy coats as we moved everything out of the apartment.

We started with the sofa. "You know you owe me big-time for this," Erik said. The sofa was heavy, which was not helping his attitude. Yet his complete disregard for how difficult this was for me was making it hard for me to stay calm.

"I can't believe I'm doing this."

I stayed quiet. I didn't have the emotional ability to fire back. Yet I was boiling. At one point, I lightly tossed a plant holder that landed on his foot.

"You did that on purpose!" he steamed.

"Accident," I replied.

He turned away, unconvinced. Maybe subconsciously, I wanted him to be in a little pain.

We took everything to the AIDS Center where an older gentleman checked in our donations. "Thank you. The hospice will use his furniture. It looks like your friend had excellent taste."

I wasn't sure about that, but I was feeling good that someone could appreciate what he had.

We unloaded everything. Erik did more grunting. We didn't talk much throughout the process. We headed back to our apartment, and all the bottled-up anger exploded.

"This is the last straw, Todd!" he yelled as he walked through the door.

"What the fuck is your problem?" I shouted. "All I asked was for you to help out. My friend is dead, and the whole time, you made this an affront to our relationship!"

"I think you care more for your dead friend than you do me."

"You don't have to worry any more about that. He's completely gone now, and soon his ashes will be in the ocean. So no worries!"

"I'm going to the bar!" He walked out.

"Have fun!" I replied to the empty space.

I went to the couch and watched television. That day, I had managed to load what was left of my friend's life onto a truck and give it away. In the process, I found out that my lover was an uncaring son of a bitch who was now looking for dick on Saturday night while I watched television.

Time for me to move out. We probably both knew it. Our relationship couldn't survive Rick's death.

THE NEXT MORNING over coffee, I said, "I think our relationship is over."

Erik stared at me and said simply, "Fine." He gathered his briefcase and his coat and headed to the door. He turned to me, opened his mouth, and then paused.

This was what I was waiting for: A comment on what went wrong. But he said nothing. He looked at me, then turned away and slammed the door behind him.

It was his pride in the end. He couldn't admit that he made mistakes. I knew I had let Rick's death consume me, but he could have been there for me. He could have been human. Instead, he didn't want to deal with it.

I decided that maybe Rick's death had been the best thing for our relationship. I learned quickly that Erik couldn't be counted on.

After a cup of coffee, I called Neely, and after explaining the situation, she agreed to let me use her truck to move out.

That weekend, I found a studio apartment near Neely and closer to the office. Erik didn't even want to be around when I moved out. He was "out" again. We had spent the last week doing the best we could at avoiding each other.

Neely showed up at 8:00 a.m. on Sunday morning with her truck. She smiled and hugged me.

"I can always count on you, Neely," I said as I gathered up an overstuffed box.

"So where is your ass of a man?" she said.

"Being more of a dick than an ass," I answered with a larger smile than I'd had in a long time. I had already gone to the truck and back for another box. I wanted this done and over as quickly as possible.

"That happens, Todd," she added with the self-assuredness that she always seemed to have.

"I know. It's not my only breakup, sadly enough," I said. "I wanted it to work out this time. Maybe if Rick hadn't died..."

"At least you know what kind of person he is," she countered.

Piece by piece, my belongings were emptied out of his apartment. I was now out of his life and back on my own. I felt a big surge of relief.

"It's strange how quickly you can come together with someone, and when it is all said and done, it's sad how easily you can leave them behind," I said.

We unloaded everything at my new place. It didn't take that long, really. I still had not acquired much stuff. I'd been in bedroom prior to moving into Erik's small place.

I looked at Neely; she was wiping sweat from her brow. It meant a lot to me that she helped me with the use of her truck.

"Would you like to go and get a beer?" I asked. "I can put everything in order in the apartment over the next few days."

"Sure," she said.

"Let's go to the lesbian bar. I don't want to risk the chance of running into Erik. Not now, at least."

THE BAR WAS packed. It had two pool tables in back, and in front was a large dance floor with lights flashing throughout. There were two large older women manning the bar and doing a good job of slinging the drinks.

"What would you like to have," I asked Neely.

"Get me a Bud Light," she answered.

"I'll have a Tequila Sunrise." I said. It would be the start of many drinks that night.

I danced with her and a girl she met. I hadn't felt that carefree in a long time. This was a moment that I needed in order to get myself back on track.

"I like how you danced with her," I said, a little drunk. "You were cheek to cheek. No space. That is the way it should be, in each other's arms."

The girl whose name I couldn't remember laughed at me.

"He's really harmless," Neely said, as she and the girl moved across the floor.

They came back to me still arm in arm. I thought it might be best to head back to my new place.

"I should probably head out. Time to leave you two lovebirds alone," I said.

I fell a sleep a little after I arrived home. I was relaxed again. I was moving on once more, but this time without Rick or Erik in my life, hurting from the loss of the one, relieved at the loss of the other.

I HUNG OUT with Neely a lot over the next few weeks. I didn't want to date anyone for a while. I was in an in-between place in my life and I needed to live on my own terms.

Neely, on the other hand, was beginning a strong relationship with Amanda, the girl she'd met at the bar that night and who was now living with her. Amanda had dyed-blonde hair and wore baggy jeans and a different tie-dyed T-shirt every day. Amanda was an artist, so Neely's apartment had been transformed into an artist's studio with wet paint and works of soon-to-be art everywhere.

Yet, there was bad news was on the job front. The newspaper's revenue was down, according to Oscar. We were waiting for what he referred to as a "big announcement." This was either going to be really good, with the newspaper possibly being sold, or really bad. I was thinking that, since we hadn't heard much from our publisher lately, it was probably the latter.

If the news was indeed bad, it might be time for me to move on again. I had taken my career and relationship as far as I could in Kansas City. Maybe I should think about a new beginning in a different city.

Before work, Amanda wanted to show me a painting she had done for Neely.

"What do you think?" She put down a brush and walked to the side so I could obtain a full view of it.

She had painted a portrait of Neely, including her narrow-framed glasses, leather jacket, white T-shirt, and her rainbow-colored tennis shoes.

"What does Neely think?" I asked.

"I haven't shown it to her yet. I've been keeping it covered. It's a surprise," she said.

I studied it for a bit. It was quite magical the way she had captured the essence of Neely in the painting.

"I'm impressed," I said. "I wish I could paint like that."

It was nice that she had shared this with me. Neely had really found a keeper.

After seeing her, I headed to work to await the announcement.

OUR LOCATION WAS a satellite office of the newspaper, with the headquarters in St. Louis. I had only met Oscar once, at an AIDS fundraiser in which he received an award. Most of the time, this was a *Charlie's Angels* enterprise. We would do correspondence by email, fax, and phone. When we needed a conference call, we would put him on speakerphone. He was always the boss I knew more by voice than sight.

Yet on this particular day, Oscar was coming in person. We knew this was serious. When I came into the office, Neely was busy cleaning. I joined in by vacuuming and organizing my desk to be presentable for the announcement.

I dusted a photo of Rick and me at a winery. Rick's memory was keeping me company at my desk, and I hoped his killers would soon be found.

The desk had also held a picture of Erik, which I threw in the dumpster out back. I'd already heard he'd met an Asian guy in his early twenties at the bar, and the guy had already moved in with him.

At about 11:00 a.m., Oscar came in. He was in his fifties, balding, and slightly overweight. He seemed out of sorts, frowning. This was not a good sign.

"I know the two of you have been anxious about the announcement. I really hate saying this, but I don't have a choice. My partner of ten years, Desmond, received a job offer in New York to manage a large theater. It's his dream. We are going to be heading out there together."

He took a deep breath and said, "So, this means that I'm closing down the newspaper I've managed for the last twenty years. I tried selling it, but no bites. The issue we are working on will be the last."

Tears welled up. Neely and I hugged each other. This was the worst possible news.

Oscar kept apologizing, but he could do little to comfort either of us. We didn't have any money to buy the newspaper and were living paycheck to paycheck. The newspaper had been our lives. It'd given me strength following a very dark chapter in my life.

Oscar glanced around the office. "It will take a month before operations are shut down. We will use that time to finalize the business, alert our clients, and pay off any bills due. We want to close this operation the right way. I also need you and Neely to gather up records."

He hugged us both. He was crying too. "I'm really sorry. I know how much this newspaper means to all of us. But I love him...and I want to be with him in New York."

"I understand that feeling Oscar. Amanda, my new girlfriend, is really starting to mean a lot to me," Neely said.

"I hope someone will come into my life and mean that much to me." I looked around too. It had meant everything to me, and now this was over. I kept telling myself I had to stay positive.

AMANDA, NEELY, AND I decided to go out together the night before the close of the newspaper.

I had made a last-ditch call to the police department for an update on the search for Rick's killers.

The cop came onto the phone and said point-blank, "We have no new leads on possible suspects and are still going off the vague description of the white truck he was last seen in."

"Call me if you hear anything new," I said.

"I will." His voice was soft and considerate, but I was left with the feeling that no resolution would be found.

I wished deep down I could do more. This would most likely go unsolved, like the shooting in Delaware.

I went to the bar in a pretty low state of mind, bought a beer, and sat down with them.

"How are you holding up, Todd?" Neely asked as she lit up a cigarette and offered me one.

I took it. "There are no new leads on Rick's killers and this is the end of my era as a gay journalist, I think. Life could be better."

"Come on, Todd. Join us on the dance floor. It's better than being all mopey!" Neely suggested, trying to cheer me up. I followed both of them out onto it.

We spent the night laughing and talking about all the happy times we'd had at the newspaper. I looked on as Neely laid her head on Amanda's shoulder while they danced closely together to Jewel's "Have a Little Faith in Me." She gave Amanda a light kiss and put her head back down. I would find out later Amanda had requested the song for her.

I was happy that Neely had found Amanda. Neely had spoken with the owner of the gay video store around the corner from our office, and he'd told her she could work for them. She told me that at least this would keep her involved in the gay community.

We all walked out of the bar together, my thoughts centered on the last day on the job.

"Tomorrow's going to be tough. I'm going to miss it. We did the best we could, but Oscar has every right to live his life with Desmond. Everyone does once they find someone they deeply care about," Neely said.

WORDLESSLY WE CLEANED the office. Neely kept flipping through old newspapers, finding stories she had written and telling me some of her best memories. She seemed happiest when she pulled out an article and told me details on her interviews.

Oscar came by the office in grubby jeans and an old red shirt that read "Gay Pride Festival 1995." He offered us office furniture, and Neely claimed a desk and a filing cabinet. He packed up the two computers that held all the records. When the office was cleared, we all took a moment and sighed.

"I'll write recommendation letters for both of you," he offered, and we thanked him.

As we left, Oscar turned off the light and locked the door. The name of the newspaper was still painted on the glass of the door. Someone would eventually flake off the letters, but for the moment, it held all the power of the gay rights movement that we had striven for.

My car was loaded up with copies of the newspapers in which my articles had appeared. I was left with a sense of accomplishment, but still felt I could have done more. I wished I had known someone who'd have taken over the publication.

I'd been sending out my resume to newspapers throughout the Midwest since Oscar gave us the news. In short order, I interviewed for and was offered a reporter job in Tulsa, Oklahoma, which I accepted.

I found it hard saying goodbye to Amanda and Neely. They had been friends I could rely on during a trying time in my life. Yet, they had built a home together, and I needed to move on.

During the last week I was living in Kansas City, I called the police station handling Rick's case. Again, nothing. It would be harder to keep pushing for them to solve the case if I was no longer involved in the local gay and lesbian community. But I didn't know what more I could do. Neely promised she would tell me if she heard anything.

On that last day, my car was full to the brim with my stuff.

Amanda came running out of their place holding a small painting. "Here, I did this for you."

A painting of Rick, all in blue. He was looking into a large orange ocean.

Amanda didn't know Rick. She only knew him by the photo I'd had of him on my desk and my talks with Neely. Yet even with these few brush strokes, she had captured him beautifully. I loved this view of him.

"Be careful out there. Don't get shot again," Neely said.

I hugged them both and put the painting in the front seat of the car. Rick would have a front row seat to my new life, which I was set on finding for myself and on my terms.

Second Shooting

Chapter Ten

2006

I drove to St. Louis by myself. After five years at a newspaper in Tulsa, I was interviewing for a job in my home state. Moving back felt better this time. The traumatic memories were now further in my past. The pain of my leg and Rick's death were still with me, but neither was as sharp or as constant. Also, Kevin had moved to St. Louis too.

I was going to interview for a reporter's position that I'd seen in the *St. Louis Post-Dispatch*. To locate the newspaper office, I had to first find my way around a small industrial park. My directions led to a gray-painted two-story brick building with a long warehouse near a railroad overpass.

I was buzzed in by a receptionist with long blonde hair and glasses who gestured me to seat on a plastic chair. "Wait out here."

I looked through the newspapers to gain an idea of their coverage. Eventually, the editor appeared: a tall older man with a long mustache and small black-framed glasses, who introduced himself as Tom Montgomery. He reminded me a bit of the actor Sam Elliott.

During the interview, he asked me the usual questions about my experience as a news reporter, looked over my writing, and said that I wrote thoughtfully and intelligently. I thanked him for the compliment.

"Your credentials and experience all look good. When can you start?" he asked.

"Uh...probably in two weeks at the earliest. I need to find an apartment here, move everything out of my current place, and give notice to my current employer."

"If it takes any longer, let me know. You have the job if you want it."

"Yes. I'll take it," I said.

I was filled with joy. Kevin and I had a chance to rekindle our friendship in a new city. My family would be closer and that would allow me to build a stronger relationship with them. Maybe even eventually come out to them. So many new possibilities, the future looked bright.

KEVIN HAD ASSISTED me in finding the place. He introduced me to a gay man and his boyfriend who owned a few apartment buildings in the city and I exchanged email correspondence to line up my new place.

My parents helped me move into an upper-story apartment in the transitional neighborhood of McKinley Heights in St. Louis. It was a duplex with a young lady with aqua-blue hair who wore a lot of black dresses living below me. I had only met her briefly, and we exchanged greetings as she headed out for the day. I would soon find that she stayed with her boyfriend most of the time while I lived there.

My landlords only lived down the road and I would drop my rent check off through a mail slot in the door. I rarely saw them in person.

Mom was helping me unpack when she asked, "You're in the middle of the city. Are you sure about this?"

"It will all be fine, Mom. The door has a deadbolt lock. And best of all, I'm only fifteen minutes from work."

My dad inspected it. "Make sure to lock it even when your home."

"I appreciate your concern, but you're worrying over nothing. I know I was shot once, but what are the chances of being shot again?"

After an afternoon of moving my things, they were ready to head home. They both hugged me and made me promise that I would be careful and not walk alone late at night in the neighborhood. I rolled my eyes—out of their view.

Their truck pulled away, and I stared at the mountain of boxes that now decorated my new digs. It was larger than I needed; my stuff only filled it by half. But I had no plans to move anytime soon, so I would have time to add to it.

The back balcony was the best part. The sun was going down, and as I looked out, city lights flickered in the distance. I could see across the wide Mississippi River. Two churches were in sight, one an old Eastern Orthodox with a dome and the other a large Catholic church. I always wanted an apartment with a view.

And with a bakery across the street, I could easily get a danish to nibble on in the morning. I lay down on the bed that Dad had put together and quickly fell asleep.

BEFORE THE MOVE, I had been chatting online with a St. Louis guy named David. We messaged each other and talked about our lives.

My first communication to him was the generic *I liked your profile*.

I learned from the profile that he was Jewish, thirty-something like me, and a professor at a university in St.

Louis. He enjoyed traveling, long walks, reading, and, most of all, cuddling with masculine-looking guys.

From his profile photo, I gleaned he had a stocky build, a well-trimmed beard, and there was a tiny bit of fur coming out of the top of his sky-blue polo shirt, which I always found attractive.

He responded by saying that he liked mine as well.

His father was a prominent optometrist in the New York area and his mother had stayed home to raise the kids. He'd come out to them when he was in college.

I told him my parents were Midwestern. My father worked in agribusiness and my mother worked in food service at school. They did not know I was gay.

I shared the fact that I came out to my sister right after my friend, Rick, had been killed in a gay bashing. It had been too painful not to at least share with someone in my family. She was actually not surprised since I had not had a girlfriend since high school along with the fact that I enjoyed choir and theater in school.

David: *I'm sorry to hear about the tragic death of your friend. That must have been horrible. I'm glad that someone in your family knows. Yet, you should come out to your parents. It took awhile for my parents to be on board with it. This was back in the 1990s before actors even came out. But now, we have a close relationship that only grew after I came out to them.*

Todd: *I know. I will. It's just hard.*

I told him my parents were religious and I loved them, but I wasn't ready to do that just yet. My sister wasn't in favor of also it either. Living in Oklahoma for a while had put some distance between my family and me.

He changed the subject to my favorite topic.

David: *I went to Italy and saw Florence and Siena, where I was able to watch the Palio, a horse race that goes around the center of town. It's an amazing sight.*

Todd: *Wow. All I did was go to Arkansas this past summer. I guess that counts for something, right?* I laughed at myself as I messaged that.

David: *Italy was for a conference.*

Todd: *Europe would be super cool someday. I so want to see the world.*

Todd: *What do you want in a guy?*

David: *I would like someone to come home to and care about my needs as much as I care about his.*

I thought for a moment. That was very valid.

Todd: *I envision a relationship like Luke and Lorelai in* Gilmore Girls. *Of course, she is a bit over-the-top at times, but I think her heart is in the right place. It's tough to let the right one in.*

David: *I don't watch the show.*

I was aghast.

Todd: *You should check it out.*

David: *I will for you.*

My heart melted just a little and then after we chatted, I went to watch *Gilmore Girls*. She was giving poor Luke more trouble. If only Lorelai realized how Luke was such a great catch.

I DECIDED IT was time to meet up with David in person. But I wanted to tread slowly as we got to know each other. My past relationships, Erik being a bastard and Aaron cheating on me, and even the death of Rick, a friend that I had turned to for advice, always made me cautious in dating.

I looked at Rick's photo near my home desk, and thought he would agree that it was time for me to take a leap of faith and see what happens.

I turned on my computer, took a deep breath, and messaged David.

Todd: *Let's meet up.*

David: *I live nearby in Benton Park. We can take my dog Frankie for a walk.*

Todd: *Sounds great.*

I could see my breath hanging in the air, the day we met. I knocked on his door and it opened up a bit. A Siberian Husky appeared and licked my hand and sniffed me a little.

David grabbed his coat while I waited. His profile was true to fact; he was a bearish guy wearing a button-down shirt. His hair was coal black, eyes the color of autumn leaves, arms like Hercules, and a broad chest. He reminded me of a shorter version of Gerard Butler and his broad smile gave me comfort.

"What do you think of your new workplace?" David asked, pushing a muscled arm into the sleeve of his coat.

"They seem nice enough, but I was only introduced briefly after I accepted the position."

"I've lived in St. Louis for about three years," David said. "I enjoy being a teacher, but I'm at a point in my life where it would be nice to settle down with someone."

He looked at me and lightly touched my hand, which caused my heart to race.

The Husky, named Frankie, was excited to be out in the cold air, and David used his strong-arm strength to keep her in line.

We talked more about traveling, which was something I'd always enjoyed.

"What have you seen of the US?" I asked.

"I've been to a few states," he said.

"I've been to all forty-eight, just missing Alaska and Hawaii."

"Those would be quite an adventure to see with someone who loved to travel as much as I do."

"Yes, it would be."

Snowflakes began to collect on the ground as we walked.

"I love the snow, just not the cold," I said.

"Ah. But it's great snuggling weather."

I burst out laughing.

Our walk ended in front of David's house. He asked me to come in.

I looked away from his gaze, trying not become enticed by them and said, "I need to head home and prepare for my first day on the job."

"That makes sense," he said. "Would you like to meet up again?"

"Yes. That would be great. I don't know my schedule yet, but I'll give you a call."

"So would we call our next time together a date?"

I shuffled my feet, "I...I'm brand new to the city. Let's hang out again and go from there."

Then he surprised me with a quick kiss on the cheek. "I normally don't do that."

I blushed. "I enjoyed the kiss, but let's take this slow."

David said, "I think we can do that" before he closed the door, but I had the sneaking feeling I was being difficult. Yet, I only wanted to be cautious with my heart this time.

THE FOLLOWING MORNING, I headed over to the bakery for my danish. I also picked up a copy of the newspaper where I'd be working. Now I would have a byline in the largest newspaper for which I had ever written for.

I was nervous as I sat at my assigned computer. It was obvious that it hadn't been used in a while, but I was determined to make it my own and do some of my best work with it. I gathered my pens together in a cup and checked out the writing software.

A stout and wavy-haired blond guy and a skinny younger woman approached.

"Hi, I'm Stephen," he said.

"And, I'm Beth," she said.

"So, would you like to go out to eat?" Stephen asked. Beth stood behind him, beaming.

"Sure."

In an unfamiliar town, it was a nice gesture to be invited out. I went with them to the deli counter in a grocery store called Le Grand's, which had some tables and metal chairs scattered about for customers to scarf down sandwiches. We waited in a long line of people, construction workers, men in suits, a mom or two with kids running around them. It seemed to be a popular place.

"You'll like working at the paper," Stephen said as he went up to place his order.

"What do you think of the office?" Beth asked.

"Quite the ramshackle warehouse," I said.

"It would be nice if it had more windows," Stephen said.

We all laughed. I sat back in my chair and relaxed as we talked.

"James Marlowe is the copy editor. If you want to improve your writing skills, he's the guy to turn to. He's worked here for years and knows everything," Stephen informed me.

"You should try to follow his advice," Beth said.

"Also, don't worry if the sports people don't seem too friendly. They tend to keep to themselves in the back," Stephen added.

Later, after I'd returned to my desk, I put up a small calendar with pictures of Kansas City, adding a piece of my past into my future.

KEVIN HAD MOVED to St. Louis following his breakup with Roger, and I hoped that living in the same city would allow us to renew our friendship.

After the first week of work, Kevin and I decided to go out. He was excited that we would be living close to each other again, a bright spot since I was nervous about starting a new job and a new life.

We met at a nearby gay bar in Soulard called the Bastille, which reflected St. Louis's heritage as a French colony. The bar was brick inside and out. It had a cozy feel with a long wooden counter and a mirrored wall behind. I checked out the men in the bar as I waited for him. It was a lively crowd with some older gents in leather attire, a lesbian couple, and a bouncy young gay guy and his muscle-bound boyfriend, who sat kissing next to me.

I found myself missing David as they interact with each other. He was out of town that weekend, so I thought this would allow me some time to get reacquainted with Kevin. I was having trouble following my "taking it slow" motto.

We hugged hello when Kevin arrived. After ordering our drinks, he grabbed my hand and tugged me toward the dance floor.

"Let's dance," he shouted over the music as he shuffled toward the writhing mass of people.

When we sat back down, he asked, "Do you want another drink?"

"No. Not right now." I became serious. "Kevin, I'm sorry about what happened between you and Roger. You were always too good for him."

"I was, wasn't I?" He beamed. "The worst part was when he was cheating on me. He was doing it right under my nose."

"But the relationship was good for a while, right?"

"It had its ups and downs," he said. "The cheating was unforgivable."

Kevin showed me a photo of a small white dog with lots of fur. "You should get a dog. They don't ever cheat on you. They're compassionate and the occasional lick on the face is all I need at the moment."

I laughed at him. "Maybe I should think about being on my own for a while. Take my time." Although thoughts of David kept flashing through my mind, I wasn't ready to talk about him yet. I wondered if he was thinking about me.

WHEN DAVID GOT back, we had dinner at a Thai restaurant on South Grand with his closest friend, Mark, who had a stocky build like David, chestnut-brown hair, a well-trimmed beard, and thin wire-framed glasses. He was studying to be a pastor for a gay-friendly church.

Mark shook my hand firmly. "I've been hearing a lot about you."

"All good, I hope," I said.

We sat down in the eclectically decorated restaurant.

David talked about work and dealing with students on their cell phones in class. "I always have to watch out for them texting."

"I only hope that my sermons keep them from doing that," Mark said. "So where are you from, Todd?"

"From all over. My parents moved a lot when we were kids, although we always stayed in the Midwest." I clenched my teeth a bit as I waited for the next question.

"So do you go to church?" Mark asked.

"No, I don't," I said sharply. I wasn't comfortable talking about God. I still had issues with the heavenly father and the religious right. Lately, it seemed as though most people who claimed to be God-fearing were also the ones who were vehemently anti-gay. At the time, this included my folks.

"Let's order dinner," David intervened, cutting off any further discussion about God.

The rest of the night went more smoothly. David and Mark were old friends, so they had a lot to talk about. I remained quiet through most of the evening.

They hugged goodbye, and we headed back toward David's place.

"You could have been nicer," David said. "He only wanted to learn a little about you, but you rebutted him. Should I know something?"

"I was the problem," I admitted.

"Yes, you were. You can relax a bit."

"I'm not comfortable talking about myself," I said.

I was tired and was not at a point where I wanted to share more about my past.

"You know you're going to have to open up if you want to keep dating," David said.

"I will. Just not today."

He kissed me gently. "You don't have to be so tough."

I returned the kiss. "I want to take it slow, like I've said."

We stopped out in front of his place.

"I know I can be difficult," I said. "I've had my heart stomped on a lot over the past few years and...it takes time to get over it. I know that's not fair to you, but it's the truth."

"It's okay, Todd. I'm not going anywhere." David kissed me once more. I turned a bit red. I hoped he didn't notice.

Back at my apartment, I stared up at the whitewashed ceiling as I lay in bed. I thought about David for a long time, his hairy body and the way his eyes seemed to stay focused on me. Maybe he really did like me and I was being hardheaded. I decided to give him a chance, but not without some reservation. I wanted to make sure that this time I was going into a relationship that might last. A gay man can dream, right?

I HAD BEEN seeing David for a few weeks. We'd even gone on a short road trip together to a nearby town. We checked out an antique store, and he bought a small wooden desk at one of the shops.

"What do you think?" he had asked.

"It looks sturdy, and it would be nice to have a desk to work from when I stay over."

He put it in the upstairs room that I used as part of a makeshift office when I worked on my news stories at his house. This was our first purchase together. We were becoming closer with each new day. Even Mark seemed to approve.

But I still had not talked to Kevin about David. I didn't want to have the conversation until I was sure David and I were a couple, which was quickly becoming the case.

Kevin and I went out to our usual gay bar one night. This time, I didn't even notice the men going in and out. I had begun to focus my life on David.

He arrived late; he had some last-minute stuff to take care of at his job. He kindly bought my favorite drink, Tequila Sunrise.

"I've been seeing this guy named David and he seems nice," I blurted. He must have sensed my reservations.

"What's the issue you're having with him?" Kevin asked as he sucked on his straw.

"It's all happening so fast," I said. "I really like him. But...my history with men, my past...I always end up in a mess. He seems sweet. I enjoy the simple moments, lying down on the couch with him and watching *Doctor Who* on Friday nights. That's it. Pretty boring, right? Is this good or bad?"

"I don't have the answers when it comes to relationships. I thought Roger and I would be together longer... Forever, maybe. But it all fell apart."

I heard the pain in his voice. I was more confused than ever.

He looked at me straight in the eye. "If you really are falling in love, you're enjoying it, so go for it. Yes, it can all come crashing down. We've both been through that. But after everything, it's still worth taking the leap for love."

He took me back onto the small dance floor. We were the only ones on the floor dancing to Cher's "Song for the Lonely." Afterward, I headed home and thought about calling David but looked at the time and noticed that it was past one in the morning.

It was a good sign that I was thinking about him at the end of the night after being at a bar surrounded by half-naked men and ignoring the ones that wanted my attention. My thoughts went to what was becoming my favorite pastime, being on the couch, my head on his lap and Frankie down below us on the floor.

DAVID AND I were on that couch when my sister called one day.

"What are you up to?" she asked.

"We're just watching television," I answered reflexively.

"Who's we?"

I hesitated. I hadn't told her about David yet. He could hear both sides of the conversation from where he sat. He knew I was hesitating about admitting I was there with him.

"Well...?" Darn, now she was intrigued.

Between that and the look David gave me, I knew that I needed to tell her. So I did. "David's here."

"David who?"

"He's the guy I'm seeing." I exhaled.

"You hardly ever talk to me about guys. He must be something special."

"He is."

"I'm glad that you're seeing someone."

"Really?" I couldn't hide my surprise. I knew she loved me, but I was still uncertain how cool she was with my being gay.

"Yes, really." She had some annoyance in her voice. "It might not be how we were raised, but I want you to be happy."

"I am. Thanks."

But before I could say anything more, she continued, "I have to check to see what the kids are up to, but I do want to meet him. We'll have to make a date for that in the near future."

It was great to hear this from my sister.

AFTER A FEW months of dating, David and I decided to move in together, which made getting to know him a priority for Kevin. He constantly questioned me about why I was doing this and said that, in his opinion, we were moving too fast.

He was right. We had only known each other a few months, but in my thirties, I had a better sense of who I was. If David was willing to take on my craziness, I was fine with that. Besides, I was spending most of my time at his place, and my apartment had a refrigerator full of food that had gone bad since I was hardly ever there.

Kevin volunteered to help me move in after borrowing a truck from a friend of his. David and I only lived a few blocks away from each other so it was quick move.

Kevin and David had met a few times over the past few months. They weren't friends as much as people who knew each other through me. Kevin liked him all right, but had said David wasn't someone he would date. That was fine, since all the people that Kevin had been with were people I would never have dated either. Kevin and I had a lot of things in common, but dating preferences were not among them.

Kevin flat-out told David, "You be careful with him. He's had his heart broken before when he moved in with someone."

I changed the subject without giving David a chance to respond. "We need to get moving since there's a chance of rain this afternoon."

As we packed, I pulled out a box filled with old videocassettes. "These are the old horror movies that Kevin and I used to stay up late watching as kids. I used to head over to Kevin's house and show him the latest one I'd picked up."

Even though we weren't out to each other, much less ourselves, we'd quietly enjoyed watching these shows for the sex scenes that always included hunky guys with their clothes off.

It was always strange to look back at my life and understand what was left unspoken. David rolled his eyes at us as he looked through the titles.

"I don't need to watch these anymore since I have a hottie like David in my life," I said. David kissed me lightly enjoying my flattery.

Kevin rolled his eyes this time. When we finished moving my stuff, we went to our regular bar in Soulard for a drink.

Kevin seemed tense, and when I questioned him, he exclaimed, "I didn't talk with you about this before, but I'm considering doing drag." He downed a beer.

"It's fine. If you want to explore a new avenue for yourself, I support it."

Then I glanced at David, who seemed unsure of what to say. He turned to Kevin and said, "Yes, Todd and I will stand behind you one hundred percent."

I gave David an odd look, not expecting the one hundred percent part. But Kevin was my closest friend. We were going to support him.

"I perform in a month at Big J's Big, Big Gay Show. Do you mind coming out and watching?" Kevin looked at us both with uncertainty.

"Sure thing," David said.

I almost laughed. David was really being a good sport about this.

Kevin spent the rest of the evening telling us about the Britney Spears number he was going to do.He stood up to show us some dance numbers, got into the act, and almost hit a waiter who was bringing some beer to a table. Kevin apologized profusely, and I fought hard to keep from laughing. He seemed so excited about this new step in his life. This was the happiest I had seen him in a long time.

We headed out late. Kevin was still talking about the outfit he was going to wear and how many people he needed to call. He wanted a large audience for his debut. I assured him that they would all show up. We kissed and hugged goodbye, and I wished him good luck.

David and I headed for bed and talked for a while.

"Thanks for your support of Kevin," I said.

"You owe me, you know," David said.

"How do I pay up?"

He waggled his brows. "You know."

We began to kiss. It seemed like life was finally going in the right direction, for Kevin and for me.

Still, I kept waking up at night, hearing sirens in the distance. I lived in the city so this was normal. But something crept in the back of my mind, as though dark days lay ahead. I couldn't shake it, no matter how hard I tried to bury my face in David's furry chest.

I DECIDED TO come out to Stephen and Beth. This was not something I normally did unless I felt I could trust someone, but over the last few months, I'd begun to feel that I could. I told them I wanted to share something personal with them over dinner, and we went out to eat at a nearby Mexican restaurant. It had a festive atmosphere with large murals of pueblos everywhere and even piñatas hung about.

"So what is the announcement?" Stephen asked. "It's not like you to arrange a dinner outing."

"I know," I said. "First, I thought you should know that I'm gay. I've wanted to tell you since we've all become so close."

They didn't say a word at first. Normally, I didn't come out to people in such a direct way.

"No big deal," Stephen said, clearing the air.

"I have no problem with that." Beth nodded.

"I have a question to follow up on my announcement. My best friend Kevin is becoming a drag performer. His first performance is in two weeks. I want to have a big crowd there for him. Would you two be interested in going?"

They stared at each other, then said, "Yes."

"It sounds like great fun," said Stephen. "Okay, it's our turn to make—what did you call it—an announcement? Beth and I have started seeing each other." To add emphasis, he gave Beth a long, full-on smooch.

She blinked in shock. After gaining back her composure, she said, "You know, you could have warned me, Stephen."

"I just wanted him to see how in love we are," he said.

"Okay, but next time you feel like giving me a huge kiss, let me know in advance. Now, I have to go see if you messed up my makeup."

She walked away to a restroom, and Stephen said, "As a gay man, do you understand women more than I do? I thought showing affection would make her happy, not upset her."

"Sorry, I'm not the one to give advice about women. I mostly hang out with gay men, and I still seem to be doing that wrong a lot of the time," I said.

It seemed we were both learning what it was to be in a relationship. It was also nice to know I had friends I could talk to who were okay with me being gay. It had been rough since I'd left the gay paper. I had shied away from getting close to people while I lived in Tulsa. Losing Rick and the shooting in Delaware had made me uncomfortable with gaining new friends. Yet now I was making it in a more diverse city with Kevin close by and newfound love. It was good to move on.

MY SISTER KAREN'S excuse for coming to see me was to deliver some boxes filled with stuff that I had been storing at her house and do some shopping in the big city, but I knew the truth. She wanted to check out David. Especially after I'd told her we moved in together.

When she knocked on the door, Frankie came running and I followed. I was nervous.

"Nice house," she said.

David came up behind me.

"This is David," I introduced.

I gave her a small tour. The downstairs included a living room with a small sofa and settees in beige and burgundy, each with an Indian scene on them. This space was only separated by pocket doors to a TV room with a large leather couch and soft leather chair. The kitchen was in the back of the house with a long center aisle and a huge dark wooden table with chairs. Upstairs included two bedrooms, a master bathroom, and an office area.

We sat down and talked in the living room.

"Todd has talked a lot about you," she said. "Are you being good to my little brother?"

David seemed taken by surprise. I couldn't help but smirk to see my boyfriend at a loss for words in front of my loving but overprotective sister.

"Karen, be nice," I said.

"Of course." He wrapped his arms around me in a hug.

Before things could really get awkward, I said, "Let's eat. We can talk more when we go get to the restaurant."

It was a short walk to a neighborhood spot that was well known for its fried chicken. It was a down-home sort of place in the middle of the city with a low-hanging ceiling, checkered tablecloths, and red metallic chairs.

When my sister finished her piece of chicken, I asked, "What do you think?"

"Pretty good. Do you come here much?"

"Every once in a while," David said. "Todd thought you would like it. What other questions do you have for me?"

"Have you found Todd to be difficult at times?" she asked, smirking.

Suddenly, I was on the spot.

David laughed. "Todd has his moments...but he has a good heart and I know he loves me."

"Good answer," she said.

"What did you tell Mom and Dad when you moved in with David?"

"The usual, that we are roommates."

"I wish he would come out," David said.

My sister was taken aback for a moment, and said, "It will be hard for them."

I could tell that my sister was ready to go when she kept checking her phone for the time.

Although I sensed some uneasiness from her, she hugged David as we headed out. "Remember, you be good to him," she said before leaving.

DAVID AND I walked into the crowded Grey Fox Pub to see Kevin's big drag debut. The bar had a stage with stairs that would allow a drag queen to walk out to greet fans seated in small round tables. We were early so we were able to find a table close to the stage.

I was excited for Kevin.

"I'm going to check and see how he is doing," I said to David.

Behind the stage was a large room filled with assorted costumes that included "Madonna cones" and a short

Wonder Woman dress with a magic lasso. I thought to myself I would love to try the lasso out.

In the farthest corner of the room sat Kevin in a long blonde wig.

He signaled me to come over. "How do I look?"

He was wearing a strapless black dress, black heels, and a good bit of blue eye shadow. His blonde wig flowed down his back in loose waves.

I had trouble wrapping my mind around his whole look. I was amazed and shocked at the same time that the friend I had known since high school could be so stunning in a dress. I was speechless.

"Todd, are you there?"

"Sorry, you just look so... Madonna would cry with joy at how you look," I said.

"Thanks. Do you really think so?"

"So, what are you filled with on top?" I touched where his boobs were. They felt soft and squishy.

He pulled them out. "Fake boobs, of course. I don't naturally have these, Todd."

"I know. I think what you're doing takes a lot of balls."

"Actually those are tucked away." He laughed, and we hugged.

"I have to practice," he said. "Thanks for coming. It means so much to me."

I walked back out to the club. I was proud of him for taking a chance like this. He seemed to glow. I was pretty sure he was walking higher than even those six-inch heels elevated him.

Almost as soon as I started looking for Beth and Stephen, they entered the bar behind two tall drag queens.

"It's a busy night," Stephen said. "It took us a while to find a parking. I guess that bodes well for your friend."

As we headed toward where David and I were sitting, the lights went low and a large African-American drag queen sauntered onstage. The show was about to begin.

"I'm Monica Daniels, and these ladies are ready to showcase their talents. Tonight, we are welcoming a newbie. Her name is Jade Sinclair, and you are going to be blown away by the performance she has planned for you!"

Kevin-as-Jade came onstage, throwing her hair back. She pranced and posed, and with each successive song, we could feel her becoming Madonna. She used each step, each movement to convey the character she had become. Each beat was perfectly timed, each note perfectly played to show Jade's talent. Her performance was met with thunderous applause. Jade was a hit. I was so proud of Kevin.

Jade even gave Stephen a kiss on his cheek, leaving red lipstick smeared on his face, during one of her sets. Stephen blushed and laughed.

"He is something," Stephen said. "I wasn't expecting this. I've never gone to drag shows before. This is fun."

The performance ended with all of the players on stage. I presented Kevin with a bouquet roses and a kiss on the cheek.

"Thank you so much, Todd." He beamed as he headed backstage.

"So what did you think of it?" I asked as I sat back down at the table.

"He was fabulous," said Stephen. "That is the right thing to say, right?" He looked around the table, questioning.

I smiled. "Good job with your gay slang. I didn't know what to expect, but he outperformed my expectations."

"She looked amazing," Beth said.

"Now, you don't have any inclinations to do the same thing, do you?" David asked me.

"And what if I do?" I answered. I wasn't interested in doing it, but it was fun to tease him.

"I hope not. You know I couldn't handle all that makeup and fingernails," David said.

"That's why you're with me, right?" I said.

"Whatever you say, butch." He winked at Stephen and Beth as he said it.

Kevin came up to our table with most of his makeup gone and his wig off. "How am I as Jade?"

"You were stupendous. You're going to do more shows, right?" I asked.

"Well, of course, dear," he said.

"That was quite the performance," Stephen said.

"Let us know next time you're back on that stage," Beth added.

"Love it, just loovvve it, as they say in show business," I said, trying to be funny and give Kevin more of a boost of support.

David rolled his eyes at me, which conveyed the message "Don't overdo it, hon."

Yet David added, "An admirable job, Jade."

It meant a lot to me that David and my new friends supported Kevin. It had been difficult for Kevin coming back to the Midwest after Roger and now taking on the persona of Jade Sinclair.

As we headed back home, I mused, "Wow, life is finally together. Thanks for doing this. It meant a lot to me. I really do love you."

He tickled me, so I tickled him back. He kissed me and I snuggled close to him.

I wanted so much for the night to last forever. Everything seemed perfect. I had a man I loved, my best friend was a star, and Stephen and Beth enhanced my work life. Things couldn't be better.

Chapter Eleven

I HAD BEEN at my job for almost a year, and then one day, I came into the office and found out that my happy world was ending. All the staff were brought into a small back room, and a man that I had never seen before walked in.

"He's James McDonald, the publisher," Stephen whispered.

"We're changing management. I'm sorry to say, Tom Montgomery has been let go. Also, we will be making some other tweaks to the operation shortly," he said.

Everyone looked at each other. This was not good. We knew to read between the lines. Some of us were probably not going to be around tomorrow.

I stayed quiet. I was the new guy. If I was laid off, I would take it. I would rather it be me than someone who had worked for the newspaper for most of their lives.

In the end, we found out that the people on the printing side were losing their jobs and not us in the newsroom. I was happy for all the workers in my department but sad for everyone else.

A few days later, I was called in to what had been Tom's office. I had liked Tom. I remembered once when I asked about a large rock that had been in the office.

He'd said, "The rock... We're not in the best part of town. I came into the office last winter and this rock was on the floor, along with glass from the shattered window behind me. Someone had broken in. I keep this rock so that if they return, at least I have something to fight back with."

That was the type of person he was. Now, someone new was in his office—a tall woman with long raven-black hair and small glasses that partially hid her narrow eyes.

She indicated the chair in front of her desk. After I was seated, she began by introducing herself. "I'm Harper Candley and I'm the new manager of both our city office and the suburban office. We've decided to transfer you to cover the news at our suburban branch."

I didn't know what to say. It didn't seem to be up to me. "When do I start out there?"

"Next Monday," she said.

I thought the suburban office should at least be a safer place to work. But I was going to miss my friends, and I wasn't sure what this new location meant for me.

ON FRIDAY, I went out to dinner with Stephen and Beth at a bar and restaurant that had lots of TVs playing sports shows, sort of an Irish pub on steroids with an expansive patio in the Dogtown area of St. Louis.

"We'll miss you," Stephen said.

"The same here. I was just getting used to this place." I was scarfing down a huge plate nachos with all the fixin's. I loved going out to a brewpub with them after work.

"How do you feel about this?" Beth said.

"I don't know. But I'm at least still employed," I said, shrugging my shoulders. That was the best I could come up with. "We'll still have to hang out even if it isn't at work."

When I went to my car, I felt a little more alone. I hoped I would meet a great workforce at the other office. Working in the suburbs—so what could go wrong? Yet I had this nagging feeling that life wasn't going to be the same. A crack now existed in the world that I had built. At least I still had my job and David. I kept trying to comfort myself in that statement.

I WAS OUT of my element as I walked up to the large glass-and-metal office building where I'd been moved for my new position.

I went up the elevator, carrying a box filled with mementos from my former desk, then approached the receptionist on the fourth floor. "I'm Todd Smith. I was a reporter at the city office and have been transferred here. I was wondering where my workspace is."

The receptionist turned. She seemed preoccupied, and I'd taken her away from whatever she'd been doing. She simply said, "Just a minute."

I waited as she made a phone call, then told me, "Harper will escort you to your desk."

As quickly as she said that, she was back on the phone. The box was feeling a little heavy. I should have thought about this before bringing everything with me.

A woman I assumed was Harper came out of her office and signaled for me to follow. "You'll be over by Sara. You'll like her, I'm sure."

I followed her down a long corridor filled with cubicles until she showed me mine. I put the heavy box down, and Harper went back to her office as I turned on the computer and settled in.

A petite woman with shoulder-length blonde hair popped her head around the corner of my cubicle. "Hi, I'm Sara. I'm the online editor. If you need anything, just let me know." At least she was friendly.

"Thanks." I was assigned to cover the suburbs now. This included city council meetings and school boards. Same job, only new digs.

MY ASSIGNTMENT WAS the city council meeting in Kirkwood, an upper-class suburb with a small working-class population. The agenda had the usual items relating to zoning, and I would write a story based on what seemed to get the citizens most excited.

I walked into the chambers, and Helen Regis, an older city councilwoman, introduced herself. She was tall with long brown hair and glasses. She was forthright and obviously had the ability to put people at ease.

"A lot of the time, it can be difficult to get to know what is going on in a new town," she said to me. "If you ever have questions or want to know more, feel free to talk with me. Here's my phone number."

The first time I took her up on the offer, she suggested we meet for coffee. Helen was happy to talk about her own years as a journalist. It was one of the warmest welcomes I've had in my career. That coffee was followed up by many productive conversations where Helen provided answers to my questions and context to my stories.

AFTER SEVERAL MONTHS, I became more comfortable with attending the meetings and following what was going on. One week's meeting started like any other one. I said my hellos to all and made conversation with Helen.

"It's a warm night for fall," I said.

"Yes, it is. I don't think tonight's going to go too late," she commented.

"Thanks for the update." I nodded as we all sat down.

The front of the room had a raised dais and a long crescent-shaped table where the council sat. Citizens who wanted to address the council would come forward through the middle aisle.

The mayor, an older gentleman with glasses and white hair with a comb-over, sat in the middle of the table, and the other council members, including Helen, surrounded him.

A tall man that I had only seen once before came into the room. He was in back, wearing a large wooden sign around his neck reading, "Kirkwood City Council says only lies."

Then he came forward during the meeting and talked with a loud voice.

I struggled to understand his angry, yet animated speech.

His time was limited by the period allowed for open comments. Once the clock buzzed, the time to talk ended. He was signaled by one of the council members to leave the podium. He walked away, muttering to himself.

I approached him, curious what his concerns were. "Can I ask your name, sir?"

He stared at me. "I'm Raymond Wilkes. And you are?"

"Todd Smith. I'm with the *County Times*."

"They're all crooks," he said.

"Who?"

"The city council."

"What's your complaint?"

"They screwed me over. That's my complaint." He went on about his problems with the council. I feverishly wrote down notes of what he said. It included a long list of all the ways that the city was singling him out and treating him unfairly and how it was hurting his business. I stayed with him until he was ready to leave the council meeting.

I wasn't sure what to think. His eyes seemed to be glazed over as he talked. Something didn't feel quite right. The wooden sign around his neck didn't help me feel more comfortable about him. But I let it go.

The council meeting included other issues that more citizens seemed interested in. I put my notes into my pack. It might be a future story, but his frustration seemed very personal.

I headed out, thinking about other people's concerns relating to zoning and a new fast-food joint coming into a close-knit neighborhood. The citizens didn't want the noise or traffic it would cause. This seemed to have more people riled up.

Yet, I still had this feeling that Raymond did have a legitimate issue, although I could feel that there was something deeper and darker in the way he had spoken to me. It scared me.

I considered staying longer and asking Helen about the man. I felt nervous about the whole situation. I didn't know what to do about it, so I focused on zoning instead.

I WASN'T REALLY getting to know my fellow reporters but was more confident in my work as I went along.

One day, I learned that Sara was leaving and her position managing the newspaper's website would be open. I decided to apply for it.

I checked with Harper about it. "I did online work for the newspaper in college and for the newspaper I worked for in Tulsa. I was wondering if I could apply for her position."

She thought for a moment. "Yes, you can do that."

"Thanks." I then planned to discuss it with David when I went home.

I explained the position to him as he put together a meal of spaghetti. "I think it will be a good thing. Why is Sara leaving?"

"I think she's getting married and moving to where her fiancé lives. They have a long-distance relationship."

"Ahh love," he said and kissed me.

"Love, right," I said.

"Does it pay more?" he asked.

"A little."

"Even better." He put the plates on the table. "Dinner is ready."

We ate and watched television. Frankie sat at our feet. I was becoming comfortable in our everyday life.

A few weeks later, Harper asked me to come into her office. "You can take over the position, although you'll need to do both jobs until we hire a new reporter."

I was happy to be moving up.

IN FEBRUARY, I was still doing double-duty as a reporter and online editor. I headed to another city council meeting in Kirkwood.

I kept having this weird feeling that I shouldn't go, that I should skip it. It tugged at the back of my mind. I couldn't understand why. Nothing on the printed agenda indicated anything to worry about. I sat in my car and took a moment to think. I rarely missed city council meetings. Why would I miss this one?

The city council's agenda contained mostly concerns relating again to zoning. That would be the bulk of the evening's issues. I spoke to a few people prior to the start of the meeting. Their issues were understandable; they just wanted the city council to consider their neighborhood before putting in a new business.

I sat near the front of the city council room.

Helen was in attendance, and I had greeted her earlier when I came in. I thought about giving her a call after the meeting to get the real scoop on some concerns I'd heard discussed.

We stood up to recite the Pledge of Allegiance, and within seconds after doing that, Raymond Wilkes showed up, his wooden sign hanging around his neck. He was a regular, becoming a mundane sight at meetings. I had learned over time that he was just a part of covering Kirkwood. Wilkes walked forward on the far right side of the room. He seemed to be going in an odd direction if he wanted to address the city council properly. I sat back down after the pledge with my computer on my lap, ready to type notes of the meeting.

"Shoot the mayor!" Wilkes shouted.

There was instant chaos.

A loud pop sounded and Rich Mull, a tall, gray-haired police officer, collapsed onto the floor. Blood gushed from of a hole in his head. I don't think my mind even had time to register that he was dead.

I started to stand up, but Raymond pointed his gun in my direction. His eyes were dark, glazed. Rage radiated from his face. He appeared committed to shooting again without regard of the consequences.

I heard more bangs. A bullet hit my hand and grazed my chest. Blood seeped out of me now. I was still standing, in complete shock, and said to no one, "Oh my God, I've been shot again." My thoughts briefly flashed back to the first time I was shot. The fear. The adrenaline. The sense that my life was in danger.

My next thought, weirdly but understandably, was *I can't write*. My hand was bleeding, the main tool of my trade as a journalist. Everything focused down to one thing, much like my previous shooting. I needed to get away in order to survive. I had been shot twice, and a third bullet might be my last.

I cautiously staggered toward the back of the room. I only concentrated on this movement. Other pops sounded behind me, but I didn't turn around. If I stopped to look, I might see the gun, his eyes, and his anger. I might freeze and wind up being shot again, either purposely or accidentally. Each step was one closer to the door, to the hallway, to the stairs. As if I had blinders on. I opened the door quietly and walked through. I didn't notice others around me. I headed down the stairs, touching the banister with my intact left hand and the wall with my right, not thinking that I was leaving a bloodstained trail behind.

My hand was bleeding, but there wasn't much pain since the wound was so deep, much like the last time. It was a constant stream of blood. A hole had opened up and was free to bleed down my fingers.

My mind was in a haze of shock. Stumbling outside, I approached an EMT, took a deep breath, and said to the uniformed man with a short beard, "I've been shot in the hand."

The scene was chaotic with police officers, EMTs, and people everywhere.

He stared at me for a moment, then handed me a cloth. "I know you are injured, but you're stable. Just sit here until we can get you an ambulance."

I don't think he comprehended how seriously wounded the hand was. Later, I would understand that the EMTs were hoping they could save more lives. The mayor had been critically wounded.

I waited with my bleeding hand, but I couldn't stand still. I walked around aimlessly. I stood for a moment, lost in thought. It seemed like a war zone. Emergency personnel streamed into City Hall. There were people talking, shouting, and crying around me. I didn't say a word. I felt lost.

Much like the first shooting, a man came up to me, a complete stranger. "Are you all right?"

I pointed to my hand, the bloody cloth.

"Here, take my sweater. You need to stay warm," he said.

I'd walked outside into the cold February night without a coat. He put it on me. I suddenly realized I hadn't told David what had happened. I put my hand to my pocket, hoping I hadn't lost my phone. I found it, told the man I had to make a phone call, and thanked him. This kind person disappeared into the night, like the man who had helped me during the first shooting.

I dialed David. "Come and get me."

"Where are you?" he asked.

"Come and get me."

David repeated, "Where are you?"

This exchange kept repeating until I finally said, "Kirkwood City Hall."

"I don't know where that is," he said.

This was before you could check your phone or GPS to find a location, but I couldn't think clearly enough to provide directions. We were silent for a moment as we were figuring out what to say.

Finally David said, "I...I have a friend who lives nearby. I'll send her to get you. Are you...all right?"

I wasn't sure what to say. Should I tell him the truth, that I was covered in blood and wasn't sure? No. I didn't want him to panic.

"I love you," I said.

"I don't want to do this...but I've got get off the phone to reach her to get you. I love you too."

The phone clicked off. I decided that I should call Harper, my managing editor.

"This is Todd and I've been shot."

"You what?"

"Shot. I won't be able to write what happened. I was shot in my right hand, sorry."

"What happened?" she asked.

"A disgruntled citizen—his name was Raymond, I think—started shooting at council members. A police officer was shot...and others... It was all so fast...such a blur. All I can really say is that I won't be able to write this with my hand at the moment. Again, sorry."

"You should probably get to the hospital... Oh! I'm seeing it on the news... Are you okay?"

"I think so... Just my hand is bleeding right now. I'm trying to keep as much pressure on it as I can. It's all pretty crazy," I said.

Silence.

"Yes...it is. You should probably get the hand looked at. Don't worry about writing up the story. We'll send another reporter. Just hang in there. You get help now," she said.

"I will."

Instinctively, I went to slip the phone into my coat pocket, only to realize my coat along with my computer was still in the council room. The relief of another reporter taking over was quickly replaced with anxiety over my possessions. The laptop was brand new and I didn't have the money to replace it.

The decision to retrieve my computer wasn't just a financial one. It held a repository of all my writing, which as a journalist was my identity. Without it, I was adrift, but focusing on it reduced the insanity of the scene around me.

As I looked around to ask someone if it was safe to retrieve my stuff, I noticed a large number of cops everywhere. Surveying this scene, I concluded that whatever had happened with Wilkes was probably over.

No one challenged me as I walked toward the doors of City Hall. Taking a deep breath, I headed up the stairs. I cautiously walked into the council chambers.

Two people lay on the floor. The lack of movement and blood could only mean one thing, but I couldn't allow myself to think about it. Shifting my gaze from the bodies to where I had been sitting, I found my computer; a splatter of blood marred its crisp white shell. My efforts to wipe away the blood only served to smear it. I was equally unsuccessful as I tried to turn it off.

One of the city council members who I sort of knew was in the room. He was an older man with black hair. He was talking with others. I made eye contact with him.

"I can't get...the computer to turn off," I said.

He stared at my wrapped, bleeding hand. "You should probably get that hand checked out."

I agreed.

He took the laptop but couldn't get it to turn off either. I finally was able to shut it down and put it in my now-bloodstained computer bag. I walked back down the stairs in a daze. My hand was still numb to the pain, but I couldn't walk around bleeding forever.

I returned to the ambulance, hoping that I could be helped out this time.

One of the paramedics asked, "Are you hurt?"

I nodded.

"We should take you to the hospital," he said.

"Thanks." I got in the ambulance.

The paramedic grabbed for the laptop bag, but I clutched it tighter. If I let it go, I would fall apart. It was as if I needed the laptop as some sort of token of normality. It should have been a part of another routine city council meeting. That's what I was supposed to be reporting on. Not this.

They put an IV in me, and we headed for a nearby hospital with blazing lights all around and the sirens sounding. I clutched my laptop even tighter.

I WAS WHEELED past the main emergency room toward a private room to be examined. While there were plenty of people coming in to check on me, it seemed calm compared to what I had left.

David entered as the emergency room doctor was explaining how they were going to bring in a hand specialist. He stayed with me as I waited and held my good hand when they probed my wound and I winced in pain. He only left my side when it came time for more X-rays. This was followed by the elevator ride to the hospital room that would be home for the next few days.

I STARED UP at the ceiling, contemplating the déjà vu of the situation. This time, I had been shot in the hand, and at least I had David in my life. So that much was different.

IV tubes and needles surrounded me. I was waiting on news of my hand; I would probably find out more soon. I might end up a one-handed journalist.

"I hate to bother you with this," David said to me when I awoke. He had brought in a breakfast tray and put it on the sliding table. "A police officer wanted to call you this morning to confirm a detail. They wanted to determine the origin of a blood trail." He grimaced as he spoke.

I called after eating breakfast.

"This is Officer Jarrod Tinson" was the greeting when he picked up the phone.

"This is Todd Smith. I was told you had some questions."

"We followed a blood trail last night," Tinson said. "We need to verify whose blood it is."

"Okay," I said.

"Did you go up and down the stairs last night?"

"Yes, that's me bleeding."

"Did you walk around outside City Hall?" he asked.

"Me again. I was having trouble just standing around and...I was a bit out of my mind."

"That's understandable," he said.

"Sorry about that."

"We just needed to confirm that info. Thanks for your cooperation."

"You're welcome," I said.

David looked at me as I hung up. "What happened?"

"They were checking to see if I was the one who left the blood trail everywhere. I hope I'm not asked to clean it up." I smirked.

"I think they'll understand," David said, patting my arm with fake solicitation.

"Only *I* could leave a blood trail."

"It happens, right?"

We both kind of chuckled. At least for the moment, I could smile at the situation. *Maybe next time I get shot. I'll try to stay in one place.*

David told me my family had been notified and were on their way. He was still wearing the same clothes that he'd had on when he arrived yesterday.

"Did you stay the night?"

"Like I was going home after everything that happened," he said.

Nudging my chin in the direction of the ugly brown chair in the corner, I asked, "Did you fall asleep in that uncomfortable-looking chair?"

He sighed and said, "Yep."

"You're probably in as much pain as I am."

"Yes, but I didn't want to leave your side."

A nurse came in to give me shots and pills and explained the extent of the damage. The bones in my hand were shattered; surgery was scheduled for the next day to put it back together with pins.

David warned me that the broadcast news and newspapers wanted to interview me. The hospital would set up a press conference after surgery if I wanted it.

I thought about it for a moment. I had a few messages on the hospital phone from TV news reporters wanting to talk to me. At least this way, I could get it over with all at once.

"The shooting has been all over the news. Do you want to know everything that happened?" David asked.

"I'm sure...I...I saw someone die, might have been others... To be honest, I'm not ready to think about it yet."

"It's okay. You went through a lot last night," he said.

He held my hand as I fell asleep.

THE ROOM WAS filled with flowers and family. Everything was fuzzy, but I saw my mom.

"How are you doing?" she asked as she kissed me. I felt a little uncertain about how to answer the question. I was in a hospital room following a shooting. Things could probably be better.

I simply said, "Still a little sore."

"He's doing all right for right now, but they will have to do surgery on his hand," David added.

Then my mother said, "Everybody's here." I stared around to see my sister, brothers, their wives and kids. I'd managed to have a family reunion in my hospital room. As great as it was to see everybody, I was groggy.

"I guess you can't get taken down by bullets," my sister quipped as she came up to me.

"Yeah, so far two of them haven't managed to do it," I said.

"How are you feeling?" my dad asked.

"I've felt better, a little sickly, probably due to the medication. Other than that, as fine as anyone who has been shot in the hand."

My brothers both came up and hugged me, along with my nieces and nephews.

"You all didn't have to come. It's just a flesh wound," I said, trying to lighten the mood.

My oldest nephew said, "I thought you were going to die this time."

"I get wounded every couple of years, but never taken down completely." I was using my strange sense of humor to lessen the overwhelming concern choking me in the small hospital room.

We talked for a while, relaxing friendly banter. I was still mostly in a hazy fog from whatever they had me on to help in my recovery.

David was by my side the whole time, holding my good hand. The elephant in the room, given the fact that I was still not out to my parents and family. My sister knew, of course. I'm sure my parents and brothers suspected something. I would have to face that issue eventually, considering that

David was providing answers to questions about how I was doing, since I was still dopey from the medications I was on. It wouldn't be hard to guess that he was more than just a friend.

As we talked, it was decided that my mother was going to help take care of me at our house in the coming week since David still had to go to work.

While my mom was out of the room, my sister said, "I wish I could be helping out instead of Mom...since you are not out to her, but it would be a lot for my husband to handle the kids all week on his own."

"I know, Karen, it should be...interesting," I said.

"Yeah, it definitely should be, but she's a good mother and she should be a big help for you. She always felt bad that she couldn't make it out to Delaware the first time you were shot."

"I know, and now she has a chance to help take care of me this time. I can't believe I'm even saying that...but here we are."

"Get better soon. It should all be good with Mom," she said.

They all said their goodbyes, and I fell fast asleep due to all the medication I was on.

When I woke up, I decided I needed to know more details about the shooting. "I am certain that I saw one police officer killed," I told David. "The night is still a blur in my mind. Who else...died?"

He looked away from me, as though trying to shield me from all the details. "Do you really want to know?"

"I saw these people at each meeting. Helen...I was close to her. Was she..."

His expression became completely serious before I even finished the sentence. He nodded.

"Oh God!" I was crying. He held me. "She always helped me find the answers I needed for stories on the city. It's not right."

"I know," he said. "There was another police officer who was killed, along with a city official and another city council member. The mayor was shot several times, but he is still alive."

I turned on the television, and what happened at Kirkwood City Hall was everywhere. Suddenly, I realized I had been swept into a major news event. I felt I was on the outside looking in as I watched the news, though I had been in the middle of it.

"TODAY IS THE big day, surgery." He was trying to lighten the mood as he held my left hand.

A doctor came in and explained what would happen. "You will be put to sleep and Dr. Carruthers is going to perform a procedure to reconnect the damaged bone and then put a cast on it."

This was more than fine with me. I had no interest in being awake while they put my hand back together.

David followed alongside the gurney down to surgery.

"I thought I saw the mayor passing in the hallway on a stretcher," I said to David as we waited outside the surgical room.

David told me as delicately as he could, "The mayor was shot twice in the head. He is stable but still in critical condition."

"I hope he gets better soon." I didn't know the mayor well. I had seen him numerous times while covering the city council, had even shaken his hand a few times. I could only think of him leading meetings. But he was personable and had taken my phone calls when I wanted questions answered.

The drugs were kicking in. Everything was becoming fuzzy. I asked David to come close. "Thanks for everything... Also..." I hesitated.

"What?" he asked.

"Will you marry me?" I asked.

I'd given him a straight-up proposal. At the moment, I wanted to know he loved me. I was a little crazed, frightened, thinking I might not survive. People can die for the strangest of reasons. But what if they missed something in examining me?

"Oh, so you say this before going into surgery," David said.

"Yes, I know, awkward timing. Just being here throughout this. No one has ever done this for me. And I love you."

"I will be truly honored to marry you." David kissed my forehead and caressed my cheek, and we both began to cry.

"I'll see you after surgery." I searched his face.

"Of course. We have a wedding to plan," he said firmly and held my hand.

I struggled to find the strength to let him go as they came for me. I kept staring at him as I was rolled into surgery.

I STARED DOWN at my arm as David signed my cast. I had now managed to have two bullets go through my body. My luck or dumb luck, I wasn't sure.

"I wanted to be the first." He finished his signature and looked directly at me. "Do you still want to do the press conference?"

I was nervous, but this was the best way of getting it over with all at once.

"If it helps, Stephen will also be there," he said.

Knowing this made me feel better. Yet I was still uncertain.

"Do you think I can do this?" I asked David.

"If you don't want to do it, don't, but the media will probably keep hounding us," he said.

"You're right. Let's get it over with. Although it's not going to be easy. That night was so horrible."

David steered my wheelchair out of the room.

Before we entered the hospital conference room where the news media was waiting on me, Stephen and Beth stopped and asked how I was doing.

I told them that, of course, I had been better and that I was nervous about the press conference.

"You'll do fine. It's good to see you...alive." Beth gave me a hug, seemed uncertain, and added, "It must have been crazy."

"It was. Thanks for coming, guys," I said.

David guided the wheelchair up to a table surrounded by microphones. There was press from everywhere: local and national TV stations, newspapers, and radio stations. I stared into the bright camera lights. I thought that maybe I shouldn't do this, yet there I was, in a wheelchair with a cast, and they were asking questions. I was at the point of no return.

I told them what I remembered. "Raymond entered the council room. He had a sign strapped to him, this time he shouted 'shoot the mayor,' and pulled out two guns from behind the sign and suddenly I heard a pop-pop. I saw a police officer go down instantly."

I quivered and hesitated for a moment. It was hard to describe the sudden death of a person right before my eyes, no matter how it had burned an image in my mind.

"I saw pure rage in his eyes. There was chaos as he began shooting. I had no idea where all the shots went. It was horrible to find out that Helen was killed and to learn how many others were shot. So senseless." I was almost in tears. I was finding it difficult to relate the loss with just words.

One of the reporters asked, "How is your recovery?"

I raised my cast as much as I could to show them where I had been shot. Flashbulbs went off, and I was able to leave but was at the point of exhaustion. This had been the hardest part so far, facing up to what had happened to others and to me.

After wheeling me back to the room, David lay down in bed with me. It gave me such comfort to be held by him as I drifted off into dreamland.

KEVIN CAME TO visit me in the hospital.

"So is David taking good care of you?" he asked. David was out getting lunch. It was nice to see Kevin alone so we could talk privately.

"Of course he is," I said, fighting lingering memories of the first shooting.

"Is he doing a better job than I did in Delaware?" Kevin asked, looking into my eyes. I knew that this was a difficult thing for him—to come to terms with what went wrong the first time this happened. Even stranger to be facing a second shooting.

Kevin bit his lip slightly.

"He's been with me every step of the way so far," I said. "We both know the hard part begins during recovery."

This was more difficult than I thought it would be. We were in a small hospital room with walls that seemed to reflect past wrongs all around us.

"I'm sorry about everything that happened before." Kevin was on the verge of tears.

I decided to change the subject. "I was right about Roger. You were too good for him."

Kevin touched my good hand, and I held his close, a sense of closure between us, to let the past wrongs fall away and allow us to move on.

"You know I will always love you," he said.

"I know that for sure. How many friends go through two shootings?" I said. We both laughed.

"You promise, not another one, right?" he said.

"I can't make that promise. I thought the first one would be the only one. But I'm hoping this is the last one," I said.

He lightly kissed me.

David came in with two Boston crème donuts for me, my favorites, not what I was supposed to be eating, but he knew that donuts make me happy in the morning. Especially ones with cream filling.

"I brought extra," he said.

I knew David was sometimes uncomfortable about my relationship with Kevin. But I think he knew that right then, I needed to feel loved and not alone.

We munched on the donuts. I hadn't eaten such a sugary concoction in a while. For a moment, we laughed and talked, and I felt normal.

BEFORE I WENT home with him, David had a surprise for me. He thought I needed an evening in which I wasn't thinking about the shooting and my hand, now plastered to my side.

"I bought us tickets to see Kathy Griffin," he said as he helped get me out of the wheelchair and into the car. I was shocked. I had heard she was coming to town, but with the shooting, I thought that seeing her was an impossibility.

He had another surprise. "You're going to be able to meet her backstage. The only catch is we have to head out pretty quickly in order to see her before the show."

This was the most exciting thing to ever happen to me. I hadn't ever met a celebrity before.

At the theater, we were able to meet her in the green room, a lounge area for performers before and after the show. It had large comfy red couches and plush chairs, which was nice since I could sit while we waited a short time for her to come on back.

She was all dolled up with her curly auburn hair, dark eyelashes, and bright crimson lipstick for her performance that night. Kathy was definitely prettier in person than she was on television.

She sat down with us. "How are you?"

"Fine." I didn't know really what to say. I was still filled with painkillers and medication.

"He's kinda doped up. Surgery wasn't too long ago," David told her.

"It must have been scary," she said.

"Yeah," I said in a whisper.

"We both love you on television," David said.

"Thanks! How are you holding up?" she asked as she signed a small poster for us.

"Things have been better." I partially held up my cast. "On the plus side, I made it out alive."

She smiled. "It's always good when that happens."

We all huddled together for a picture.

"You have an awesome boyfriend to do this for you," she said.

"Yes, I'm lucky to have him."

She gave David and me a hug.

"I really appreciate you taking the time to do this," David said as we left. She hugged me one more time and headed for the stage.

I tried my best to follow the show. I laughed a few times, but the drugs I was on didn't make it easy to register all the jokes. She was her usual, outstandingly funny self. I wish I could have been more into it, but at least I was able to meet her in person.

She made a short announcement during the performance, "Tonight we have a special guest. A survivor of the Kirkwood shooting is here. Stand up."

I was a bit embarrassed but played along and stood up to applause, amazing and scary at the same time in such a large crowd.

David held my hand the whole time. I couldn't believe he had done this for me. It was really the sweetest thing anyone had ever done. But I knew the next months would be difficult. I had gone through this before, so I was aware I had a long recovery ahead. Instead of a leg, I had a hand to rebuild. *That's life. It always throws something at you that you aren't expecting to happen—at least not twice.*

Chapter Twelve

COMING HOME WAS strange. My work life was on hold while I recovered. Flowers were everywhere from family and friends, which made me feel a bit like someone had died, but I knew they meant well.

The pain in my hand was controlled by the pills the doctor had given me, but they also made me sick. David called the doctor so I could obtain a change in prescription.

I was not supposed to move my cast around much at first, and I had to elevate it at night. This also meant I needed to sleep separately in the guest bedroom since I needed room to comfortably position it. That fact made it less awkward to pretend we were only roommates while my mom was staying with us.

The doctor had also thought it was best for someone to be at home with me while David was at work in case something they had missed caused problems.

David prepared for the day while I was still in bed. I felt lethargic from the medication and even with the change in prescription my stomach was off.

I watched him as he dressed. "So just me and Mom today. This should be fun."

"I feel bad that I have to leave you. I haven't left your side since the shooting. Are you sure you're going to be okay?" he asked, tying his tie.

"One of us has to go to work." I was on medical leave without any idea of when I could return. I'd told my boss that I wouldn't be in on Monday, not realizing that this was bigger than a day or two out of the office. This was to be weeks of recovery. The shooting would have a long-term effect on my life.

"Just relax. You got this." He gave me a quick peck on the forehead and then headed out the door for his job.

I went back to sleep and had a nightmare. In the dream, Raymond was hunting me down as I kept running through hallway after hallway, seeing those dark piercing eyes as he shot me over and over. Bullets tore through my body. Not only me, but also friends and family were shot in front of me.

I awoke sweating and in pain. Groggily, I walked to the bathroom and found my pills, which I couldn't open.

"Mom, I can't get the lid off the pill bottle. Can you help?" I felt like a little kid again.

"Sure, Todd." She came upstairs from the living room, where she had been watching *The Price Is Right*. She opened the bottle for me and brought me water as I sat on the bed.

"So how are you feeling?" She handed me the small glass.

"The pain should go away in a few days. It did with the first shooting."

"Oh."

I knew I shouldn't have said it that way. "I was trying to say that I've done this before... I can survive it." I wanted to comfort her, since she still felt bad about not being in Delaware the first time I was shot. "I'm going to go back to sleep. It helps me get past the pain."

She gave me a kiss on the forehead, like I was three years old, and headed back down the stairs.

The next few days were a mix of this. Finally, I felt a little better and wanted a bath. I hadn't had a real chance to clean up since the shooting. I still had dried blood on me.

Mom called the doctor, and he said that as long as my cast was out of the water, it would be fine and the flesh wound on my chest should be healed enough for water.

At first, I asked her if she wanted to help me, but it felt odd, since I was a grown man. "Actually, I think David will be home early today. He can help."

"If you want him to do it, that's fine," she said.

David arrived and came up the stairs to kissed me. "How are things?" he said as he changed out of his work clothes.

"I was hoping to take a bath, but I'll need help."

This turned out to be a lot of work. He helped me into the tub, but it was harder than I thought to keep my arm out of the water.

"I feel like an invalid," I told him.

"It's sort of romantic in a way," he said as he sponged me.

He ducked my head under the faucet to wash my hair. He cleaned off the blood that still clung to my body.

"I wonder if this is all my blood."

"Hope so," he said as he scrubbed.

I used his arm for support in getting out of the tub, and then he toweled me dry and put me into bed.

"I need more of the pills," I said.

He handed them to me before I fell asleep to more nightmares of being chased.

I awoke in the middle of the night with chills, but this time, it wasn't the dream. I was really sick. For whatever reason, these pills also bothered me. I hoped it wouldn't be long before I could stop taking them.

AFTER A FEW days at home, I was moving around a little more easily and my mom said, "Your dad has been on his own for a while and has probably made a mess of the house. I think it's time for me to head back."

I agreed.

"Thanks for coming. This really helped us out," David told her as he poured milk into my bowl of raisin bran.

"I...I feel that David can take care of you," my mother said.

It felt as though there was a deeper thought behind what she said. But I left it at that. David and I had decided that this was not the time for me to come out to her. It had been a difficult period for all of us.

"I'll be home early today to take care of him," he added.

"I feel better than I have since the shooting. I really haven't been able to eat much, but today, I'm able to eat my cereal. Hopefully, I can keep it down," I said.

"That's good to hear." After eating, she headed into the living room to watch another episode of *The Price Is Right*.

I hugged David. "Do you think she knows about us?"

"I'm sure she is aware of something between us." He kissed me lightly and headed out the door.

I went into the living room area and watched TV with her.

I stared at her for a moment, thinking a bit about telling her. I looked down at my lap and thought of how worried she'd been about me being shot again and decided against it.

She kept asking if I would really be fine for her to go that day. I comforted her by saying I would be okay. Before she left, she gave me a hug.

"If you need anything at all, don't hesitate to call."

"I'll be fine," I said once more. "I've got David here."

"I wish I could do more," she said, holding back tears.

"I just need time to recover."

"Don't hesitate, if you need anything...anything at all...you let me know," she said again.

I watched her leave and was happy when David showed up only a half hour later. He made late lunch for me, and I spent the rest of the day watching TV while David did some grading upstairs.

Frankie slept at my feet, which comforted me.

SPENDING THE FIRST whole day alone was not easy, even having Frankie on the couch with me, making me feel a little safer. I made sure all the doors were locked.

David had lunches prepared for me, so I didn't have to face that chore. Everything was a bit difficult because I only had one useful hand. I hated my newfound tendency to drop everything. Eating was always fun, since it all seemed to dribble down onto my shirt.

I looked over my right hand, completely shrouded in a cast. It seemed important to remember my past abilities with my hands and arms. I pulled out photos of the summer in Colorado, where I did rock climbing. In those photos, I used my hand strength and arm muscles together to climb up a sheer cliff.

I'd hung off a mountainside and pulled myself up, surprising a friend. He had almost fell down cursing at me, having no idea that I could crawl around the cliff side like a monkey. I was short and stout and could pull my own weight.

David and I had talked about going out to Colorado the following summer. I wasn't sure if I wanted to after the surgery.

Like an echo, I heard the doctor say, "We'll try to get as much normal movement out of the hand that we can, but no promises."

"No promises." That was not a prescription for complete recovery, although better than losing my life. But I still hated the fact that bullets had made a permanent difference in my life.

Raymond was dead after being shot by the police that night and would never face what he had done to me. I wished that I could tell him in person what I had lost, the pain he'd put me through, and the constant fear I lived in now.

Time alone was not helpful to my psyche. I was flipping through the channels when I found the funeral notices for the people who were killed at City Hall.

I couldn't seem to find my way past that night. The coverage of the shooting kept surrounding me. Alone, I didn't feel right about myself. Why had I survived? I read other accounts of that night and became more depressed.

I called David. "They have a whole section on me in the online paper. I feel like they're exploiting my pain. They say horrible things about me in comments."

"You shouldn't read that stuff," he said.

"I know. It feels strange to see all those funerals and not attend. I can't even leave the house without you. It's like I did something wrong by being hit by a bullet. Like it was my fault for being at City Hall that night and doing my job." I began to cry.

"It's all right, Todd," he said. "Let it out."

"I want things to be normal again," I said, even though I knew that wasn't possible.

"I wish they could be."

"I can barely sleep at night."

"I have the same trouble," David confided. "I wish I could have been in that room that night and protected you from the bullet. I know that's crazy. Right? I wish you weren't feeling all this pain. Most of all, I want you to know that we will both find our way through this together. I wish I could be home right now for you, but I have to get ready to teach class."

"Thank you for giving me a moment to clear my mind, hon. I do love you. And you're right; we'll get through this." I kept reading up on the shooting and watching the TV reports. I wanted to know everything. Maybe seeing the funerals made me feel less alone. I don't know. But I didn't really know most of the people very well who were shot. Which made me feel even worse.

I had been swept into something I wasn't truly a part of. I was totally secluded, stuck in the house, wishing it would all go away.

When David came home that day, he could tell I had been crying. He put me in bed, held me, and stroked my hair. He kept telling me that everything would be all right.

I wished I could believe him, but a man with a gun had blown apart my sense of what was right in the world.

"I NEED TO make an appearance at a wedding reception for some coworkers of mine. Do you want to go, or should I attend without you?" David said.

It would be the first time I'd left the house. I thought I needed to see how I was progressing. "Yes, I think I'll be okay to go along."

"This might also be a good way to get your mind off the shooting," he said.

When we arrived and I found a nicely decorated condominium with floor-to-ceiling windows, golden-brown couches, and modern art paintings throughout. Yet, I discovered that the few people I knew from his job hadn't made it and it was mostly strangers that surrounded me.

David introduced me to people, and someone asked, "How are things going?"

"I'm fine; doing better," I said. I was beginning to feel uncomfortable.

Then I started to feel pain throb in my hand. *Shoot, I forgot to bring my pain pills.*

David came by to check on me. "Are you okay?"

I smiled and nodded, because I knew how important this was to him. He worked closely with these people. I lay back on one of the couches, trying to gently massage around my hand as he talked with others. I was doing my best to alleviate the pain.

One of his coworkers came up to ask, "How are you doing following the shooting?"

"I'm okay." I slouched down farther on the couch between pain and conversation.

"It must have been rough with him coming in and shooting like that. It had to be difficult to see," the coworker said. I didn't recognize him.

"Yeah. Getting better, though."

"You hang in there, kiddo," he said as he walked away.

The pain in my hand was worse. I was becoming dizzy and my face felt as bright as a red balloon. My eyes glazed and I was wet with perspiration. It had been too much, too soon.

David came over. "You look flushed."

"I'm going to throw up. Help me to the bathroom," I said.

He helped me to it. I threw up and struggled to clean the vomit off my face. "I...I need to go." I was a mess.

"Okay, okay," David said. "Let me say goodbye to everybody."

I slunk out the door without him, I needed air. I must have seemed irrational to them, crazy to say the least. *What's wrong with me, God? I'm losing it.*

We headed to the car. I was in tears as he held me. "I'm sorry."

"What's wrong?" he asked.

"They meant well. My hand was hurting bad. I forgot the pills, and everyone kept bringing up the shooting. It made me sick to think about it. I'm not ready yet, David."

"Okay...okay. You only need to tell me these things. I won't put you through anything like that again. You'll be ready when you are."

"I'm sorry I'm like this," I said.

"You went through hell that night. What should people expect?"

We didn't talk on the car ride home. I think David felt guilty about bringing me out too early in the process. I was only beginning to feel better about leaving the house. I still had fear of being among people, and then I was still recovering from the surgery. The fear was irrational, but this was what I was feeling. God, I hoped I would get past this.

THAT NIGHT, I didn't gain refuge in sleep. In this nightmare, I was going up creaky stairs in complete darkness. I opened a door to a room and it slammed shut behind me.

Then I heard a voice. "I'm coming in!"

My heart jumped. Nowhere to run. Standing in front of me was a line of people I hadn't seen before.

Blood splattered everywhere. I yelled at them, "Get out of the way. He has a gun!"

No one heard me.

I tried to shield one of them, but heat radiated as the bullet entered me and went through my hand. Blood began to spew. Instant pain.

The shooter was gone just as suddenly as he had appeared. I followed, looking for him, but he was nowhere to be found. Blood trickled out of me leaving a trail behind.

Dead bodies surrounded me. Nothing I could do for them or myself. When I looked down, my chest was gushing blood. I crumpled to the ground.

I wanted to sleep and never wake up again. I didn't want death surrounding me; I only wanted to be dead like them. My heartbeat slowed.

A bright light shone but then was blocked.

It was him, the shooter, his face right over me, smelling me. I tried to move away from him, but he was smothering me, choking me. I couldn't breathe. My throat became tight.

I pulled and struggled. All I could hear was his laughter as I found it harder and harder to breathe.

I sat straight up in bed, panting.

David reached out for me. "What is it?"

"They're all dead!" I shouted.

"I know. It's okay. You're safe now." He held me for a while, before finding me some sleeping pills. "These will help."

He was trying his best, I knew. I finally fell into a half sleep. I wondered if the dead bodies would return when I closed my eyes and if the gunman would be lurking in the shadows.

THE PSYCHIATRIST I was sent to was a lanky man by the name of John Witman. I didn't know what to say to him. I wasn't comfortable talking to anyone about what had happened. I wanted to forget it, not deal with it. The memories of that night filled me with revulsion and horror. I was fidgeting as he looked through his paperwork on me. I stared at all his credentials that hung on the walls around me. He had stacks of books everywhere, it seemed like what I always pictured a psychiatrist room would look like, complete with an uncomfortable leather couch.

"How do you feel today?" he asked.

"Fine." I had filled out a long psychological assessment that was pages and pages long. It had pained my left hand something awful to fill out. I wasn't used to writing with it.

"It's understandable if you do not want to talk," Dr. Witman said.

"Okay."

"I have a friend who is a therapist. I think it would be good for you to talk with him."

"Oh, that's right, you provide the pills," I said.

He waited for me to speak again, unfazed by my blunted reaction. When I didn't, he said, "I can prescribe some medications that can relax you. Do you feel anxious or depressed?"

I wasn't sure which I felt more. "Both." I wasn't certain how I was supposed to feel after watching people get killed in cold blood.

"If you need more, call our office," he said, offering the prescriptions.

I took them. "I will."

"How are you doing with sleeping?"

"I have nightmares every night."

"Hmmm...I can prescribe you some other pills to help you sleep."

"That sounds fine." I became quiet.

"Have you been suicidal?" he asked.

"No, not really. I have David, my partner, who helps me with the day-to-day life and the anxieties that I'm facing," I said.

"When it comes to tragic events, it's always good to have someone close by that you can count on. How's your family?"

"They've been a great help, well, as much as they can be."

"It sounds like you have a support network." Dr. Witman took down more notes on his pad.

I had been very uncertain about seeing him, but it seemed to go all right. I stared down at the prescriptions. I guess this was to keep me from going crazy or losing it.

THE CAST WAS coming off a month after the shooting, which put me closer to going back to work. I rubbed my chin as I contemplated this change in my life. I was tired of being at home and wasn't comfortable in the house all day by myself while David was at work. Watching old black-and-white comedies with our dog Frankie next to me had provided some comfort, but I felt I was becoming a recluse.

Dr. Carruthers had done the surgery on my hand, and I would continue to see him during my recovery.

His secretary, Amanda, was an attractive blonde with amber skin. She had miniature chocolates on the counter in front of her and told us to feel free to take as many as we wanted. The treats relaxed us a bit.

David was my chauffeur now since I couldn't drive with the cast on my right hand and due to all the medication I was on as part of the healing process.

While we waited to be seen, David's eyes kept drifting closed, and he kept moving his head around to stay awake. I had to depend on him for everything: helping me get dressed, making food, taking baths. I could barely do anything without making a mess, which he would have to clean up. I was hoping that having the cast off would make his life easier.

After the first shooting, I could at least do everything with my hands. I could walk some with the crutches. But with only one hand, I felt pretty useless, especially since my right hand was the one I wrote with, and I couldn't safely lift anything with only one usable hand.

A nurse announced that Dr. Carruthers was ready to see us.

He looked over the hand and said, "The cast is ready to come off. I will prescribe some painkillers for a while. And you'll also have some more soreness as it heals in the open," he cautioned.

Dr. Carruthers carefully removed the cast, and my hand was revealed for the first time since the shooting.

Metal pins were visible in my hand that I guessed held it in place while it healed.

"You're going to have these for a few more weeks. After we take these out, you can head back to work."

"Okay." I wasn't sure how ready I was to go back since my job was all about typing. "Just make sure that I can hit the key strokes with both hands again."

"We'll probably have your newspaper start you out part-time," he said.

I agreed. He wrapped my hand in a bandage.

"It hurts again," I said as we left the office. "Damn it, I wish the pain would stop."

"It will. I promise," David said.

I winced as my muscles reacted to being released from their stiff position.

David quickly found me the pain pills. I kept picturing myself lying on the beach with a margarita, hoping that would help. This was all I could do to keep from focusing on the throbbing.

You never see what it's really like to be shot on cop shows. It seems that the person can take two bullets, jump back up again, fire his gun once more at the bad guys, and even manage to bring one down. They make it look so easy, but it's not like that, not in real life. It takes a long time to physically heal. The mental part is a whole different story.

THE PINS WERE ready to come out. We went into the doctor's office in the middle of the day.

"How are the both of you?" Amanda inquired. We had become friendly with each other over the multiple visits we'd made to Dr. Carruthers.

"It's going to be a fun one. I'm getting the pins taken out," I said with my overstated enthusiasm for this possibly unpleasant procedure.

"Here, have a sucker. That makes it better, right?" She handed me more than one from a basket she kept by her desk. I liked her attitude, though I was pretty sure suckers wouldn't help.

We sat in the small waiting room. I tapped my foot on the floor anxiously.

"It'll be all right," David said and held my hand tight.

"It will be what it will be."

The doctor came out and asked, "Are you ready?"

"I guess," I said simply as we headed back.

The doctor first touched my hand and checked out how it was working. He kept asking to know if this hurt or if that hurt.

I kept saying, "Just a little."

Every spot on my hand was examined before he grabbed pliers.

"Aren't these better suited for home repair?" I cracked.

"Not today, Todd. Today these are specially made to pull out pins. One warning...it's going to hurt a bit after this."

Great.

He pulled hard with the pliers and gave a few big tugs before the first one came out. A second tug, and the next one was out. My hand went limp.

"You can move it." The doctor gave me the look that said I needed to.

I shifted my hand around. Strong sensations of prickliness and stinging spread as I moved. My hand had not been in motion for about two months. I was amazed to see the fingers flexing again. The bullet had taken motion away from me for such a long time.

I asked my usual question. "Will I get it back to normal?"

Dr. Carruthers hesitated, and then said, "With physical therapy, you can gain a higher percentage of ability with the hand."

That was at least something, although not the answer I was hoping for.

"It looks like you're ready to go," he said.

As we left, I asked David, "What do you think about the prognosis?"

"I know it's tough to hear," he said as he started the car. "I wish you could have complete movement with your hand again."

This was hard to face, these new limitations.

Silence filled the car on the way home. Excruciating pain hit me. This was a delayed reaction to the loss of the pins in my hand.

"Pills, please."

He handed them to me. I was once again trying to imagine the beach scene.

PHYSICAL THERAPY HAD to start before I could return to work. The wound had healed so the doctor felt it was time. Here, they could gauge how I was progressing. I had already been out for a little over two months.

I wasn't sure if I was ready. I was still uncomfortable with people after the shooting.

A brunette lady came out front and said, "You will need to start by soaking your hand in hot wax."

I looked at her with uncertainty.

"Paraffin wax therapy helps in healing, moisturizes the skin, and soothes it before you start your hand exercises," she told me.

So I let her take my hand and put into the wax. This was like dipping your hand in a shallow wax candle and making a mold. The heat felt warm and comforting.

"Now, we'll put a towel around your hand and let the wax soothe it," she said.

This was all new to me. With each injury, I had different procedures for physical therapy.

After a few minutes, a woman with long flowing hair entered the room. "So are you Todd?"

"Yep, that's me."

"I'm Angela. Let's get that wax off and we'll massage your hand."

Angela had curly ginger-brown hair, a comely figure, a button nose, and a friendly demeanor. She could have easily been an extra on *Scrubs*.

Her tender touch felt good. I didn't even ask David to do this for me. Actually, I had never asked anyone to do this, so it was the first time someone had ever massaged my hand.

"That feels nice," I said.

"It should." She kept pressing along my hand at different points. "What brings you here for physical therapy?" She ran her fingers around my healing scar. It looked like someone had tried to rip off my hand and only a long scar was left.

"Did you hear about the Kirkwood shooting?" I tried not to look at her eyes. I didn't want to give a long detailed description. "I was the reporter, and this is my memento."

"At least you can have a sense of humor about it."

"I have to. Otherwise, I would sink into..." I didn't go further.

Angela changed the subject. "Are you ready for some muscle workouts for the hand?"

I shrugged.

Hand physical therapy reminded me of games for adults. The first activity was to put pegs into a board over and over. I felt a bit like a kid.

"So does it matter how the colors are arranged?" I said.

"Oh, you think you're being cute. No, this isn't elementary school. We need you to put all your effort into it in order to build up your hand strength."

I moved up to a big wad of clay that she made me take out of a plastic bucket. She brought out a small container of marbles and told me to put them in the clay and wad it up. Then I was supposed to take the marbles out.

"Can I make a castle with the clay?" I said.

"Only on your own time," she said with a smile. I hadn't really bantered with anyone in a long time, and I was happy that Angela played along.

I did the marble exercise, and she brought out another gadget.

"We need to see how your muscles are doing," she said. "Now press hard."

I pressed and pressed, and by the end, my hand was limp from the workout.

Angela made notes. "I will send this on to the doctor. Now, one last hand massage for you."

My hand ached now, but at least I had made some progress.

"Over the next few weeks, they will evaluate my progress and make a decision of whether I will be able to go back to work and drive," I said to David when he picked me up.

"Are you ready, do you think?" he asked.

"Yeah. I need to at some point, right?"

Heading back to work was going to be tough. I hadn't been out of the house much since the shooting. I didn't even know how to really deal with other people, besides David. I had been in my own little world. Soon I would have to leave the cocoon I'd built around me.

Chapter Thirteen

I WAS CLEARED to drive and go back to work. David had my lunch packed and ready to go my first morning back. I tried out my hand, exercising it and moving my fingers back and forth. *I'll be able to do this, right?*

"Are you ready?" David asked, seemingly reading my mind.

"As ready as I'll ever be," I answered.

"You'll do fine," he said. "Remember, just take your time and ease into it. If you feel tired, let them know. You don't want a setback."

I was a bit nervous on the freeway, hoping that my reflexes would be fast enough for the commute. Of course, the first thing I encountered was someone cutting me off on the interstate. Followed by backed-up traffic and a construction zone. I survived it all, but I was late.

I walked in and sat in my cubicle. I looked through a stack of letters and cards. Along with this came a full email box that would take me days to go through. Work had begun again.

Harper came by and asked, "Are you getting back into the swing of things?"

She noticed all the emails on the computer and the blinking phone indicator.

"You know, don't worry about getting to everything today."

I thanked her. Eventually, other employees came by to give me condolences for what I had gone through, and said that if I needed anything, they would be happy to help.

I didn't know how to take this. I really didn't know all the people in the office. I thanked them all for their concern and assistance.

Just before lunch, the publisher came in and everyone gathered around. "Based on his bravery on the job, Todd Smith is now an employee of the month." Everyone around me clapped and smiled.

I had been hurt doing my job, shot in the hand, and unable to write due to the injury. Was that brave? I wasn't sure.

I sat back down and began to go through everything that was on my desk and computer.

The day went by as normal as possible. I didn't have Sara to talk to since she'd left, so I was mostly on my own, tucked away in my cubicle, which was fine with me.

Eventually I would learn that this was a part of post-traumatic stress disorder, sort of withdrawing from people. I could be pleasant with people and smile at appropriate times, but I wasn't good at going past that point. I was unable to trust others; it was a lingering mental hurt I just couldn't get past.

I came home that night and only wanted to go to sleep. "It was exhausting."

He came up behind me and held me. "I'm sure. How were they?"

"Well-meaning."

"People don't know what to say and it's probably hard for them too."

"You're right."

Later that first week, I learned that more than one person was nominated for employee of the month and my name was put into a pool to win a prize. My name wasn't chosen, and a secretary in another department received the prize.

A friend from my old office called me after that announcement. "I guess getting shot on the job isn't good enough."

I had to chuckle to myself. *I guess not.*

I WENT TO my first appointment with the therapist a week after returning to work. Charlie Stemmer was a fifty-five-year-old man with long blond hair wearing a Hawaiian shirt.

Around his office, he had framed tropical photos of plunging waterfalls in a vast green jungle canopy and beaches surrounded by palm trees.

"How is life going for you?" he asked from behind a large wooden desk, a small notebook in his hand. While the decor might have been assembled to calm any nervousness, it didn't seem to be working for me since I was flushed and sweating, my nerves working overtime.

I thought for a moment; I wondered what therapists or psychiatrists really write down. Were they actually scribbling out strange pieces of ballpoint pen art? That's what I did in school if I lost interest in the discussion.

"I'm back at work. My coworkers are well meaning. They ask a lot about how I'm doing and if I am feeling okay. And I answer that everything is fine. Although, the constant checking on me makes me a bit uncomfortable."

He lingered a bit on my answers. "People want to know that you're all right, considering what happened to you. So, how are you feeling?"

"Not altogether normal." I tried to look away from him and lose myself in the tropical pictures.

"It can be difficult to get back into the flow of things. I think you should take it one day at a time," he said.

"I'm trying. I don't know how I feel about people now. What a weird statement, right? How can people become such a stumbling block? I have a hard time trusting. I feel alone, because I survived all this. The others who got shot...most of them died, and the mayor is still recovering. I...I don't know who to go to."

"What do you want or need?" he said.

"Space. I might need some time on my own. My partner has been great through all this, but I'm still processing it all."

"It's a lot. Reach out to friends and family and not only him. Also, don't go inward," he said.

"I know I should be over this. I'm having trouble getting back on track. I keep wondering what's wrong with me."

"That's normal. Let your feelings out. Let it go. Eventually you'll be past this."

I wasn't sure. "I hope you're right."

He told me to look at one of the tropical pictures in the room. I chose the waterfall one, and he told me to relax my breathing.

I tried to comply, but staring at me from the painting was a figure that I could barely see, pointing a gun at me through the tropical foliage.

Great. I still wasn't over seeing his image everywhere. I didn't tell the therapist that. I didn't want him to commit me, and I wanted badly for everything to be normal.

AS TIME PASSED after the shooting, David and I began to have fights.

"You forgot to pick up groceries," David said as he was going through the cabinets.

"I know," I snapped. "But that's me, right? Forgetting to do everything lately."

"I was wanting a little help." He finally clawed his way to the bottom of the freezer, finding frozen fish.

"I know. I'm useless," I said.

"You're not. I need little help is all, Todd. I can't keep doing everything on my own. You go into this little world of yours. You're ignoring what needs to be taken care of in the house."

"I agree," I said quietly, turned on the television for an old episode of *Two and a Half Men,* and went about ignoring him.

He came into the living room from the kitchen. "Are you even paying attention to me?"

"No, I'm not. Leave me alone," I grumbled, then ran upstairs to the bedroom and slammed the door.

I kept forgetting everything lately. He had asked for me to pick up milk, coffee, and a few other groceries after work. But I couldn't seem to focus on anything.

I locked the door to the bedroom and turned up the stereo loud, listening to Carly Simon.

David kept knocking, but I ignored him. Eventually, he stormed out of the house.

I kept mimicking the words over and over that Carly sang. I wasn't really mad at David. I was mad at myself for having trouble putting my life back together. My world was dissolving around me; I was losing my mind.

I played the same songs over and over and wept. I needed to cry.

I had to stop seeing dead bodies every time I closed my eyes. I had to stop seeing the blood flowing everywhere. So much blood. Blood flowing out of the bodies and me.

I didn't want to hear the screams in my mind as the gun went off.

I was beginning to remember things. Horrible things. I knew that if I listened to the lyrics loudly enough, the ghosts of that night would go away.

The words began to comfort and relax me. The music coursed through the room. Her soothing voice caused me to sniffle. Then I stopped. It was over. I turned off the stereo and unlocked the door.

He was on the other side of the door, sitting on the floor and crying. He'd come back for me.

"I'm sorry," he said.

"I am too," I replied.

He held me as we slept that night. I felt better, but I was involuntarily lashing out at the only person in the house instead of fighting the madman in my nightmares.

DESPITE THE LINGERING tension between us, David and I decided to go out to see Kevin's drag show. I think I was trying to return to that moment of normalcy I'd felt in the hospital room, when Kevin had come to see me.

Kevin came up to us as Jade Sinclair, all decked out in a long flowing black dress, high heels, a curly brunette wig, and a darker tone of makeup. He looked even more a woman than when he'd first donned the wig and begun performing.

"We're supposed to have a full house tonight," Kevin said.

"Thanks for inviting us out. It's nice to be up close to see you in all your goddessness," I said with a slight chuckle.

"You always have a way of putting things," Kevin said.

When the lights went up on stage, Jade came out doing Cher's "If I Could Turn Back Time." Only my drag queen best friend could take an 80s Cher hit and turn it into an onstage apology.

Jade danced like I had never seen before. I felt like I was part of the performance. Jade kept coming up to me and dancing around me during the song. David touched my fingers, each one feeling the warmth and enjoyment I was experiencing that night.

As her number drew to a close, Jade glided back to the stage. I went up to give a large tip and we hugged.

"You always have a way of making a statement," I said in his ear.

"That's what I do." Jade kissed me on the cheek, leaving a large spot of lipstick before heading offstage as the next performer came out.

David shook his head with amusement.

"I know." I hadn't felt that glimmer of enjoyment for such a long time. This was what we all needed, a moment to forget what had happened to me. I didn't think about my hand all night, and that had not happened in far too long.

THE HARDEST PART of returning to work was the breaking crime stories. This macabre world of danger was a constant reality that had to be covered. I never looked forward to writing these. It was a hard fact of life that I no longer wanted to face.

I was hit with a particularly nasty story the minute I walked in one morning. A man had walked into a bar and shot someone, according to the police report. I looked around the office for another reporter, but everyone else was out covering other stories.

Harper came by and suggested that it would be a good start for me to go out and take a photo.

I didn't want to tell her I wasn't up for this. I wanted to be strong. So I told her I would do the photo and a short write-up for the website until another reporter could follow the story further.

I gathered more information for the report. The shooting happened at 1:00 a.m. The bartender had been in the middle of closing down when the shooter came back into the bar and shot the bartender two times. One bullet hit his chest, and another hit his head.

Money was taken from the cash register. An older model Chevrolet was seen leaving the scene. The police were still trying to determine what the perpetrator looked like, and though this appeared to have started as a robbery, they needed to find out what had gone wrong.

I headed to the bar; yellow tape was all around the outside of the business, with police milling about. I couldn't get too close. At least all this was at a distance.

I clicked photos with a small camera. A hint of fog hung in the air, making the scene more dreary and haunting.

I decided to gather a few details from a nearby cop.

The officer was an older man with a short beard.

"Do they know what set off the robber?" I asked as I took out a small notepad.

"All we know is that there was shouting. Afterward, the suspect ran out and drove away. Nearby neighbors heard the gunfire and reported it," he said with a gruff voice.

"Any more facts available?" I asked.

"We are not releasing the details yet on the suspect, but will later in the day. This is all we have at this time."

I thanked him, wrote down what he told me, and looked around a bit. I couldn't see much inside the bar. I found out the bartender's name was Howard and was well liked.

At least I was coming back with a photo of the bar surrounded in police tape and a few details from the police officer.

I went back to my car and headed for the office. I mostly felt numb. I thought I would be scared, but at least I didn't know the person who was shot and didn't have enough information on the suspect to be scared of him.

Once I was back at work, I quickly wrote it up and sent it on to the editor. Another reporter would have to go in and find more details.

Later that day, the suspect was found, and my anxiety about him on the streets was calmed. The police emailed me a picture of a disheveled individual with a long nose in a white T-shirt and jeans. His name was Leroy Jones. I attached the picture to the online story right before I headed home that day.

I told David about covering the crime.

"Those bastards." He blurted out his annoyance at my boss. "How are you dealing with it?"

"I'm fine. Numb. Is that a good thing?"

"Not sure. Maybe you're getting over it."

"That's possible," I said.

In the back of my mind, I was afraid that feeling nothing was more worrisome. I didn't want to become one of those people who bury emotions and, later on, lose it completely. Maybe the numb was the calm that I shouldn't be feeling, like I should have more emotion to keep being normal.

ANOTHER DAY SEEING the therapist. He was always pleasant and friendly when I saw him and of course filled with questions I needed to answer.

"How are you today? How's the hand?" Charlie asked.

"I'm doing better. I'm still on the prescription from the psychiatrist, so that keeps me in check some."

"Do you think you still need the medications?" he asked.

"For right now." I hated this interrogation about needing the pills. It made me feel like a druggie. I changed the subject, "The mayor is not doing well the last I heard."

"What do you think about that?" He seemed to want a long answer.

I only provided him a short one. "Alone, but I'm trying not to let that bother me." I didn't want to think more about the mayor who I felt truly sad for, having survived this but still in such dire straits from the shooting.

"How's your relationship with David?" Charlie asked.

"Rocky. You know, he went through the same thing I did with the shooting. He feels some anger against everyone for not understanding how painful this was for the both of us. I wish I could do more, but I'm still recovering."

I stopped for a moment and stared out the window, taking my thoughts off David. "One good thing, I'm making progress with the hand now. I'm gaining back the ability to use it, mostly. Yet I keep having pain with it. If it doesn't get better, I'll have to have a second surgery, go through a whole new recovery period and more physical therapy. It's never over." My hand was feeling sore as we talked.

"How do you feel about possible surgery?"

"If it makes it better, I'm for it. Yet, it's been several months since the shooting and I still have all these lingering issues. This is like the first one, a lost year of my life. I never get ahead. I'm struggling again, even with David's help. Why is that?"

Charlie took a moment to think of an answer, then said, "Because it is a lot to take in for someone—anyone, for that matter."

He had a point.

"How's work?"

I didn't really want to talk about work, but since he asked the question, I felt I was obligated to reply. "Work is... I do my job and try to stay focused. A few times, I have found it rough, especially covering incidents that involve gunfire. Part of my job is to follow crime. I try not to think about it too much. I remind myself that these are people I don't know. Although, I find at times when I write up the reports I have to stop myself from getting lost in the horrible details."

"How do you stay positive?"

"I wish I could do more for society and not just write up the who, what, when, and where. I'm always a witness to these horrible events, yet never making a difference. Too many bad things happen every night on the evening news, and all we do is watch."

"What do you wish you could do?"

"I think that at some point I should find a way to help others. For every crime, there is a victim. Too often, we blame the victim for what happened to them. That they should have had a gun, or they shouldn't have been where they were, or it was the lifestyle they lived."

I flashed back to Rick for a moment and how Erik always blamed Rick for his own death, which he said was due to his drinking.

Charlie pulled me out of my deep thoughts. "Sounds like maybe you should eventually find a job helping crime victims."

"Something to think about," I said.

Again, he ended the session with me looking at the tropical print. This time, I pictured myself helping a man who had been shot by the sniper in the woods.

Maybe this was a possible future, a step away from being the victim.

DAVID AND I went out with Beth and Stephen.

"So how's work going?" Stephen asked.

"I'm fine with it. Still getting used to the daily grind," I said.

"Is your hand better?" Beth inquired.

"It's healing."

David stepped in. "He's doing physical therapy for it, and he's gaining strength slowly but surely."

"Angela, my physical therapist, has been a sweetheart to work with," I added. "She's really tender with her touch."

"Not too tender, right?" David said. "I don't want to be outdone by her." We all chuckled.

I excused myself to use the bathroom. The restaurant was in a rehabbed building and had exposed bricks everywhere. The latch on the bathroom door was a bit difficult to turn, but I didn't think anything of it.

I did my business and tried to unlock the door. I couldn't turn it. I kept trying, but I only had one hand that could complete this task. I used all my strength. My right hand was of no use.

I didn't know what to do. So embarrassing. I looked around for anything that I could use to gain a stronger grip. Nothing was available. I took a moment and gave it another hard turn. No budging.

I sat down on the toilet and tried to fight my growing panic.

I finally called David with my cell phone from the bathroom. "This is so wrong. I can't get out of the bathroom. I don't have enough strength with my right hand to do it. I've tried everything," I said quietly, not wanting to announce my predicament.

"I'll be right back. Have to take this call," he said to Beth and Stephen.

David came to the bathroom door. "Todd, just relax. Now, try it again."

"I will, but it will be the same thing," I said, feeling defeated.

I gave it the best tug that I could. Whether it was to prove me wrong or I had somehow loosened whatever mechanism that had locked it, it finally worked.

I opened the door, exhausted. "I can be a crazy mess, right?"

"Yes, but I love my crazy mess," David said.

We walked back to the table, not saying a word. I went on talking with them as if it never happened. It seemed that every time I tried to make it to normal, something stupid got in the way.

WE WERE SUPPOSED to have a day of fun at an art fair. We looked at paintings, glasswork, and all sorts of artistic endeavors. I gazed at a large painting of a blue sky with lifelike clouds scattered about and the sun trying to peek through them.

"What do you think?" I asked David.

David examined the painting closer. "I'm not sure, almost too much blue for me."

"I like how the clouds have shapes. One looks like a puppy dog," I said.

"Hmmm. I see more of a wolf than a dog," he said.

I asked the artist, "What's the price?"

He was working on a painting in front of me; it was red on the edges and went to a black in the middle. "The painting is $700."

I whispered the price to David.

"Yeah... out of our price range," he said.

I asked for the artist's card and we left. We were about to head for a makeshift food court when I received a phone call from Harper's assistant at the newspaper.

"Did you hear? The mayor has died," she said. "We should probably put something up on the website."

I was in shock. I was now the only surviving victim. I hadn't seen the mayor since we were both in the hospital, passing on gurneys; he had been in and out of the hospital.

I stood motionless. I didn't know how to feel, how to take this news.

"What's wrong?" asked David.

"The mayor...has...died," I said.

I wanted the mayor to keep up the fight and survive. I didn't want to be the only one. Against my will, I was brought back to that night. It didn't feel like it had been months. Suddenly, it felt like it only happened yesterday.

"I'm supposed to check with Harper to see if she knew about this. The website should be updated," I said.

"Let your boss take care of it. You're too emotionally involved."

"I...I know...but..." I keyed in Harper's number.

"I heard about the mayor's death. Do you need me to file a story? We're at an art festival, so I'm not near the computer."

Harper answered, "We have a story up on the site already."

"That's cool, thanks."

I didn't feel like I could deal with this properly anyway.

We were still near the food court, but I'd lost my appetite. "I don't feel like eating."

"That makes sense," he said. "Do you want to look at more artwork?"

"No. I want to go now."

We headed home. The news talked about the shooting again and the mayor's death. I followed it all. I wanted to feel like I knew him, but all we really had in common was what happened in the Kirkwood City Council chambers only a few months ago.

"What can I do?" David asked.

"Hold me. I know that this is stupid. Feeling messed up about this after so many months. But I do," I said.

"You have a right to feel that way."

The mayor's funeral was in a few days. Harper sent another reporter because if I had gone, I would have been a mess. I didn't know the mayor personally; only a few words of friendly conversation had transpired between us prior to him being shot. Yet being shot like he was shouldn't happen to anybody. And now he was dead. It was so wrong. I held tight to David as I struggled to sleep.

Chapter Fourteen

DR. CARRUTHERS RECOMMENDED that I have the second surgery, but this one would be as an outpatient. I would go to sleep and they would reshape my hand with an artificial joint in my thumb. I would be back to doing physical therapy again.

I was up for anything to stop frequent bouts of pain and gain more use of my hand. But he cautioned that motion in my hand would not be like it was before the shooting.

"You won't have a complete recovery, but it will be as close as we can make it," he said. "And understand that you could have early arthritis in the future. But we will do our best."

I wanted things to be normal. I wanted to be rid of the strange stiffness that at times kept me up at night. I didn't want to have a constant reminder of that night, besides the mental pictures.

David was uncertain about it, only because he didn't like the idea of me having a second surgery, but he supported my decision.

A week later, I was in the outpatient clinic. David gave me a kiss as I headed into the operating room.

"This will be the last one, right, Doc?" I asked Dr. Carruthers.

"It is all we can do for the hand," he said.

"Too bad this isn't the future where I can get a mechanical one, like in Star Wars," I said to both of them.

"I wish they had the technology for that," David said.

They wheeled me off into surgery. It only took a few hours. When I woke, my hand was bandaged up again. I would have to be off from work for a few weeks and return to physical rehabilitation.

"At least I have a chance to visit with Angela again. I enjoyed her hand massages," I said.

"Oh, you did? Am I going to have to worry about you with her?" David teased.

"Only when it comes to hand massages."

"Maybe I should come with you next time."

"I don't think you're allowed back," I said.

"I guess I'll let it go, as long as it doesn't go any further."

I WAITED IN the front room of the physical therapy clinic to give Angela an update about how the job was going and my last surgery. I hoped that I could really move forward now.

But when they called me back from the waiting room, I didn't see Angela. Eventually, an older woman with dark black hair came up and massaged my hand.

"What happened to Angela?" I asked.

"She started her own physical therapy service," she said.

"Oh, good for her." And I meant it. Angela had talked about starting her own business.

The new lady was pleasant enough. But it wasn't the same without Angela. I had enjoyed talking with her about David. I didn't volunteer information to the new lady about the shooting. I'm sure the whole ugly past was in their paperwork. I gave her fake smiles as we went through the motions.

I should not have become accustomed to Angela. I sighed to myself.

I did all the exercises for the new lady. I barely caught her name. Part of me didn't want to learn it. I'm not the best with change.

"We'll work you back to what you were doing before," she said as I left.

That was it, back to my current level with my hand. It hurt after the workout. That was normal—the new normal.

I drove back home, where David had made dinner—chicken and rice. I barely tasted it. I sat down and watched some comedy. I didn't want to think about anything for a while.

The world had moved on. I hadn't. Angela had started a new business in the short time between my first surgery and the second. Where was my life going?

I MADE IT through physical therapy, and David and I were cruising along after our lost year. Now, we were in a new year and heading for the one-year anniversary of the shooting.

I went to work and did my job without a thought. I was living as best I could. I was getting by, but that was the problem.

With the one-year anniversary, the City of Kirkwood had decided to have a memorial ceremony at City Hall. I was invited. Not directly by anybody, but by a card in the mail that had arrived only a day before the ceremony. Almost like I had been an afterthought on their part.

David was not happy when he saw the belated card. "It's almost like you were forgotten." He reminded me that during my recovery, the city never sent a get-well card, never acknowledged what I had gone through.

I saw pain in his eyes. It was true. But I thought I should go. I wasn't sure why—maybe because that moment had utterly changed my life.

I discussed my need to go to the ceremony when I went to the therapist the next day. "What do you think? Should I do it?"

"I think you should attend. You need to move past how you feel about Kirkwood."

"Is it helpful to go back?"

"Yes, you can face your demons in the place that you still fear. Have you been in Kirkwood City Hall since it happened?"

"No, to be honest, I do my best not to visit the town. I still have this lingering uneasiness about the place," I said. "I can't even imagine going anywhere nearby to eat. It makes me almost throw up thinking about it. Crazy, huh?"

"No, not crazy. Normal reactions to what happened to you. I think it would do a lot for your recovery not to see the place as a nightmare," he countered.

"If you think it will be good for me, I'll go," I said.

WE PREPARED FOR the memorial together. It was held on a freezing cold night. I dressed up in some new brown pants and a dark-blue button-down shirt. I kept staring at myself in the mirror. It felt like I was heading for work, instead of facing a nightmare.

"Should I wear a tie?" I asked.

"Sure. You look hot all dressed up," David said.

"Thanks, but I find nothing sexy about doing this. I'm so far away from that mentally."

"I know. I was trying to make it better for you," he said.

The area around the building was packed. We found a spot up the block to park and headed toward Kirkwood City Hall in silence.

The building was ornate with a small tower. It was everything a town hall should be, at least for a Midwestern city of 20,000 people. Yet that didn't comfort me that night.

I held David tight. I felt like something was going to happen, a fear that I couldn't quite explain.

A man was seated behind a table inside the entrance, and we checked in with him before we went into the chambers.

The man running check-in went through his papers, "I-I can't seem to find your name."

I was shocked. He stepped away for a moment, went to talk to someone else, and came back. "You can come on up."

I didn't know what say. It was too shocking. I let it go. The therapist said I needed to face my fears. So for the first time since the shooting, I turned to go upstairs with David. It was where I had left a blood path. If I closed my eyes, I could still see my hand dripping blood on the stairs. The whole place smelled of fresh paint.

David wanted to head to the right, to find a seat in the chambers.

"I can't. It's crazy, I know, but he ran down the right when he started shooting. I still feel a sense of something evil on that side."

We stood for a moment, then headed to the left. He could not have known. It was something I hadn't told him until that moment.

I couldn't shake the feeling that death was in this place. I was shocked to see cookies and punch up front. People were gathering around, talking and even laughing.

All I felt was dread. I kept thinking, *I shouldn't have done this. It's all too much.*

A few people came up to me and asked how I was doing. I simply said, "I'm doing fine." I could barely speak. I was too disturbed to say much more.

The remembrance service included a small ceremony inside and then a memorial service outside in the front of the building.

Everyone was given candles. I had trouble with mine, of course. We were to light them in memory of those who'd died that night. I lost my ability to focus. I thought I could move past this a year later, but I was still floating along.

Wax dripped all over me. We had paper to try to keep it from doing this, but I didn't seem to be able to make it work right. I ended up with wax all over me.

It was like the universe itself was in flux. The wax became the blood shed that night, which had stained my clothes as it had my mind.

We shook hands with some of the surviving council members. David talked for me. I kept looking behind everyone. In the back of my mind, I saw him everywhere. He was pointing a gun, and this time, he was not going to miss.

That thought blared through my mind even after we left. I couldn't get his face out of my mind, and that night again, my sleep was filled with nightmares. It was as though the shooting had just happened, time once more had stopped, and that fateful day was being relived over and over in my head. Only this time, I was one of the dead.

Chapter Fifteen

ONE OF THE reporters in our main office had received an award for our coverage of the shooting. My boss had told me she wanted to see me, and I thought possibly I was going to receive something related to that.

I was very much mistaken. The human resources person was waiting for me in Harper's office with a large folder.

"This does not reflect on your work," Harper said. "We're downsizing due to the economy."

I stared at them both. I blinked. I couldn't believe this was happening.

The human resources director said, "You need to sign these papers and you can receive your unemployment, severance, and COBRA your benefits."

She seemed as disappointed to do this, as I was to receive the news.

Behind her lay a large pile of similar packets. At least I wasn't alone.

I left the room and walked out into the long hallway of cubicles. The first few were newly empty.

I was mentally and physically wounded. And now I was jobless.

I gathered all my things, which did not include a lot. I was never comfortable putting up a photo of David. I stared at the certificate for employee of the month for a moment. *I guess that doesn't save you in the end.*

It was the economy, I knew. Nothing personal. It never was. The shootings, the deaths that seemed to fill my past, none of it was personal.

I said goodbye to the other reporters. I got the usual responses: *stay strong, sorry to see you go.* Others were being let go. One said it had been a pleasure working with me.

My box was filled at 10:00 a.m. exactly. I completely cleaned the desk, mostly by throwing things away. I took some copies of the papers my writing had appeared in.

I remembered layoffs in the past. I had coasted through them before, but now it was my turn. I had this vague expectation that the shooting would have made a difference.

I was wrong—foolish, foolish thoughts. I was another casualty of the times.

I DROVE AROUND St. Louis most of the day until I could arrive home at my usual time from work. I didn't want to be home without him.

"I've been laid off," I said as I walked in the door. I hadn't had the strength to tell him by phone. And I had been crying.

"Are you fucking kidding me?" David said. "No way. After every fucking thing that's happened?"

"I know," I said.

"How are you doing?"

Tears welled up in my eyes. "I'm holding up as best I can."

He kissed me and took me in his arms.

But I pulled away. "I can't do this. I'm sorry."

"I want to be here for you, Todd. Why won't you let me in?"

"I can't. Not right now." I walked out of the house, got into the car, and headed out. He only wanted to hold me, and I was pulling away. I didn't know why I'd walked in the door and then left once I told him. I was acting crazy. Insane.

I went to visit with Kevin. He was at the Grey Fox Pub, getting ready for a performance.

"We need to talk."

Kevin was lathering on makeup. "Do you mind helping?"

"Sure," I said.

"I usually have Larry do this."

I didn't know Larry very well. All I knew was that he helped Kevin prepare for performances.

"He's late, of course, and I have an early number to do tonight." Kevin had not put on his wig. He was bald now. My hair was also receding. *Maybe I should think about cutting it all off.* We were both aging.

"I was laid off today," I blurted out.

"I wondered why you called up wanting to see me right away. Come here. You need a hug from your oldest and dearest friend."

Kevin was always more relaxed when he was Jade Sinclair. I needed a little honey for the bitter fruit I had tasted today.

"Can you grab that eye shadow and help me put it on?"

"I'll have to do it with my left hand, the non-bullet one." I did the best I could.

"That looks gorgeous," he said as he gazed into the mirror at himself.

I hadn't realized I could do that with my left hand. It seemed to be taking on a stronger role as time moved on.

"I know the economy is rocky, but it was hard to take just a year after the shooting. And fuck, I got shot in the line of duty," I said.

He looked at himself again for a moment. "Life does suck. Can you be a dear and put a bit of base makeup on me? Spread it around lightly."

I grabbed the foundation and smeared it around lightly like he said.

"I can never understand why people can't do right by each other," he said. "I always think that if you work hard and do your job well, that you can move ahead."

I smeared the foundation. "You know, the night of the shooting, I kept feeling I shouldn't go to the meeting and thinking that something bad was going to happen...like a weird whisper. And now, look what I get for all my trouble. A swift kick in the ass. Am I right?"

"You're really good at this. Maybe you should get a job doing makeup."

"Uh...thanks." At least I had some sort of accomplishment today.

He turned away from the mirror. "How do I look?"

I actually did do a fantastic job on the makeup: the right amount of rouge, foundation, and eyeliner.

"At least I can put on a drag queen's makeup." I laughed.

"Let me tell you something," Kevin said. "I think you should find what makes you happy in life. It could be another reporter job or writing a book. Find what you really enjoy and go all the way with it. If you enjoy something, it will work out. It always does. Not that life isn't going to throw shit at it, but at least if your day-to-day life is filled with something you love, it's all worth it."

He slipped on the wig. "Performing is the highest moment of any day for me. The crowd wants me. They, dare I say it, love me. Maybe not as Kevin, but as Jade Sinclair. That, my friend, is worth going home at 2:00 a.m. completely exhausted. Now, I have to perform Cher's 'Gypsies, Tramps and Thieves.'"

A few minutes later, I heard applause as Jade took to the stage and opened with "Who wants old-school Cher tonight?"

He had them enthralled.

Jade said every word with gripping intensity. He received loud applause and laughs as he danced from the stage and into the crowd. Most everyone knew the words. Jade now had a following. He was a goddess when he performed. He had found his calling. I only had to find mine.

I walked away, knowing he was right. I needed to figure out what to do next. The show must go on, so to speak.

FIGHTING HAD BECOME the new norm since I had lost my job. It wasn't really anyone's fault. I was depressed and lashing out, and David was sadly the most likely target. I was all anger and spite and falling apart.

David was making eggs while I was looking through want ads in the paper. I felt like time had stopped. When the newspaper had shut down in Kansas City, I'd easily found a job in Tulsa. Now nothing.

David put eggs on my plate. "Did you check out the small weekly that we get dropped on the porch?"

"Of course I did. You think I didn't think of that one?" I wasn't really sure what I was angry at. I was flailing big-time.

"I was only checking, no reason to get bitchy about it," he fired back. "Do you have any interviews today? I was hoping that you could go by the store."

He sat down and ate the eggs that he'd made.

"No, no interviews. Not this week, not last week, and probably not next week," I snapped again.

David shook his head at me. The tension in the air was lingering like the smell of the toast I had burned moments ago.

David walked out of the kitchen. He seemed to need some time to clear his frustration with me.

The phone rang and I answered it.

"Hi, I'm a reporter with the *New York Times*," the voice on the line said.

"Uh, who? Is this a joke? Is someone fucking with me?" I said.

A moment of silence. "Uh, I'm with the *New York Times*. Are you the reporter who was fired after being shot while covering the Kirkwood City Council meeting?"

I stopped for a moment. *Oh, this is real.* I sucked air back into my lungs, then said, "Yes, that's me. Why?"

"Do you mind if I call you this afternoon to do an over-the-phone interview about your layoff?"

"That would be fine. Sorry, I wasn't sure if this was for real. We've had prank calls after the shooting. You know, how I should have had a gun that day." I had gotten such calls even though having a gun would probably have caused me to get shot, since when the police came in, they wouldn't have known who the shooter was.

"How does 3:00 p.m. sound?"

"Sounds great." I hung up.

David came back into the room. "Who was that?"

"The *New York Times*," I said.

"Really?" he said.

"Yeah. I guess getting shot and laid off is enough to have someone at the *New York Times* take notice."

The reporter called me back that afternoon. I related life after the shooting and about being laid-off.

He ended by asking, "How are you getting along now?"

"I'm getting along as best I can. Each shooting has its own problems and issues I have to face," I said, matter-of-fact.

The reporter said my story would be part of an article about a person in Arizona who was laid-off after receiving a Pulitzer Prize.

"That is rough, to be such an honored writer and shown the door."

He thanked me for my time. I hung up and went back to looking for jobs. This was my life once more—a search for employment.

The article appeared in the *New York Times* a few days after the interview. David found a print edition at a nearby Barnes and Noble.

I read through it. "Well, at least I had my fifteen minutes of fame."

"The reporter did an excellent job of capturing what happened to you," David added.

Although the article didn't change the friction between us, it gave us a moment to pause. At least the unfairness of it was recognized. But this did nothing for my present circumstances or lead to any jobs.

David's father, Saul, called after seeing the *Times* article. I always felt a bit uncomfortable talking with him since he was such a well-known optometrist in New York.

David had me take the phone. Saul read excerpts for me. "How do you feel their coverage was?"

"I think they wrote a piece that captured the heart of the issue." I hoped that sounded intelligent. It was the *New York Times*; I wasn't going to criticize them. Also, this would probably be my only chance to be mentioned in the *Times* unless I was shot again. Which, considering the trajectory of my life had become all too possible.

"How's the job search going?" Saul said.

"It's a tough economy, but hopefully, I will find something."

"You will. Keep looking. And most of all I love you both," he said.

It was nice to hear encouraging words from him. But at the same time, I felt loss now that I had been let go from my job. What was I to do next? I just didn't know.

SOMETIMES, A PERSON hits rock bottom in life, a point where everything weighs them down. I was sinking fast without seeing a way I could turn back. I was going inward and turning my anger onto others and myself. I was not in a good place. David and I were constantly fighting. I think it was basically the same fight over and over.

I went to talk to Kevin about it one night. We met for a beer at the gay bar in Soulard that we frequented. That night there were only a few regulars there, which gave us some quiet to have a serious conversation about David and me.

"I'm going to have to leave town for a while," I said to him as he got a beer.

"What do you mean by that?" he asked.

"I'm going to spend some time with my sister so I can pull my thoughts together about my life."

"What about you and David?" he asked.

"I...I need a break: The shooting, the recovery, the layoff. It's all been one thing after another. He's been great, but I need time away from the relationship for a while. What do you think?"

"You need to talk to him about it." Kevin snagged another beer. "Are you two breaking up?"

"No. Yes. I don't know. I need to leave...to get myself together."

"Why?" he asked.

I chugged down a big gulp before answering. "I...I just need it."

"I must say this," Kevin said. "Make sure you're able to handle the consequences. David might not be waiting for you if you step out of the relationship. He might move on. You can't expect him to wait for you to get your act together."

I agreed with him, yet I still needed some time to reflect on my life, to think about how I felt about everything.

"So are you going to go out and party it up?"

"I don't know. Again, not the reason I'm doing this."

"Make sure to use protection."

"I will. I promise. Although, again, that isn't the reason for this." I changed the subject. "How is dating going for you?"

"I've gone on a few dates," Kevin said. "Nothing long-lasting yet. I'm still performing drag with the anthem of a lonely diva being thrown into the cold world of men with sequined hearts." He laughed.

"Oh, really? Let's dance, to all the horrible bastards out there!" I shouted.

We went up to the dance floor and Cher's "Song for the Lonely" came on. *How appropriate.*

Suddenly, I was alive with my best friend, before I had to face the music with my boyfriend.

I TOLD DAVID we had to have a serious discussion. I didn't give him a lot of specifics. I kept going over what I was going to say in my mind.

It was going to hurt me as much as him. But it had to be said. I knew what I wanted was asking a lot. He had every right to hate me and move on.

I didn't want to do it, but I needed some time to reflect on what I wanted to do next with my life. I had grown so dependent on him, like I couldn't do anything on my own anymore.

The shooting had caused me to question my ability to survive on my own. Now, I wanted to know if I really loved him or I only needed him. I had a thousand questions about the relationship, and I needed them answered. The only way our relationship was going to work was if I had this break.

What if he found another? That was a risk I was taking. And he had every right to do that. Who was I to stop him?

David came home as it became dark and found me sitting in the living room. It was early fall, and each day ended sooner. On this particular day, I hadn't even noticed it.

"Why are you sitting in here without a light on?" he asked.

"We need to talk," I said. "Do you mind if we go out to the Brazilian restaurant?"

His stare bored into me. "What is it?"

"Let's talk over dinner." I knew telling him what I had to do was a conversation that needed to be accompanied by a beer.

The place was almost empty when we walked in, too early for an after-work dinner.

I first ordered a beer and chugged it down. He gave me an odd look. I called the waitress again and asked her to bring me another one.

I started to say. "The thing is..."

"What's the problem?" he said.

"I need to spend some time with my sister," I said.

"Sure, visiting her a few days would be great," he said, not understanding the full implications.

"I know. That's why I'm considering..." I paused as I chugged more beer.

He interrupted again, "What are you thinking about doing? Explain."

"I think I'm going to stay up there for a while."

"How long?" he asked.

"David, I don't really know how to tell you this."

"What is going through your mind, Todd?"

He searched my face for clues. He obviously knew something was wrong. We had been together for almost three years. Half the time, he knew my thoughts before they were even spoken.

"I...I need a break," I said.

"What do you mean by a break?"

"I feel that I need to be on my own for a while."

"Explain. I'm not understanding."

"It's been a difficult time for me, the shooting, surgery, recovery, surgery, recovery, layoff. It's a lot to bear. It's been so much that I'm not exactly sure who the heck I am right now. If I take this break, I can think through these things." I paused. "I'm not going to see you for a while. I might call once a week, maybe. I need to know that I really love you, that I'm not just dependent on you. I know that's a lot to ask. I'm not sure if, after this break, we'll still be together. Maybe.

"And if you find someone else while I'm getting my act together, that's understandable. Makes total sense. That's my fuckup. I wish I could be clearer, but I don't know who I am right now. I just really need time off from the engagement."

David didn't say a word. He got up from the table and walked out of the restaurant.

I signaled the waiter that we were leaving.

David's actions made sense to me. He now needed some time to think about the bombshell I'd dropped. I squeezed my eyes shut, took a deep breath, swigged down one last beer, and then quickly paid the check.

For the first time, I walked home from the restaurant alone. A cold chill followed me as I headed down the block. I was lost in a complete and utter disarray of emotion. I knew what I had done was rough but necessary.

I stayed awake in bed all night. He didn't come home until the sun came up on Saturday morning. The door slammed, and he came up the stairs.

He had been drinking. He never went to the bar without me. This was unusual behavior. He got into bed.

"I'm sorry," I said.

"That doesn't help. Did you even want to ask me first?" He wouldn't even look at me.

"I...I needed to do this on my own. Like I said, I don't think this means it's over for us. I need time...with my thoughts." I was trying to comfort him.

He didn't go along with it. "When are you leaving?"

"On Monday," I said. "I will spend Sunday getting everything ready. I don't have a lot of stuff."

He looked me straight in the eye. "Are you sure you want to do this?"

"Yes. Again, I don't think the relationship is over. I..."

He stopped me. "You do realize that once you walk out of the house, that could be it. Is that the risk you're willing to take for this *break*?"

"I still love you. I just need...some time away, okay?"

"It's not okay. We've been through so much. How can you walk out on us?"

"I'm not walking out. I'm taking..."

He stopped me again. "A break. I get it. I'm going to stay with Mark until you leave. I can't be here while you're here."

He kissed me. I just stared at him...knowing I needed to do this. My jaw was clenched and I narrowed my vision trying to hold my own against the pain I had caused.

He turned away. He packed up a suitcase. I stayed in bed while the door slammed shut. I stared up at the ceiling as tears filled my eyes.

"I just need a break." Kept saying this over and over in my mind. And I wondered what that really meant. Were we breaking up or only separating? What was I doing? I wasn't even sure at that moment if I was making the right choice...for now, maybe forever, who knows.

I tried to fall asleep, but I couldn't take my eyes off the picture on the nightstand of us together in front of the Arch. I finally had to turn it around.

I lay on my left side, turned away from the photo, hoping to ignore the pain I was feeling. But I was facing a photo of us before I had been shot on top of a mountain in Colorado.

I turned it around and spent the night staring up at the ceiling.

LEAVING DAY. I walked out of the house without ever speaking a word to David. Mark had become an intermediary between us.

He said, "David will come back once you're gone. He doesn't want to face you right now."

I got into my overfilled car. I kept staring at the house as I stood out front. Was this the last time I was going to see this place? Would I be back? I didn't know how the future would play out. If it would play out.

I thought about the relationship I had with my sister— we'd become closer when I came out to her after Rick's death.

Besides Kevin, she was the only one I could turn to in times of trouble like this. After everything that had happened in Delaware, I wasn't comfortable living with Kevin again. It was also one of those times I wished Rick was still alive for advice about relationships.

My sister was still the only one in the family who I'd told I was gay.

I turned to her now when I was uncertain of my current relationship. I had only let her know by phone a few days before about my needing some time away from David. I was lucky she had an extra bedroom since my oldest nephew had moved out of the house.

"I do like David, but I understand if you need a little time on your own," she said.

"It's not that I don't still love him, but I need some time to reflect how I feel about everything—losing the job, getting shot twice. I need to figure out my life."

"I understand. That's what I'm here for, and I'm looking forward to spending time with my little brother."

I arrived at my sister's later that day. She hugged me. "How long will you be here?"

"I don't know. Thanks for doing this, Karen."

"You can stay as long as you need to," she said.

I spent a week at her place. I felt alone the most at night. I kept reaching for his hand, only to find no one to touch.

My thoughts during that week went to happier times. On a beach where we built a sand castle together and I gave it a swift kick and it all came down. He chased me and we fell on top of each other and laughed. We went to Colorado together and sat on a blanket and watched fireworks out over a lake with the Rocky Mountain National Park as the backdrop. I once had him drive three hours so I could go to the highest point in Illinois. It was mid-July, a horrendously hot day, and even though it only amounted to a slightly big hill, it was a long walk down a gravel lane with dust blowing from everywhere to finally reach the pinnacle. We were sweaty and grimy on the way back to the car. He was crazy to be in love with me.

I hadn't heard from David. I did have Mark's number and decided to call and check on him.

I took two deep breaths and asked, "How's he doing?"

"Okay. He still doesn't understand why you did this."

"I know. I need time away..."

"You know he's devastated. He didn't see this coming. He's fine with his work. But I can see that the gleam in his eye is gone. Did you take that into account when you left him?" Mark asked with a harsh tone. He was right to be mad at me.

I think Mark was hoping to get it through to me that what I'd done was wrong, so I did an about-face.

"Tell him I still care for him deeply. And this was just as hard for me." I hoped he could tell from my soft, strained voice that I was serious.

"You should call him," Mark said. "He's not going to call you. This was your decision, remember?"

"I know."

We left it at that. I tried to go to sleep that night, but I stayed awake the whole night staring at the ceiling and wondering if I had made the right decision.

KEVIN CAME UP the second weekend that I was at my sister's to go out with me. "Have you talked to David?"

"No, not since we separated. Have you heard from him?"

"No. Were you hoping?" he asked. "You know you wanted the separation."

"I know."

We headed out to a gay bar that was near my sister's house. It was older with wood paneling, round metal tables and chairs, but still had the strobe lights blinking on the hardwood dance floor. We went to the back area, where it was quieter and away from those trying to find someone for the night. I ordered beer for the both of us.

"So how's it going with David?" Kevin asked.

"I think I'm missing him." I peeled some of the label off the beer bottle.

"Call him up and tell him." Kevin tried to get me to stop making a mess.

"But after all that I did, can I do that?" I pulled off the final bit of paper from the front.

"Sure," he said.

"What should I say?"

"Todd, I'm your oldest friend. Cut the shit."

"I think I made a mistake. But I don't know what to do about it." I finished the beer and ordered another.

"I think you should call him. See how he's doing. It doesn't hurt to reach out. He might be feeling the same thing," Kevin said.

"Do you think I went too far?"

"Maybe. But you might still be able to fix this."

"But what if he's given up on me?"

"Sometimes, Todd, you have to take a chance. If he moved on, maybe he never really loved you or you messed it up. That's a possibility. You don't know, but the only way you will, is if you call him and see."

"You're right. You know, I'm going to head on back to my sister's house and give him a call. Can't do this in a gay bar with people trying to hook up all around me..."

"Giving you positive vibes," he said with a smirk.

I headed out to see if David still loved me or if it was over.

IT WAS ABOUT midnight when I walked quietly to the bedroom. I thought to myself that he should be asleep by now. Part of me hoped that he was. I could leave a message telling him I wanted to talk. It would be a weak way of handling this, but right then, that was fine with me.

I dialed. First ring, second ring, third ring...I was almost home free for the answering machine to pick up.

"Hello, Todd," David said.

What should I say?

I blurted it out, "I fucked up." I started crying. This was the rawest emotion I had ever felt in my life. "I'm sorry. I know that doesn't cut it. But I am. Will you forgive me? Can you forgive me, please...?"

Dead space—the seconds slowed to a crawl.

Waiting.

Waiting.

Nothing.

Really? Nothing.

God, please...

Nothing.

I was going crazy with silence. No answer. Not good. Not good. Oh God, it's over.

"Todd," he finally said.

"Yes, I'm here."

"You put me through hell. You walked out on me. You're an asshole, you know."

"I know, I know. I'm still sorry," I said.

"Sorry doesn't fix this. Why?"

"I wanted to see if I really loved you. It was wrong, I know. But I wanted to make sure this was real."

"Remember the hospital. You asked me to marry me. What happened to that, Todd? Why did you leave me?"

"I know this isn't the answer you wanted. But I don't know..."

"I'll need to think about this," he said.

"Really? I want you back. Now."

"I'm sure you do," he said. "But now I need some time to myself. That's all I can offer right now. You did this. I didn't. Were you expecting me to take you back in one drunken phone call, Todd? That's not how it works. Now, it's my turn. I might take you back and I might not. That's where we stand right now."

The phone clicked.

We were somewhere in the middle ground between starting over again or never. Not the answer I wanted, but something. A starting point. I had let David slip away because of my own stubbornness. It was wrong, and now I was paying for it.

Chapter Sixteen

DAVID AND I decided to go on a date. We were heading back into relationship mode, but it was a slow process. After many phone calls, trying to figure out how to go back to the way we were, he decided to come up to Quincy, the town nearest my sister's house.

It was strange to call it such a thing—a date. We had been together for three years, and in this fourth year, we were going on a date.

I decided to take him out to a restaurant that featured romantic candlelight dinners. Maybe this would reignite the relationship that I had taken apart.

David wore a crimson red long-sleeve shirt with brown khakis and a *Simpsons* tie. I was boring, in a white long-sleeve shirt with blue pants and a green tie.

My sister was out for the night with the kids and her husband to give me some time alone with David. "He will take you back. If he doesn't, I'll beat him up," she had said.

I answered the door, and we gave each other an awkward hug, then headed to the bedroom.

"Strange to be in your nephew's former bedroom, even if it is decorated as your bedroom now." He picked up a picture of Kevin and me at our high school graduation. I had wanted to put a photo of both of us out, but I didn't want to push things. He laughed at all my crazy superhero stuff. I had never done this in our house. I limited myself to color prints of Spiderman, Hulk, and the X-Men.

He picked up a small metal sculpture of the Empire State Building." Do you remember when we were in New York City?"

"Yeah. It was cold that day, but I couldn't get past needing to take photo after photo, even at the top." I pointed to the statue. David had yelled at me to stop. We were both about frozen. He had signaled me to come close and kissed me. "You kept kissing me until that security guy came by to tell us to get a room."

"It was a fantastic moment," he said.

"It was." I looked down at my watch.

"Oh, we need to head out," I said.

He didn't seem ready at first, but reluctantly, he said, "You're right."

The restaurant was packed. Luckily, I'd remembered to make a reservation. Not something I'd normally think to do. I tended to do things last minute.

"Order what you like, my treat," I said.

He had a steak dinner and I had a seafood and pasta dish. We both ate slowly and talked about the last few years, right up until the separation.

He finally asked the question I knew was coming. "Why did you feel you needed to step away?"

"I wanted to know that I really loved you. That seems crazy, but so much of what happened to us recently has been about surviving the shooting. It was wrong, but I wanted to make sure that what we have is real."

"What did you learn?" He stared into my eyes.

I fidgeted with the cloth napkin. I hoped the next words out of my mouth would show how much it was killing me to be without him.

"I...still love you. More than I ever did." I was about to lose my composure. Not something I normally did in a nice restaurant. "I'm sorry. I made a big mistake."

Now, I was searching his eyes for an expression of understanding.

He wasn't fidgeting with anything. He cut into the last piece of the steak and swallowed it with some wine.

He was savoring this. Giving me a moment to sweat. I deserved it. I had left him, not the other way around. "I still love you. We can work toward getting back together. Let's go from there."

I wanted to reach across the table and touch his hand at that moment, but didn't. I wanted to take it slow and let him lead the way. Instead, I signaled the waiter that we were ready to go.

"Was this a good choice as a restaurant?" I asked.

"Not as good as the one a few blocks away from my house."

I knew what he was getting at. He was pushing my buttons a little. We walked out to snow coming down in waves.

We headed back to my sister's house and sat on the couch. I was lucky my sister and her family were still out to a movie. I lay close to him, but not touching. Just being near him felt great.

It was getting late.

"I would have you stay the night, but it might be awkward with my sister and the kids," I said.

"I wish I could too...but I need to get back."

I gave him a kiss before he finished talking. A long one. He kissed back just the same. "Sorry I've been away."

"All that matters is that we're back together," he said.

We snuggled closer and closer. The phone rang. I thought it was my sister telling me they would be back soon.

It was Kevin. He sounded out of sorts.

"What's wrong?" I asked.

"It's my mom. She...has cancer."

"Oh my God!"

"She...she only has a short time to live."

"What do you need me to do?"

"Do you mind coming up to my mom's house on Sunday? If it's possible...I don't want to be alone," he said.

"No problem at all."

"Thanks."

"What's going on?" David was trying to figure out what was happening from only half the conversation.

"Kevin's mom has cancer, and the prognosis isn't good," I said. "David, I hope you understand that I have to be there for him. But once I'm back, I want home to be Saint Louis with you."

"Of course."

We kissed and he headed out. I wished I could have gone home with him, but my focus now had to be on helping Kevin.

I must have been lost in thought because I didn't realize my sister had come home until she plopped down beside me on the bed.

"Are you and David getting back together?" she asked.

"Yes, but I have sad news to share."

"What?"

"Kevin's mom has cancer, and she's not doing well. I'm going to spend some time with him."

"That's good," she said. "He will need you."

She left me alone in my thoughts. It was painful to know what my best friend was going through. I looked at the photo of us together and noticed his parents in the background smiling. *I have to be there for him.*

STANDING IN FRONT of Kevin's home felt like I was in high school again. The redbrick house looked exactly the same as when I'd left to go to college. Now I was back in the town I had went to high school in for the all-but-certain funeral of my best friend's mother.

Kevin's oldest sister Jamie answered the door, looking exhausted. She led me to the family room. It was as I remembered: a large space with a tall stone fireplace, two couches that had been in the room since the first time I met Kevin, a table beneath large windows that let in light from a now-brown field outside.

Kevin was in the kitchen, next to the family room.

"How are you?" I hoped that was the right question to ask.

"I'm doing okay." He was going through the cabinets. "I haven't been able to eat anything all day, and now suddenly I'm hungry."

He went to the refrigerator and pulled out some ham, cheese, and bread. He put a sandwich together and grabbed chips. Kevin seemed to be ignoring me at first. Maybe my visit was making it too real.

He sat down on the couch closest to the TV. "Mom's upstairs in bed. She has hardly said a word. The cancer has spread... I..." He stopped. He seemed to lose his appetite, went to the kitchen, and threw out the sandwich. "It's damn hard, you know."

"I know. What do you need me to do?"

"Do you mind going out to the bar here in town? We can walk," he offered.

Kevin and I sat at the long wooden counter facing an array of liquor bottles and taps and bought a beer. "She's been so quiet. Her hair is gone because of the chemo. I'm sorry I didn't tell you sooner. I've been keeping this in the family. I didn't want to deal with it. The chemo didn't work. The prognosis isn't good."

"It's all right." I held him as he cried on my shoulder.

He let go and ordered another drink, trying to change the subject. "What do you think of the bar?"

"It's nice, a lot of wood. Quite different from the restaurant we always ate in after church," I said.

He talked about doing a drag performance up at the Drake in nearby Quincy, which was only about thirty minutes from where we had gone to high school together.

"What's it like to perform so close to home?"

"It's really cool actually, I make good money when I perform there. I'm gaining a following up here." He was being modest. He had recently been crowned Miss Gay Missouri America and was going up for a national competition.

"You're becoming quite the star," I said.

He laughed at that. It was the first time he had smiled since we arrived.

We left the bar late. Kevin offered me a bedroom at the house. I declined at first, but he insisted. I stayed in the green room upstairs, which had been one of his sisters.

The next morning, Kevin invited me into his mother's room. A heart monitor was hooked up to her as she lay sleeping. She had only woken up a few times since she'd left the hospital, he'd said. They let her sleep as much as she wanted.

I touched her hand. It was the most caring thing that I could do. Her hand felt cold to the touch and I became misty-eyed. I silently said a prayer, wishing that her passage into the hereafter would be without pain and she would find peace.

Kevin led me out. "It's hard to see her that way." Tears moistened his eyes. I held out my arm to console him. I was weeping now. It was difficult to watch him go through this, and nothing I said or did made it any easier.

His mom passed away the next day, and though expected, it was devastating for everyone.

I remembered that she would come down the stairs with popcorn for us and see how we were doing. She had even liked the rom-coms or horror movies Kevin rented and watched them with us.

It felt like yesterday. Where had the time gone?

Kevin once more wanted to go out. "Let's head to the bar again."

I said that was fine, whatever he wanted to do was what I would be doing.

Kevin spent the night talking about his mom, how only a few days before she'd wished that he would find a nice guy to settle down with.

"I promised her I would," he said. "Now, I only have to find this guy. Simple, right?"

"Well, it's still work once you find them," I said.

"Oh, how are you and David?"

I drank my beer. "We're working on it. I made a mistake in taking the break. I know that now. At the time, I thought it was the right thing to do, but I was wrong. Now we're slowly putting it back together. In time, I think we'll get it right."

He completely changed direction. "Do your parents know about him and you being gay?"

"No, not yet."

"You need to cross that bridge," he said. "You need to tell them everything. You need to have the relationship with them. You don't know, one day they might be gone and what are you left with? They never really knew who you were."

"You're right."

We went back to the house and he took a shower while I was in his room. Kevin had been the youngest and kept his room the same as I remembered it. I snooped around. I had been doing this since I was in my teens. I went through old photos he'd left out: us together wearing vests for a school dance, standing next to our parents at graduation, and on a roller coaster at Six Flags with our hands up in the air. A lot of good times to remember.

I went through his records. I found an old Cher record as he came into the room from the shower and put on his clothes.

"I know this is not appropriate, but growing up, you loved this." And with a flick of the needle the "The Shoop Shoop Song" began to play.

"Do you think I really feel like dancing?" he asked.

"No, but sometimes, you just have to. Come on." He knew the song by heart as much as I did. We were dancing around the room like when we were kids. If anyone was upstairs while the music was blaring, they must have thought that we had both lost it.

I matched him in lockstep. We bopped around to the point of exhaustion.

Finally, I asked him, "Are you going to be okay?"

"Um...I'll make it through this." He kissed me on the forehead and gave me a big hug.

Hopefully, I did something right tonight, I thought as I fell asleep.

THE DAY OF the funeral was cold and clear. I stood next to Kevin, and he held my hand as tightly as he could at the burial site. I remember him holding my hand that tightly when they were pulling the first bullet out of me.

But the pain I felt that day was nowhere near what he was feeling. Everyone was shedding tears.

Kevin had spoken earlier at the visitation about how much his mom had meant to him, that even passed from this earth, she would still be watching him. She had always been there for him, no matter what happened.

He had told me about telling her he was gay while she was putting dinner on the plate. She kept right on laying out the spaghetti and said, "I always knew. It doesn't matter to me. I love you. Now, it's hot, so give it a minute to cool down. You don't want to burn your tongue."

That was his mom. I wasn't as close, but it reflected who she was and how she was with all her children. She loved them all unconditionally.

I didn't say much to Kevin throughout the day. I was the shoulder he needed to cry on.

When the casket was lowered, he held my hand tighter. Soon, it was over.

I told him I was headed back to my sister's place. "I wish I could have done more."

"You were a hand that I could hold onto when I needed you most. That's what a true friend...a best friend is for," he said.

"God, I still have to repair the damage to my relationship with David."

"It will all work out. If it doesn't, it's his loss. You are a great person, Todd. Don't let anyone tell you otherwise."

We hugged, and I headed back to Karen's house.

Chapter Seventeen

I WANTED TO talk with my sister privately so we went out to a nearby burger joint together.

"Karen, I'm going to marry David," I said as I bit into a juicy burger.

My sister stared at me for a moment. "I'm not sure if I'm comfortable with the marriage thing. It is so different."

I was a bit taken back. This was the first time I had ever seen her be unsure about something like marriage. I knew it was time for me to go. "I know this is a lot to take in."

She seemed still to be in shock with everything, so I continued on. "I am also going to come out to Mom and Dad."

"Please don't," she said.

"I understand your concerns—their religious convictions—but I have to. I know that it will take time for Mom and Dad to accept. But David means too much to me for them not to know."

She only said goodbye when I left. Coming out to my parents had made her feel uncomfortable. Maybe I had said too much about what I wanted, but making a life with David was now the most important thing to me.

DAVID AND I were on the top floor of a revolving restaurant in St. Louis. The sun was setting in a sky made up of light orange and red. The Arch was in clear view, and soon, lights would flicker on in the cityscape. I had a bottle of wine on ice.

"So, what is this all about?" he asked.

"I just wanted to take you somewhere nice."

"One of the most expensive restaurants in town with a skyline view." He kept smiling, and I tried to hide my excitement.

"Let's have a glass of wine first." I grabbed the two glasses and poured. "I would like to propose a toast, that no matter how bad things get between us, no matter what the hell life throws at us next, that we just let it roll off of us and keep going together. We've gone through everything to get to this evening, so life can only get better, right?"

We clinked glasses. I blew him a kiss and touched his leg under the table. He held my hand.

We ordered dinner and had a few more glasses of wine. Dessert was Boston cream pie, his favorite. When the plates were finally cleared, I was ready to make my move.

I went down on one knee. I kept trying to breathe easy, just like my therapist had told me to do in times of great stress. "The first time I asked this I was under the influence of a lot of drugs. This time, I want to ask it with a clear head. Will you marry me, David Kaplan?"

David didn't answer. He went back to eating his last piece of dessert. Why did he have to be so *himself* at this moment? "Did you say something?"

I was still kneeling. He let me sweat it out for a moment. He knelt, too, and opened his hand. In it was an open jewelry box with a ring for me.

I was shocked. My mouth hung open. I totally did not see this coming. I was speechless.

"First, you answer me this: Will you marry me, Todd Smith?"

I stammered out a yes.

"And I say yes to you too." David laughed. We exchanged our rings, similar gold bands.

"How did you know to get one like that?" I asked.

"You told Kevin that you were going to do this and he called me, so I found the jeweler and had mine made like yours. Sneaky of me, right?"

"Very," I said.

We had one last glass of wine. I told him that I'd also booked a room for us to stay in for the night.

"Oh, so you really had this all set up."

"Yep."

We went to the room. It had a full view of the Arch. Lights glittered in the distance. It was magical, staring eye to eye with the icon in the city I returned to for him. We lay in bed, looking out the window, not saying a word, just glad to be in the moment.

I MOVED BACK in with David. My sister and I didn't talk much after I'd made the decision to come out to Mom and Dad. It was important I do this now since we were going to be married soon. If it wasn't for David, I'm not sure if I would ever have done it, but they needed to know how important he was in my life and how important our relationship was, especially after sticking with me through my low points after the shooting.

My mom was out in the yard when we arrived. The vegetable garden was her favorite place. I always looked forward to having tomatoes, green peppers, and a Halloween pumpkin in the fall. I wasn't sure if I would receive these gifts of the earth after this conversation.

I told Mom and Dad to come inside and brought everyone together in the living room.

It took a moment to spit it out. "I'm gay," I finally said. Two simple words that together held lots of meaning for all of us.

My father said, "I...always knew, Todd. But this is hard for your mother to hear."

My mother turned to the Bible and began to read passages where it said it was wrong to be gay.

I didn't stop her. I let her read, although I wasn't paying attention really. I was too busy crying as she read them.

After she stopped reading, she said, "Why did you have to tell me this?"

"Because I love him, Mom. Because I love him!"

She headed back outside to the garden and slammed the door behind her.

I followed her out.

"I don't want to discuss it. I always thought of David as a close friend," she said as she roughly pulled weeds.

"You knew he was more than that." I stood to the side, trying my best to hold it together. Even though a part of me wanted to take it all back, but it was a little late for that.

"Why are you doing this to me?" she asked.

"I'm not doing anything *to* you, Mom. I wanted you to know how much David means to me. We've been through a lot more than most couples. From one thing to the next, he's always supported me. And we're getting married."

She gave me a stern look and shook her head. I had probably gone too far.

"I need some time to think all of this over." She walked away from me toward the outside faucet on the house.

I followed her. "What do you mean?"

"I need to discuss this with our pastor and think about this, Todd." She filled up a pail to water plants in the garden.

"Okay." I was about to walk away, somehow feeling defeated.

"It doesn't mean I don't love you. I just need to take it all in," she said.

"I understand," I said.

She stood for a moment with the pail in her hands. "You were always more sensitive than your brothers and sister... It will take time."

"Time for what?" I said.

"To face this. Can you give me that much?" She returned to the garden, moving slowly between the rows, watering the plants as she went.

"Yes." I tried to hug her, but she didn't want any of it.

I went back inside.

"How does your mother feel?" Dad asked.

"She needs some time," I answered.

"I'm not okay with this," he said. "I just knew."

"What should we do about Mom?"

"You should do what she said and give her time. And give me some time."

"I just wanted you all to know," I said.

"I understand that, but you've had years to face this. And this is the first time your mom and I have had to deal with it. So it might be best if you both head out now."

I kept staring at the house as we left. I didn't want to go. I wanted to be a kid again. I didn't know how to deal with this. At that moment, being an adult seemed too hard.

David held my hand. It didn't help. I felt alone, even with him by my side. My parents had to deal with me being gay, and I didn't like being separated from them.

I wanted to run back and tell them I wasn't gay. We were kidding. It was stupid, I know. I was an adult and in order to be with the one I loved I needed to deal with adult situations.

The hardest thing about being gay was that sometimes you had to go against society's norms. I had never felt so different. I wondered why the Christian Right felt it was so necessary to separate us from our family and friends. What kind of God would do that to people?

I kept wondering all these things as we headed to home. *What kind of God?* I cried in David's arms.

AFTER COMING OUT to my parents, it was time to plan the wedding. We decided to do it in Boston, where David's sister lived and gay marriage was legally recognized in 2009. David's whole family lived on the East Coast, and they would make up the majority of the wedding party, so it made sense.

I was uncertain if any of my family would make it to the wedding especially given their negative reaction to my coming out.

We planned to have the wedding on the anniversary of the day we first met. It would be early fall, when the trees changed with brilliant color—David's and my favorite season.

I was still unemployed. And I was trying to figure out what to do next with my life. Then it struck me. I'd wanted to write a book all my life.

It had begun as a dream when I was a kid. I wanted to write stories about superheroes; I fantasized about their strong muscular bodies, which makes more sense now, of course, once I'd realized I was gay. But maybe I could write a book based on reality.

I brought this up to David on a night we went out to a local Mexican restaurant.

"I don't think I'm going to go back to work." I took a big gulp of my margarita. "I'm going to write a book."

"What sort of book?" he asked.

"I think it will be about us, the shootings, the physical recoveries, Rick's death, my coming out, everything I went through and how it has forever changed me. Sort of a memoir."

He gave me an uncertain look. "Are you sure you want to bring up all those ghosts of the past?"

"I know that these are heavy subjects, but I feel I need to exorcize those demons." I gulped down another big swig of margarita as I waited for a response.

He looked away from me to signal the waitress for a check. She didn't seem to notice. This was always a problem; for some reason, David had a hard time getting the waitress back to the table when we were done. But this time, it would be fine, since we needed to discuss this.

"I think it's a good idea," he finally said.

"I'm glad you agree."

"What if I didn't?"

I looked at him with my determined look. "Of course, I would have done it anyway. I need to do this."

Now, all I had to do was write the book. Easy, right?

WE CHOSE A hotel that overlooked the Boston Central Library for the wedding. This seemed appropriate, since David and I were voracious readers. The trees around Copley Square outside the hotel displayed a multitude of autumn colors, a rainbow canopy.

I invited everyone that I could. Stephen and Beth made it up for the affair. I asked Kevin to walk me down the aisle. I wished I could have had my mom do this.

David's mother took me aside the night before the wedding. She was wearing a long flowing dress and seemed ready for the wedding, even though it was the night before.

"You're going to make him happy, right?" she asked, looking in my eyes.

"Of course, I will. He's the best thing that's ever happened to me," I said.

"He should be. He's my son." She smiled, and I relaxed a bit.

"Are you ready for this?" she asked.

"As ready as I'll ever be," I answered.

KEVIN AND I met for a drink in the hotel lobby the night before the wedding. David was nervous about it and kept making me reassure him that I didn't have cold feet. I wanted a moment to take everything in with my oldest and dearest friend.

I stared at Kevin as he walked into the bar. It seemed forever ago that we were kids, still dreaming about marrying a woman, not dealing with the fact that we were gay.

"Are you ready to walk down the aisle with me?" I asked.

"Yes, I can't wait," he said. "And as for my advice for the future—no more getting shot!"

"I hope it's my last time too—not sure if I can survive another one." I kicked him and thought about how quickly life can change. "I never thought—as a gay person—that I would get married. It seemed an impossibility. And here in Massachusetts, it's legal. That's the best thing. Hopefully, someday, it will be like that throughout the country."

"Well, not sure about that back in Missouri," he said.

I agreed. "Thanks for doing this. I really wish my parents and family were able to make it. They're still coping with me coming out to them. My sister wasn't happy that I'd told Mom and Dad, and I'm pretty sure my brothers know now too. It's sort of my fault. I waited too long to tell my parents. I also decided to do it right before getting married. What was I thinking?"

"Why didn't you wait to marry?" Kevin asked.

"David's parents are older and it was important to both of us that they were here to celebrate with us. Also, I'm not sure if my parents would have ever wanted to attend my gay wedding."

We walked into the room where the wedding was going to take place the next day. We did a practice run of Kevin escorting me down the aisle. The chuppah was already set up for our Jewish ceremony.

"What's that for?" Kevin asked.

"It's part of the ceremony. We get married under it. I had a lot to learn about a Jewish wedding."

Kevin picked up a cloth-encased glass. He pointed to it with an inquisitive look.

"So in addition to being married under the chuppah, we break the glass at the end of the ceremony. FYI, that's when everyone shouts *mazel tov!*"

"Anything else I should know?"

"No. Most of all...thanks for being here for me."

"I wouldn't be anywhere else."

I WENT UP to the hotel room and found David trying on the suit that he would be wearing the next day.

"What do you think?" he asked as he buttoned up the sleeves of his shirt.

"I think you look like the handsomest Jewish guy in Boston," I said.

"Just Jewish?"

"Do you have to be so difficult?"

"Always," he said with a smile.

We kissed. The following day was going to be very busy. I did my best to sleep that night, but it was hard. I finally rolled over and held him in my arms, and that helped me find some shut-eye.

I awoke to snow falling outside. Of course, it would be that sort of day.

"Glad we chose to be indoors," he said as we got ready.

Getting ready felt unreal. When I had understood that I was gay, I never thought about being able to marry and having it be recognized. It seemed so far outside what I thought would be possible.

"How do you feel?" David asked.

"Nervous."

"It will go great."

We gazed at ourselves in the mirror, all suited up. After all this time, we were finally tying the knot.

Yet, first, we had to sign the marriage contract. This was also part of Jewish tradition. His parents were already in the room.

"You plan to be a good husband to my son, correct?" His father looked seriously at me.

"Yes, I do," I said.

He grinned and laughed at me, giving me a hug. We signed the document. His father ended the signing by whispering in my ear, "Welcome to the family."

Next, I stood outside the hall to follow David down the aisle. David stood with his mom.

"I really do love you both," his mother said to us. She had a tear in her eye.

They headed down the aisle.

I took Kevin's hand. "Thanks for doing this."

"You're my closest friend. You're like a brother. I was always going to do this," he said.

I took a deep breath and we walked toward the chuppah.

When the time came for our vows, I started with:

"Between us
The past,
Moments of laughter,
The first time we stared into each other's eyes,
When we first said I love you.
Through all my life,
I have been dreaming and wishing
That someday you would be here,
To hold me in the night,
Through the darkness,
Until there is light.
I stand holding your hand,
Touching you,
Wishing and hoping you feel the same,
As when we first said I love you.
I feel the loss of you
When you are gone,
And happiness when you return.
I want you to take this ring,
Know that I think of you always,
My one true love."

Like a dancer, I fixed my gaze on his to keep my balance. By the end, I was fighting back tears, and only his smile and firm grip let me get through my vows.

As if on cue, as I ended my vows, we each took a deep breath. We shifted our grips so now I was supporting him, as he vowed:

"I never felt like I was incomplete until I met you.

But knowing you has made me feel stronger and better than I ever have.

You have made me smile every day that we have shared, and when I thought I might lose you, I learned despair.

Today I vow to always make you smile,

To be with you every day so you never know despair.

To be your strength when you need it

And to seek your strength when I do

And to forever be your beloved as you are mine."

The rest of the ceremony was a blur, until the kiss. I thought I knew his kiss, but this was different. This was my husband and I found a new strength and passion in his lips.

The rabbi's instruction to break the glass returned us to reality.

"Mazel Tov!" our friends and family shouted in unison.

After that, we walked back down the aisle and went to a side room. Waiting for us was a small meal. We would have a few minutes to ourselves before we'd join everyone at the reception hall.

"So why is this part of the tradition?" I asked as David put food on his plate.

"In the past, the bride and groom often didn't know each other before they got married. So this gave them some time to get acquainted with each other. Today, I think it is just to make sure we get a chance to eat." He leaned in to kiss me and added mischievously, "But if you want to get to know each other again, I'm game."

"I think we might need more than a few minutes," I replied with a grin.

"I'M...SORRY." WERE the first words I heard from my sister as a married man. She had called several times that weekend, but I waited until I was back in Saint Louis to speak with her.

They were the right first words, but I wasn't sure I was ready to forgive, no matter how I had been raised.

I steadied myself before responding. "That's great to hear, but you know that you hurt me deeply."

"Okay, I messed up," she said.

"Yes, you did." That was all I could say to her.

"When can I see you?"

"You can see us when you're ready to hug your brother-in-law."

She came sooner than I expected. She suggested we go back to the neighborhood chicken restaurant. But David said he was in the mood for Mexican. I knew that was a lie. David never suggested Mexican. He wasn't sure how things would end, and he didn't want to ruin one of his favorite places.

No one seemed to know how to start the conversation. To her credit, my sister began.

"How have you two been?"

"We're doing all right. David is really busy with it being close to midterms." I was looking away from her as I spoke.

"I am truly sorry. Can you forgive me?" she asked.

I was quiet for a moment. "I can't forgive what you did, but I still love you... You're my sister. If you promise to love David as much as you love me, then we have a place to start." I counted in my head as I waited for her to answer. I was almost to fourteen when she answered.

"I...I promise to love you both. I know David is good for you," she said. "Have you talked to Mom and Dad?"

"I've talked to Mom some. It will take time for us to sort through this," I said.

When it came time to say goodbye, David returned her hug. It was a new beginning for us all.

AS MY SISTER predicted, it took longer with my parents. Our first conversations were about the weather and road construction. Eventually Mom asked about Frankie. From that point on, the phone calls became warmer.

When David received a birthday card signed Mom and Dad, I told him that was a sign of acceptance. I called Mom and asked if they were free the following weekend.

Mom greeted us with some auction finds, which included a picnic basket and some neat glasses. Neither had been on our registry, but we thanked them.

We sat down at the kitchen table and Mom brought out some pie for us. She had made a banana cream for me and an apple pie for David.

As we took the first delicious bites, she said with a smile, "You both look good."

"Thanks," I said. It was hard not to love her when she was trying so hard.

"So David, how are your parents?"

"They're good."

"Did you bring pictures? We've never been to Boston."

"We left them at home," I informed her.

"Don't forget to bring them next time."

I was surprised to hear David answer. "I'll remind Todd."

The conversation shifted to what we were planning to plant in our garden this summer. Mom offered a few suggestions, but the most important seed had been planted.

OVER THE NEXT few months, we continued our support of Kevin by going to see him perform. On one such occasion, I was having him do something special. It was all for David.

Stephen and Beth and even my sister Karen made it for the show.

"It was important for all of us to be here. What's happening?" my sister asked.

"Don't worry, it will be great," I said. "Now, I'm going backstage to help Kevin."

Kevin was getting himself ready. His hair was pink that night. A photo of his mother hung above his reflection on the mirror.

"Are you sure you want to do this?" he asked.

"Just this once," I answered firmly.

Kevin spread makeup on my face and handed me a red wig to wear. I dressed in a steamy pink dress. I would be performing for the first and only time.

"You can introduce me, but I want you in the audience," I said.

"Oh, I can't wait. It will be fabulous."

The lights went low, and Kevin told everyone that I had to run an errand and would be back.

When the lights came back up, Kevin stepped onto the stage.

"Tonight, we have a special guest, Miranda Starlight, who will be performing Cyndi Lauper's 'True Colors.'"

I walked out fiercely in my heels; luckily, I'd been working on my act with the best of the best—Jade Sinclair.

As I started to sing, I stepped down off the stage and right in front of David and Kevin in his Jade persona. I gave Kevin a kiss on the cheek, but I reserved a long kiss for David. Almost losing my way through the song in the moment that our lips locked. I even surprised Stephen with a kiss on his cheek; he glowed red. Beth and my sister got up and danced with me.

When the song was coming to the close, I pulled David on stage with me and we finished it out. My mascara was running as tears flowed. He cleared them away and smiled at me.

"That was fantastic!" he said.

I held him even closer as the spotlight gradually dimmed.

Epilogue

IN 2011, MARK moved out to San Francisco and we planned to visit him. This would give me a chance to say goodbye to Rick on Half Moon Bay where his ashes had been scattered.

David and I dropped Frankie off with my parents so she wouldn't have to be kenneled while we traveled to California.

I had promised myself that if I ever made it out there, I would do this. "I have to say goodbye to a friend who was killed in a gay bashing," I told my mother. "I'm going to the beach where his ashes were scattered."

She was taken aback for a moment. I had been blunt with her about the tragedy, but it brought back a lot of painful emotions I had from his death.

"I'm sorry to hear your friend was killed in that manner. It's nice that you're making this effort." She hugged me. We were at a place where she could comfort me again.

I told her how close we had been. "I miss him when I come across old romantic comedies on television. We spent many nights watching them... I wish he was still around, and I could call him up when I'm going through a bad spell in life."

We stayed for a small lunch before heading out. They hugged us. We were a family.

"I love you both. And I made you some sandwiches for the plane," she said.

"Thanks, Mom."

"I'm truly sorry about what happened to your friend." Her eyes glistened as she hugged me again. It was nice that she had come this far with us.

I held David's hand as we left.

WE ARRIVED AT Oakland International Airport. Mark now had a boyfriend named Dean, and they lived close to Berkeley where Mark was a pastor at a church.

"It's great to see you both," he said, and introduced us to Dean. He had short-cropped hair, glasses, and a big smile.

"It's great to finally meet you in person," David said.

We all hugged and went to their home up in the hills. It had a beautiful view of San Francisco.

They were almost too nice. That morning, they made an awesome breakfast. More food than anyone could possibly eat. This included homemade bagels, lox, cream cheese along with danishes, eggs, bacon, even pancakes and freshly squeezed orange juice.

"Wow, you know how to make a spread."

"It'll be good to have a large meal before...heading to Half Moon Bay," David added.

The thought almost made me lose my appetite, but they were doing me a big favor by taking the long drive there.

"I really appreciate you all doing this," I told them. "Especially for someone you didn't even know."

"I know that losing someone you care for can be hard," Mark said.

"I know you need to do this, hon," David said. "The loss of Rick, especially the way he...died, was a lot to handle."

"Thanks, hon."

He gave me a small kiss on the forehead.

We left after breakfast. I'd wondered how I was going to honor his memory. On the way down, I noticed a small florist and had them stop. I found sunflowers, which had always been Rick's favorite flowers.

"I'm going to spread sunflower petals in his memory," I said. "He always bought a fresh sunflower if we came across one at the farmer's market. He'd place it in a small vase on his kitchen table."

"That is a great idea," David said.

THE BEACH WAS quiet, a steady wind with intermittent clouds causing moments of darkness before the sun would peek through again.

We were silent, letting ourselves absorbed the atmosphere of sun, wind, and surf.

I walked out onto the beach by myself and then to the water's edge where the chill of the wet sand seeped into my bones. I took the petals and spread them. The waves seemed to fight me; even in death, Rick struggled with finding peace.

Rick's killers were still free. They hadn't answered for their crimes. If there was a God and a hell in the hereafter, they'd have what's coming to them for the pain he must have endured.

I broke up the sunflower into smaller pieces. The seeds drifted out farther, and the waves eventually took them away. I felt that with them, his ghost was finding peace after his horrible death.

I brought out a photo that I had carried with me since his death, threw it into the water, and watched it float away.

"I'm so, so sorry, Rick." Tears rolled down my face.

David tried to comfort me, but I wasn't ready for it. The pain and frustration I still harbored over Rick's death seemed to weigh me down as I dropped to the sand.

Mark came and held me. "It's all right, Todd. He's in a better place. I can feel it."

I don't know if I believed him. Such horrible things had happened to someone who only wanted to be loved. That was what he had been searching for the night he was killed.

They held my hands. "I just don't understand. I'm sorry. I want to believe that something deeper and spiritual can be in this world. It is so hard to see that when humans do such horrible things to each other. We fight so hard against each other."

Mark leaned over and wrote letters in the sand: R-I-C-K.

The waves spread around the wording, not wiping them away. I kept staring at his name, deeply touched. I felt Rick was there, looking at us from whatever could be found beyond this world.

I called out over the crash of the waves. "I know this does not help, but you were loved!"

We walked away from the beach until I found a place to plant a few of the seeds I had kept.

"I'm not sure if they can grow here, but maybe when I return, I'll see a sunflower plant here in memory of him. Maybe whatever is out there can grant this one little miracle."

We walked back to the car, but I kept looking out over the ocean. The sun finally came out of the clouds and warmed my face. For a moment, I thought a smile was visible in the clouds before the sun slipped away, and the air grew heavy with mist.

As we drove away, the wind picked up again and dark clouds filled the sky, blocking out the sun.

Acknowledgements

This book was inspired by real events and the many people who provided me with love and support, only some of whom were reflected in these pages. In addition, many others were there for me as I wrote this book. I want to start my thank-yous with David Kaplan, the love of my life. My family, who I know has always loved me. Friends from my youth and college days: Michael Klataske, DuWayne Belles, Robert Ludwig, and David Wartman. Friends and fellow writers: Shawn Clubb, Julie Clubb, Elizabeth Donald, and the E'ville Writers. And finally, my son Drew, who reminds me every day of the wonder and hope in the world.

About the Author

Todd Smith brings a unique perspective to his writing having survived being shot twice. These shootings, along with the unsolved gay bashing murder of his friend form the basis of his first novel. While recovering in the hospital from the second shooting he proposed to his husband. Theirs is a mixed marriage of Missouri Baptist and New York Jew. Together they are raising a son and are trying to replicate his feat of travelling to all 50 states. Most of his writing career has been for newspapers, including the GLBT paper in Kansas City. He continues to work on new projects and writes with a group affectionately known as the Eville writers.

Website: www.Toddallensmith.com

Twitter: @ToddSmithSTL

Also Available from NineStar Press

Connect with NineStar Press

Website: NineStarPress.com

Facebook: NineStarPress

Facebook Reader Group: NineStarNiche

Twitter: @ninestarpress

Tumblr: NineStarPress

CPSIA information can be obtained
at www.ICGtesting.com
Printed in the USA
FFOW02n1525090618
47098758-49546FF